Doctor Hudson's
Secret Journal

Also by Lloyd C. Douglas
in Thorndike Large Print ®

Magnificent Obsession

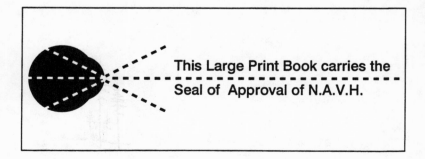

This Large Print Book carries the
Seal of Approval of N.A.V.H.

Doctor Hudson's Secret Journal

Lloyd C. Douglas

Thorndike Press • Thorndike, Maine

3 1969 00860 0586

Thorndike Large Print ® All Time Favorite Series edition published in 1993 by arrangement with Houghton Mifflin Company.

The tree indicium is a trademark of Thorndike Press.

This book is printed on acid-free, high opacity paper.∞

Set in 16 pt. News Plantin by Minnie B. Raven.

Library of Congress Cataloging in Publication Data

Douglas, Lloyd C. (Lloyd Cassel), 1877–1951.
    Doctor Hudson's secret journal / Lloyd C. Douglas.
       p.   cm.
    ISBN 1-56054-776-6 (alk. paper : lg. print)
    1. Large type books. I. Title.
    [PS3507.O7573D58   1993]
    813'.52—dc20   93-13716
                                                         CIP

GRATEFULLY DEDICATED
TO THE READERS OF
MAGNIFICENT OBSESSION

Publishers' Preface

In 1929 appeared the First Edition of a book with the odd title, *Magnificent Obsession*. Two well-known general publishing houses had declined the book — one because it was too much of a story and not sufficiently a religious book, and the other because it was too much a religious book and not sufficiently a story — and both on the ground that it was not likely to justify the expense of publication. The author had then offered the manuscript to a house that made a specialty of publishing in the religious field. There it was accepted and published. The first printing was one of three thousand copies; the second, one of fifteen hundred.

It is interesting to know that when the book was first offered to the trade it was sold as a religious work. Dealers placed it among the sermons and ethical essays. It was fully six months later before booksellers began to consider it as a novel.

Novels that appear in the Best Seller List usually achieve their popularity and their ratings immediately. If they are to become 'Best Sellers,' they give evidence of it within thirty days after publication. *Magnificent Obsession* did not reach the Best Seller List until a year after it was published; but having arrived there, it remained on the list for eighteen months. Modestly advertised in religious journals, its popularity came chiefly from the word-of-mouth publicity that it received. In this publicity the interest of several eminent clergymen in various parts of the country was strikingly effective. Those men lent their influence to the book, reviewing it before their congregations and church conventions.

After the book had been out for a year the jacket was altered slightly by the addition of this sentence: 'It has frequently been said of this strange story that the people who read it are never quite the same again.'

The book evoked an amazing flood of letters from its readers. These letters came from every state in the Union, every province in Canada, and from Great Britain. Reading clubs in Germany studied it. London preachers reviewed it in their pulpits. It has been translated into many languages. It has been on the air and on the motion-picture screen. By a highly conservative estimate two million persons have read *Magnificent Obsession*.

Among the queries presented in those letters, several constantly recurred. One almost always found was this: 'Is the complete Journal of Doctor Hudson available?'

For several years it has been Mr. Douglas's

intention to answer that question in the affirmative.

Doctor Hudson's Secret Journal is not a sequel to *Magnificent Obsession*. It is rather an expansion of the philosophy that made *Magnificent Obsession* important, illumined by other experiences of Doctor Hudson's than those recorded in the novel.

The persons who found inspiration in *Magnificent Obsession* will, we believe, feel a deep satisfaction in seeing the tenth anniversary of that extraordinary book celebrated by the publication of *Doctor Hudson's Secret Journal.*

Author's Foreword

Shortly after the quiet appearance of *Magnificent Obsession*, ten years ago, the author became aware that he had not completed his task.

The letters which began to pour in were not of the sort usually referred to as 'fan mail.' Nobody wanted an autograph, a photograph, or a lock of hair. Not many bothered to remark that they had been entertained by the story. But they all asked questions and most of the questions were serious, wistful, and challenging.

The theme of the novel had derived from a little handful of verses midway of the Sermon on the Mount, but all references to the enchanted passage were purposely vague, the author feeling that a treasure hunt in Holy Writ would probably do his customers no harm. Within the first twelve months after publication, more than two thousand people had written to inquire, 'What page of the Bible did the sculptor carry in his wallet?' We left off counting these queries, but they have continued to come, all through these intervening years.

Second in importance to this inquiry was a very searching question, phrased in terms ranging all the way from polite hinting to forthright impudence: 'Do you honestly believe in this thing — or were you just writing a story?' After a while, letters began to arrive from persons who said they had tried it, and it worked; though they were careful not to be too specific in reporting their adventures, aware that if they told they would be sorry. A few lamented the cost of unrewarded experiments and denounced the whole idea as a lot of hooey.

The task of dealing sympathetically with this strange correspondence became a grave responsibility. No stock letter, done on a mimeograph, would serve the purpose. It was necessary that individual replies be sent to all earnest inquirers. One dared not risk the accusation that, having advocated an expensive and venturesome technique for generating personal power, the author was thereafter too busy or lazy to care whether anybody benefited by such investments. It was interesting to observe how wide a variety of people came forward with questions. A single post might contain inquiries from a high school boy, a college professor, a farmer's wife, a physician, a pious old lady, an actress, a postman, a preacher, and a sailor. Some of the questions were practically unanswerable, but it wasn't quite fair to limit one's reply to a laconic 'I don't know.' Frequently one's counsel was pitiably inadequate, but not because it was coolly casual or thoughtlessly composed. I suppose that if all of these letters were compiled and printed they would fill several volumes as large as the novel which evoked them.

A third question, which began to show up promptly, inquired, 'Is the complete text of Doctor Hudson's journal available in print?' The correct answer to that was 'No.' It not only wasn't in print; it had not been written. Occasionally someone would counter, 'How were you able to quote from Doctor Hudson's journal, if there never was any such thing?' — an amusingly artless question, to be sure; but an obviously honest tribute to the realism of a document which had no existence in fact.

Readers of *Magnificent Obsession* will recall that, early in the story, an eminent brain surgeon, Doctor Wayne Hudson, lost his life by drowning. Among his effects there was found a journal containing some amazing memoirs. Because of the singular nature of these experiences, Doctor Hudson had concealed his story in a baffling code, hoping by this means to insure it against a hasty perusal by persons who might view it with careless indifference or a half-contemptuous incredulity.

Throughout the novel, 'quotations' from and adversions to this laboriously decoded journal provided the explanation of young

Merrick's belief and behavior as he endeavored to follow in his mentor's footsteps. And perhaps it is not an unreasonable request if the people who have found a measure of inspiration in those brief and detached fragments from the Hudson journal should want to see the whole of it.

This book is related to *Magnificent Obsession* as an overture rather than a sequel. Therefore it may be read without any bewilderment by persons unacquainted with the novel.

But it is only natural if, during the belated composition of this journal, the author should have visualized an audience largely composed of those to whom Doctor Hudson is no stranger. I find myself surveying this audience — however widely scattered over the earth — as an assembly of people friendly to one another — and to me. I feel that we are somehow related in a common cause, a common quest. In this audience there are many hundreds of gracious souls to whom I am indebted for confidences and comradeships which have enriched my life and emphasized for me the significance of spiritual forces.

I am particularly hopeful that this book may be approved by my friends of the clergy who were primarily responsible for the wide distribution of the novel. Too frequently one hears discrediting criticism of the ministers on

14

the ground that they are too much occupied with the material success of their own denominations; that they are inhospitable to new evaluations of enduring verities; that they are more concerned with 'churchianity' than Christianity. This indictment is, for the most part, unfair.

In *Magnificent Obsession* there was no talk about the importance of attending religious services or supporting religious institutions in any manner whatsoever. Nobody in the book ever put his nose inside a church, except on one occasion when Bobby Merrick went to hear his friend, Doctor McLaren, by special and urgent invitation.

This attitude was not intended to convey a feeling of disregard for religious organizations on the part of the author. The Church was conspicuously and willfully omitted from the story for the reason that in almost all of the 'religious' novels the Church serves as the axis on which the plot spins. It was my hope to interest not only the people who rely upon the Church for their moral and spiritual instruction but to suggest a way of life to many others — seldom approached in this manner — who have never looked to the Church for answers to their riddles.

It was with some trepidation that the author adopted this course, for he had spent most

15

of his life in the service of the Church; his closest friends were church people; he hoped they would take no offense; he wondered if they would understand. And they understood.

In spite of the fact that *Magnificent Obsession* had almost nothing to do with the Church, plus the fact that most of the people in the novel were distinctly worldly, and some were addicted to debatable habits, and a few were shockingly profane, it was the clergy of America and the British Empire who carried that novel to success. They may have wished that it contained fewer cuss-words and cocktails, but they had the sportsmanship to overlook the frailties it admitted and approve the faith it upheld. It was well worth the bother of writing a novel — just to find that out.

Facsimile of the first page of the Hudson Journal

Rae Josdrom fin u sdren
Jeyny red w Adom N Y u
preac u N C Medor Esvrns
w Hvnah E Etr bltt u Aig eivd
Haii yo w Ratibo yua eloh u
edhso Kohva ste w R G Jooasi
Mr Aos u iht PS est yron w
Front J icpew lb. u Odig hsnihr
ili co M D Pansop oed u Auliay
nvee w

Translation

READER I CONSIDER YOU MY FRIEND AND COM-
MEND YOUR PERSEVERANCE   HAVING ACHIEVED
THE ABILITY TO READ THIS BOOK YOU HAVE ALSO
THE RIGHT TO POSSESS IT   MY REASONS FOR
DOING THIS IN CIPHER WILL BE MADE PLAIN AS
YOU PROCEED

DOCTOR HUDSON'S SECRET JOURNAL

*(Decoded and typed by Robert Merrick,
assisted by Nancy Ashford.)*

Brightwood Hospital,
Detroit, Michigan

October sixth, 1913, 11 P.M.

This has been an eventful day. We formally
opened our new hospital this afternoon. The
city's medical profession was ably represented
and many of our well-to-do philanthropists
came for tea and a tour of inspection.

Everybody commented on our astounding
luck in disposing of the shabby old building
in Cadillac Square for a quarter of a million.
Lucky, they said, that our site had been chosen
for the new skyscraping office building. And
what a lucky dog I was, added the mayor,
that this exquisitely landscaped four-acre tract
came onto the market just as we had begun
to look for a new location.

I nodded an appreciative assent to all of

these pleasant comments on my good luck, but felt rather traitorous; for it wasn't luck. Nothing that has happened to me since June of 1905 could be properly called luck. I am in the grip of something that I don't understand; but, whatever it is, there's nothing capricious about it.

But if I had blurted out some such remark to the mayor or good old Mrs. Arlington or Nick Merrick, there would have been a lot of explaining to do (or dodge) so I cheerfully agreed with them that I was lucky. Had I told them the whole story about our acquirement of the new hospital, they would have thought me stark mad.

Billy Werner called up from New York, about four, to offer congratulations and regret he could not be here. He said, 'We're square now, Doc, except for the interest on that loan.' And I said, 'Don't ever try to pay that back, Billy. It might upset the apple-cart.'

Frequently, during these past few years, I have fairly burned with desire to confide in someone. The weight of my secrets has been almost crushing at times. But I have this load to carry alone as long as I live. The strange events which have come to pass through my private investments do not permit of an airing: their good results might be jeopardized. I know a few other people whom I suspect of bearing the same sort of burden, but we can't discuss it. I often wonder if it is not more difficult to suppress a great exaltation than to conceal a secret sorrow.

An hour ago, Nancy Ashford paused at my office door to say good night. She was drooping a little with fatigue from the day's unusual excitements.

'Well,' she said, wearily, 'you have put over a great project.'

I wanted to invite her in and tell her how we got this new hospital. It wouldn't have taken very long. She knows the beginning of the story. I needed only to say, 'Nancy, do you remember the woman we had with us for six months, the one with the broken neck?'

And Nancy would have replied, 'Of course — Mrs. Werner — and her husband was sore about the bills.'

I would have gone on from there. Mrs. Werner had had the best room in the hospital and a deal of extra attention, much of which was unnecessary but expensive. Everybody assumed that the Werners were wealthy. He had a big store downtown, and they lived in a beautiful home. There was a rumor that they were extravagant. She was always traveling about, and he was reputed a gambler.

It wasn't my job to supervise hospital statements, but Werner's must have been pretty high. When he was billed for the surgery, the amount was not excessive, but it was in the same general bracket with the other expenses of his wife's illness. I was not informed, until some time afterwards, that when he paid the bill he made a scene, protesting that he had been overcharged.

About that time there was a story afloat about town that Werner was in serious straits financially. He had offended the president of his bank and had been unreasonably cocky with almost everybody else. He had no one to turn to in his emergency. Perhaps his irascibility, in his dealings with us, was all of a piece with his other blunders. But — once upon a time he had been able to build up a fine business. Something had happened to him. He needed to be rehabilitated.

One morning, in *The Free Press*, I noticed a conspicuous advertisement of Werner's home for sale at a cruel sacrifice. On impulse, I went down to his office immediately. He was reluctant to see me and greeted me with a glum grunt and a surly scowl. I told him I had come to lend him twenty thousand — the amount he had asked for his house. He could put that into his business, and perhaps save his home. He was suspicious, and wanted to know what rate of interest I expected. I said I didn't want any interest because I intended to use it for another purpose. He asked me if I was feeling well, and brought me a drink of water.

Of course, that small loan wouldn't have been a drop in his dry bucket, considered as mere dollars and cents. But the fact that I had volunteered to let him have it when he was all but on the rocks, and it seemed like pouring so much money into a rat-hole — and he knew that I knew it — had the effect of a shot of strychnine.

He paced up and down the room, for a minute or two, and then snapped out, 'Thanks, Doc. You'll not regret it.'

'Not if you keep it a secret,' I replied. 'This must not be told.'

I made no effort to keep track of his activities but it was evident that Werner had gone at it again with tremendous energy. Perhaps he plunged recklessly. I do not know the details of that story. But soon he was enlarging his store and in command of his mercantile field. Three years after that, he organized the company that put up the new office building. Because he had conceived the project, his board of directors deferred to his judgment in many matters including the selection of a site. He urged the purchase of our old hospital.

So — that's the way we got the new hospital.

But I couldn't recite any of this even to Nancy, who would have been stirred and mystified by the story. I can hear the way she would have murmured, 'Well — of all things!'

I did not detain her. I simply smiled, nodded, and told her to go to bed; that she had earned a good night's rest. A remarkable woman. Sometimes I wonder how much she knows about my odd investments. She has witnessed my signature, occasionally, on papers that must have excited her curiosity. Perhaps she thinks I am living a double life. I should like to set her mind at ease about that. But it is impossible. My lips are sealed. She will have to draw her own conclusions.

I suppose I should be content with the rewards of my dynamic discovery, even if not permitted to disclose it to others. It has brought me innumerable satisfactions; an excellent rating in a difficult field of surgery, a position of influence in civic affairs, a comfortable home, and — above all — the enduring gratitude of a large number of persons whose lives have been reconditioned through these investments.

But it is a lonesome sensation, sometimes, to feel that one is in league with a catalytic force as versatile as electricity, prompt as dynamite, stirring as a symphony, warm as a handclasp — but available only on condition that one does not tell. To confide what one has done to achieve this peculiar power might be very costly, not only to oneself but to others whose welfare is integrally related to one's own success.

Not to confide it, especially to one's close and trusted friends, seems unconscionably selfish; yet there is no way — so far as I know — for confiding the theory unless one divulges the practice, which would necessitate a narrative of specific events.

But for a long time I have had it in mind to record at least a few of these facts for the guidance and encouragement of someone who might wish to experiment with this thing after I am gone. To record some of these events in a private journal and deposit the book in my safe would seem entirely feasible, except for the risk that the book might fall into the hands of some person who would read it without imagination or the slightest glimmer of sympathetic understanding. Hence my decision to write the book in cipher. I do not think that anyone will go through the drudgery of decoding it unless he is interested in the contents. Whenever he finds that the job isn't worth the bother, the reader can quit. And the sooner he quits, the safer the secret.

I would give a good deal to know — at this

writing — what sort of person will have the time, patience, and disposition to translate this book. I hope he will not be in too much of a hurry to learn the secret. I intend to approach the matter with a deliberation that may exasperate my reader. But if he isn't concerned enough to persevere, he probably would not know how to use the secret even if he discovered it.

If you have got this far, my friend, perhaps you will have decided that I am crazy. This will be incorrect. I have contrived to lay hold upon a principle that has expanded my life and multiplied my normal energies. I have a consuming curiosity to know more about this thing; and if you are still engaged in deciphering this book you share this curiosity. If I am crazy for writing it, you are equally crazy for reading it. I warn you that if you go much farther, it will get you, as it got me. But I am not crazy.

Eventually the time may come, though I shall not live to see it, when mental aberrations are regarded with the same sympathy now bestowed upon physical disabilities. As the matter stands at present, while it is no disgrace to have an ailment of the heart, you are viewed with aversion if there is anything wrong with your head. I understand this feeling; and, to a considerable extent, share it myself.

Of course, when I am dealing professionally with a brain tumor, my patient's mental disorder does not offend or annoy me, for I have a scientific interest in his dementia as an inevitable concomitant to the pressure on his brain. Indeed, the phenomena of his lunacy sometimes aid me in defining the field of the pressure.

But — professional curiosity aside — I am very uncomfortable in the society of people whose minds are upset. I dislike hysterics. I have a strong distaste for exhibitionism in any of its manifestations. I have no use for the mentality that hankers to be unique. I have no patience at all with eccentrics who go chasing about after ridiculous isms and fantastic ologies. I like normal people and I should like to be considered normal myself.

When a man tells me that his Aunt Alicia roused suddenly in the middle of the night, dressed, packed a bag, and took a train, at the behest of some esoteric hunch that her bankrupt nephew was on the brink of a tragedy, and arrived in the nick of time to talk him out of his revolver and into a new resolution, I instinctively add this fellow's name to the list of those with whom I shall not be going on a canoe-trip around the world.

I try to avoid the balmy, the monomaniacs, the religious fanatics, the obsessed, except in my hospital where it is my business to see them. I would walk a mile to escape a conversation with somebody who had gone in for spiritualism, astrology, yogism, or an expectation of the return of Christ by a week from Tuesday. I take no stock in magic. Belief in the supernatural comes hard with me. I automatically shy off at reports of miracles, both classic and contemporary.

And the reason I am so tiresomely insistent upon the orderly and conservative nature of my own mind, and my distaste for persons with odd kinks, quirks, maggots, crotchets, hallucinations, and various benign psychoses, is that I want the reader of this journal to believe that I am as sane as anybody he knows. I insist on this, at the outset, my friend, for I shall be documenting some very strange events.

It is broad daylight now, and we are both weary. I have to be in the operating chamber at ten, and I assume that you, too, have something important to do. It is unlikely that an idle person would have access to this book.

AT HOME

October tenth, 1913, 9:30 P.M.

It all began on a fine June morning in 1905. Nothing has been the same since. Life took on a new meaning, that day.

It was the first anniversary of my wife's death. I had found it hard to reconcile myself to that loss, and the recurrence of the date revived in sharp detail the whole pitiful story of Joyce's unwilling departure and my unspeakable desolation.

For some time it had been in my mind to order a suitable marker for her grave. I had been tardy about it, hoping that my financial circumstances might improve. But there was no sign of such improvement. My affairs were growing more dismaying.

Restless and lonely, I resolved to visit some concern dealing in memorial stones and see whether I could afford to honor my dear girl's grave with a little monument. It was while engaged in this errand that I came by the secret of personal power.

Joyce and I had been very companionable. Not only were we naturally congenial, but her long illness had bound us together in a tender intimacy hardly to be achieved under any other circumstance. During the last year of her life, which we spent in Tucson, I made no attempt to do anything but keep her comfortable and amused. I tried to stand between her and all the little jars and irks and shocks. When the baby cried, I promptly found out what she wanted and got it for her. I have been doing that ever since and if she isn't a spoiled child she has every right to be. I loved my wife no more for her devotion to me than my own sympathy for her. I think we love best those whom we serve most zealously. It is an ennobling experience to love anyone in need of tender ministries. The time comes when nothing else matters much but the happiness of one's beloved.

There are plenty of afflictions more difficult to deal with than pulmonary tuberculosis. The patient is usually hopeful, cheerful, wistful. As physical vitality ebbs, the psychical forces flow with the strength and speed of a harvest tide.

If it ever becomes your destiny to entertain an invalid over any considerable length of time, it will be to your advantage if the patient's disability has not struck him below the belt. Your heart and lung people are optimists.

Of course I couldn't help knowing that Joyce was doomed. Had she been only one-tenth as sweet and patient, my sense of obligation to her would have kept me by her side. But I sincerely enjoyed that final year with her. We read innumerable books, lounged in the sun, swam in the pool, played together like children; and all this at a period of my career when — under normal conditions — I should have been working eighteen hours of every twenty-four to get a start in my profession.

Once in a while I would be swept by a surge of dismay over my inability to do anything at all when it was so obvious that I should have been going forward with my vocation. But these misgivings gripped me less frequently and more feebly as the days passed. The sunshine was genial, the air was sedative, my excuse for indolence was valid. I almost forgot I wanted to be a doctor.

Even now, after more than nine years, I cannot bring myself to the point of relating the events of Joyce's last hours, the sad and all but interminable journey home, the funeral, and — afterwards — the enervating depression; the feeling that life was barely worth the bother; the almost sickening aversion to the thought of resuming the old routine in the clinic.

The people at the hospital were very kind and forbearing. I must have been a dreadful nuisance. It should have been easy enough to see that my heart wasn't in it. But they seemed to understand; Doctor Pyle, especially. Pyle had always been a bit crusty, and I hadn't known him very well. They used to say of Pyle that if you could let him do all the abdominal surgery with the understanding that the patient would never see him again, he might become popular. Next morning after removing a kidney or a gall-bladder, Pyle would call on his uncomfortable victim and offer him some such amenity as, 'What in hell are you making so much racket about? Lots of people in this hospital with more pain than you have.'

But it was good old Pyle that helped me — roughly — back into the harness. I still hated it, and it galled me, but I wore it. Pyle fitted it on me again, muttering many a what-in-hell, but apparently bent on making something of me — a very unpromising project. One day I told him I believed I had better give it all up and go into business.

'What kind of business?' he growled. 'If you went out as grim and glum and licked as you look, today, you couldn't sell silver dollars for a nickel apiece. You stick to your job, young fellow.'

So — I stuck to the job; but I didn't like it.

It was in that state of mind that I went to look for the little tombstone. I told the manager it would have to be something inexpensive. He was quite obliging, treated me as considerately as he might if I had come to spend a thousand dollars. We agreed upon a small block of granite at what I thought was a merciful price. Then he asked me what I wanted engraved on the stone. I wrote Joyce's name and the dates.

'Would you like a brief epitaph?' he asked.

'Is it necessary?' I wondered.

'It is customary,' he replied.

I told him I had nothing in mind, and he suggested that I go out into the production room where many monuments were in process. Perhaps I might see something suitable. It was a good idea.

He opened the door and considerately left me to explore on my own. Several stonecutters glanced up and nodded as I paused to watch their work. I wasn't very much impressed by the various texts they were carving. None of them sounded much like anything Joyce would have been likely to quote.

Presently I came to the half-open door of a large studio where a man was at work on an amazingly beautiful piece of statuary. High above me on the catwalk of the scaffolding, and intent upon his occupation, the man did not notice me standing there until I had time to survey his creation deliberately. This fellow was not a mere stone-cutter; he was a sculptor, and an uncommonly good one, I surmised.

The piece he was working on seemed to be nearing completion. It was a triumphant angelic figure, heroic size, gracefully poised on a marble pedestal, altar-shaped; an exquisitely modeled hand shading the eyes which gazed into the far horizon, entranced by some distant radiance. It occurred to me that no man could have invested those eyes with such an expression of serenity and certitude unless he himself was convinced, beyond all doubt, that something was to be seen Out There. The statue was august in its simplicity. It had all the combined delicacy and strength of a Canova. On the face of the altar-shaped pedestal there was engraved, in gothic lettering and in high relief, a text which was not decipherable from where I stood. My movement for a better view caught the sculptor's attention. He must have seen that I was impressed.

'Come in,' he said, cordially. 'My name is Randolph. Anything I can do for you?'

'My name is Hudson. I have been looking about for a suitable epitaph to have engraved on a tombstone.'

Randolph leaned over and pointed down with the handle of his mallet.

'How do you like this one?' he asked.

The inscription read, 'Thanks Be to God Who Giveth Us the Victory.'

'Means nothing to me!' I remarked, rather testily, I fear. 'If there is a God, He probably has no more interest in any man's so-called victory, which can always be circumstantially explained, than in the victory of a cabbage that does well in a favorable soil.'

'Then you're related to God same as a cabbage,' chuckled Randolph. 'That's good.' He resumed his work, deftly tapping his chisel. 'I used to think that,' he went on, talking half to himself. 'Made a little experiment, and changed my mind about it.' He put down the mallet, leaned far forward; and, cupping his mouth with both hands, confided, in a mysterious tone, *'I've been on the line!'*

He did not have the tone or stance of a fanatic; spoke quietly; had none of the usual tricks by which aberrations are readily identified; talked well, with absolute self-containment. 'Victory? Well — rather! I now have everything I want and can do anything I wish! So can you! So can anybody! All you have to do is follow the rules! There's a formula, you know. I came upon it by accident!' He took up his chisel again.

He was a queer one. I felt shy and embarrassed. Clearly, he was cracked, but his manner denied it. I tried to remember that he was
an artist, with permission to be eccentric; but
this was more than an eccentricity. He made
me shivery. I wanted away. So — I was back-
ing through his doorway when he called,
'Doctor — do you have victory?'

'Victory over what?' I demanded, impatiently. I had not told him I was discouraged; hadn't mentioned I was a
doctor . . . I never did find out how he
guessed that — the question being eclipsed
by more important mysteries.

'Oh — over anything — everything! Listen!' He climbed swiftly down from his
scaffolding, and gliding stealthily toward me
as if he had some great secret to impart he
whispered into my ear — his hand firmly grip-
ping my coat-lapel, somewhat to my own anxiety — 'Would you like to be the best doctor
in this town?'

So — then I knew he was crazy, and I began
tugging myself loose.

'Come to my house, tonight, about nine
o'clock,' he said, handing me his card, 'and
I'll tell you what you want to know!'

I must have looked dazed, for he laughed
hilariously, as he climbed up again. I laughed
too as I reached the street — the epitaph mat-

36

ter having completely left my mind for the time. I had never heard so much nonsense in my life. 'Like hell,' I growled, as I started my car, 'will I waste an evening with that fool!'

At Home

October 19, 1913, 8:30 P.M.

At nine o'clock I was at Randolph's door. . . . When these words are read I shall be unable to answer any queries as to my motive in going there that night. And that will be fortunate; for I have no explanation further than to say (and this will unquestionably be regarded with distrust and disappointment) that I was propelled there against my wishes. I had no thought of going; went in response to some urge over which I had no control. . . . I was downtown to dinner, that evening; returned home at eight; went immediately to bed — quite contrary to my custom, for I never retired before midnight — and began reading a book, unable to concentrate on a line of it. I could not keep my eyes off the clock. It ticked louder and louder and my heart beat faster and faster until the two of them seemed synchronized. At length, becoming so nervous I could no longer contain myself, I rose, dressed hastily, dashed out for my car, and drove to Randolph's address without regard to boulevard stops or angry traffic officers.

My mouth was dry, my heart thumping.

'You had not intended to come, had you?' inquired Randolph, taking my hat.

'No!' I replied, sourly.

'That's what I feared,' he said, gently, 'but I felt so sure you needed to have a talk with me that I —'

'That is what I want to know!' I demanded. *'What did you do?'*

He grinned slyly, rubbed his hands together softly, satisfiedly, and said, 'Well — I earnestly wanted you here; and, as I told you, this morning, whatever I earnestly want — *it comes! I wanted you here! You came!'*

He motioned me to a seat — I was glad enough to accept it for my knees were wobbly — in a living-room furnished in exquisite taste. His daughter, whom he had gracefully presented, promptly excused herself, and left us alone. Offering me a cigar, he leisurely filled a long-stemmed churchwarden pipe for himself, and drew his chair closer. In his velvet jacket, at his ease, he was all artist; quite grizzled, wore a short Van Dyke beard; had a clear, clean, gray eye that came at you a bit shyly and tentatively, but left you no way of escape.

He lost no time in preliminary maneuvers. Reaching to a small book-table, at his elbow, he took up a limp-leather Bible. I knew then that I was in for it. Impetuously, I resolved upon an immediate, if inglorious exit. Savagely, I put up a protesting hand and said firmly, 'Now — if it's that, I don't care to hear about it!'

To my surprise, he put the book back on the table, and calmly puffed at his pipe, thoughtfully, for a while; then replied, 'Well — neither do I — except as it's really an important history of a great religious system. Quite useful, I presume; but I'm not specially interested in it — except one page —' He blew a few smoke rings, his head tilted far back against his tall chair, '— And I have cut that page out. . . . I just wanted you to see this particular copy of the Bible. I was about to say — when you plunged in with your impatient remark — that this copy of the Bible lacks the secret formula for power. I keep that one page elsewhere!'

'What's on it?' I inquired, annoyed at my own confession of interest.

'Oh —' he replied casually, 'it's just the rules for getting whatever you want, and doing whatever you wish to do, and being whatever you would like to be. But — you're not interested in that; so we'll talk about something else.'

'What is on that page?' I demanded — my voice sounding rather shrill.

40

'Do you really want to know?' he challenged, leaning forward and fixing me intently with his gaze.

'Yes!' I barked.

His next words came slowly, incisively, single-file.

'More — than — you — have — ever — wanted — to — know — anything — before?'

'Yes!' I admitted — and meant it.

'Say it!' he commanded.

I repeated it: *'More — than — I — have — ever — wanted — to — know — anything — before!'*

His manner changed instantly.

'Good! Now we can talk!'

He went down into an inside pocket and produced a morocco wallet. From the wallet, he extracted a folded page.

I did not leave Randolph's house until four o'clock, and when I finally went out into the dark, considerably shaken, I was aware that my life would never be the same again. Whatever of success has come to me in my profession dates from that hour and can be explained in terms of the mysterious potentiality which Randolph communicated to me that night.

I had reached out my hand greedily for the page Randolph unfolded, but he shook his head.

'Not just yet,' he said, smiling at my eagerness. 'I mean to let you see it; but I must tell you something about it, first. This page contains the rules for generating that mysterious power I mentioned. By following these instructions to the letter, you can have anything you want, do anything you wish to do, be whatever you would like to be. I have tried it. It works. It worked for me. It will work for you!'

Combined impatience and incredulity brought a chuckle from me which he did not resent.

'You saw that piece I was working on when you came in this morning?'

'Beautiful!' I exclaimed — sincerely.

'You liked it that much?' He was pleased with my enthusiasm.

'Nothing short of a masterpiece!'

'Perhaps I should be more grateful for that compliment, doctor; but I really have had very little to do with it. . . . You may be interested to learn that I was an ordinary stone-cutter until about three years ago, hacking out stamped letters with a compression chisel. From my youth, I had cherished an ambition to do something important in stone. But there was never any money for training; never any time for experiment. Such crude and hasty attempts as I had made, from time to time, had netted nothing but discouragement.

'One day, I went to the church my little girl attended, and heard a preacher read what is on this page. It evidently meant nothing to him, for he read it in a dull, monotonous chant. And the congregation sat glassy-eyed, the words apparently making no impression. As for me, I was profoundly stirred. The remainder of the hour was torture, for I wanted out where I could think.

'Hurrying home to our bare little house, I found — with considerable difficulty, for I was not familiar with the Bible — that page from which the minister had read. There it was — in black and white — the exact process for achieving power to do, be and have what you want! I experimented.'

With that, Randolph handed me the magic page. Some twenty lines of it were heavily underscored in red ink. In silence he puffed his pipe while my eye traversed the cryptic paragraphs, and when I looked up, inquiringly, he said:

'Of course, you will not realize the full importance of all this, instantly. It seems simple because it was spoken dispassionately, with no oratorical bombast or prefatory warning that the formula he was about to state was the key to power!'

Edging his chair closer to mine, he laid a

long hand on my knee and looked me squarely in the eyes.

'Doctor Hudson — if you had a small, inadequate brick house, and decided to give yourself more room, what would you need for your building? . . . More brick. . . . If you had a small, inadequate steam-engine, you would want more steel to construct larger cylinders — not a different kind of steel to house a different kind of steam, but merely more room for expansion. . . . Now — if you had a small, inadequate personality, and wanted to give it a chance to be something more important, where would you find the building materials?'

He seemed waiting for a reply, so I humored him.

'Well — according to the drift of your argument, I presume I would have to build it out of other personalities. Is that what you're driving at?'

'Pre-cisely!' he shouted. 'But — not "out of"! . . . *Into!* . . . Glad you said that, though; for it gives me a chance to show you the exact difference between the right and wrong methods of making use of other people's personalities in improving one's own. . . . Everybody is aware, instinctively, that his personality is modified by others. Most people go about imitating various scraps and phases of the personalities that have attracted them — copying one man's walk, another's accent, another's laugh, another's trick of gesture — making mere monkeys of themselves. . . . This theory I am talking about doesn't ask you to build your personality *out of* other personalities, but *into* them!'

'I'm afraid all that's too deep for me,' I admitted befuddledly.

He rose and stamped back and forth in front of the grate, shaking his shaggy mop of grizzled hair, and waving his long-stemmed pipe as if trying to conjure a better explanation.

'See here! You know all about blood transfusion. That's in your line. Superb! . . . One man puts his life into another man. . . . Doctor — how do you accomplish a blood transfusion? Tell me in detail!'

I explained the principles of transfusion, briefly, and Randolph seemed mightily pleased, especially with that feature of it which concerned the problem of coagulation.

'You will notice there,' pointing to the page in my hand, 'that this first step toward the achievement of power is an expansion — a projection of one's self into other personalities. You will see that it has to be done with such absolute secrecy that if, by any chance, the contact is not immediate and direct — if, by any chance, there is a leak along the line of transfer — the whole effect of it is wasted! You have to do it so stealthily that even your own left hand —'

Randolph returned to his chair, and went on, in a lowered voice:

'Hudson — the first time I tried it — I can tell you the incident freely because nothing ever came of it, although it had cost me more than I could afford, at the time, to do it — the chap was so grateful he told a neighbor of mine, in spite of my swearing him in. He had been out of work and there had been a long run of sickness in the family, and he was too shabby and down at heel to make a presentable appearance in asking for a job. I outfitted him. He told it. A neighbor felicitated me, next day. So there was more than sixty dollars of my hard-earned cash squandered!'

'Squandered!' I shouted, in amazement. 'How squandered? Didn't he get the job?'

Randolph sighed.

'Oh, yes,' he said. 'He found a job. I was glad enough for that, of course. But — that didn't do *me* any good! You'd better believe — the next time I made an outlay I informed the fellow that if I ever heard of his telling anybody, I would break his neck.'

He laughed merrily at the remembrance of the incident.

'The man thought I was crazy!' he added, wiping his eyes.

'And you weren't?' I inquired, in a tone that sobered him.

'Really — it does sound foolish, doesn't it? I mean — when you first hear of it. I don't wonder you're perplexed.'

'I am worse than perplexed,' I admitted, bluntly. 'I'm disgusted!'

'You might well be,' admitted Randolph, 'if I were trying to get power, that way, to stack up a lot of money for my own pleasure. All I wanted was the effective release of my latent ability to do something fine! . . . And, as for being disgusted because I requested the man not to tell anybody what I had done for him, if that offends you, you wouldn't like the Lord himself! . . . For he often said that to people he had helped.'

'I'm sure I don't know,' I said. . . . 'Not very well acquainted with what he said. . . . Go ahead with your story.'

'Thanks. . . . But, first let me lead you just a little farther into the general philosophy of this. . . . On the night of the day I made my first successful projection of my personality — I cannot tell you what that was — I dare not — I went literally into a closet in my house, and shut the door. That's the next step in the program, as you have read there on that page. You see — I was very much in earnest about this matter; and, having already bungled one attempt, I was resolved to obey the rules to the letter. . . . Later, I discovered that the principle will work elsewhere than in a closet. Just so you're insulated.'

'Oh — Randolph — for God's sake!' I exploded. 'What manner of wild talk is this?'

'I confess I can't understand,' said Randolph, impatiently, 'why you find this so hard to accept! Why — it's in line with our experience of every other energy we use! Either we meet its terms, or we don't get the power. What did Volta's battery or Faraday's dynamo amount to, practically, until Du Fay discovered an insulation that would protect the current from being dissipated through contacts with other things than the object to be energized? . . . Most personalities are just grounded! That's all that ails them!

'So, I went into a closet; shut the door; closed my eyes; quietly put myself into a spiritually receptive mood; and said, confidently, addressing the Major Personality — *I have fulfilled all the conditions required of me for receiving power! I am ready to have it! I want it! I want the capacity to do just one creditable work of statuary!*

'Now — you may be inclined to believe that I experienced a queer delusion, at that moment. As a scientific man, you may think that my mental state can easily be accounted for by principles well known to psychology. If you think that, I have no objection. The fact that a process of achieving power by the expansion of the human personality admits of an explanation, in scientific terms, does not damage its value at all, in my opinion. I dare say the time will come when this matter is made a subject of scientific inquiry.

'But — whether it is explicable or not, I can truthfully assure you that upon finishing my experiment in that closet, I received — as definitely as one receives a shock from an electrode, or a sudden glare of light by opening a tightly shuttered room — a strange inner illumination!

'It was late in the night. I came out of that dark, stifling little closet with a curious sense of mastery. It put me erect, flexed the muscles of my jaw, made my step resilient. I wanted to laugh! I tried to sleep; and, failing of it, walked the streets until dawn. At eight-thirty, I approached the manager of the factory and asked for six months' leave. When he inquired my reason, I told him I had it in mind to attempt a piece of statuary.

' "Something we might use, perhaps?" he asked.

' "I am confident of it," I said, surprised

at my own audacity. It was enough that I had determined to survive somehow, without wages, for six months; but now I had made an extravagant promise to the manager. He was thoughtful for a while and then said:

' "I'll give you a chance to try it. For the present, you are to have your usual pay, and a studio to yourself. If you produce something we can place, you will share in the sale. Your hours will be your own business. I should be glad if you succeeded."

'I began work at once in a flutter of excitement. The clay seemed alive in my hands! That first day was a revelation. It was as if I had never really lived before! All colors were more vivid. I want you to remember that, Hudson. See if you have the same reaction. Grass is greener; the sky is bluer; you hear the birds more distinctly. It sharpens the senses — like cocaine.

'That night, I went into my closet again, and was immediately conscious of a peculiar intimacy between myself and That Other; but it was not so dynamic as on the previous night. I decided that if I was to get any more power that way, I would have to make some further adjustments of my own spiritual equipment.

'That was on a Friday, the tenth of June. On the first day of September, I invited the manager in to see the cast I had made. He looked at it for a long time without any remark. Then he said, quietly, "I have some people who may be interested in this."

'It was the figure of a child, a chubby little fellow about four years old. The boy was posed on one knee. He had just raised up from his play with a little dog that stood tensely alert, in front of him, with a ball in his mouth, waiting for the child to notice him. The boy's shirt was open at the throat. His tight little knickers were buttoned to broad suspenders. The legs were bare to the knee. He was looking straight aloft, his little face all squinted up with baffled amazement, wonderment, curiosity. His small square hand shaded his eyes against a light almost too bright for him, the head tilted at an angle indicating that he had heard something he could not quite understand and was listening for it to be repeated.

'The next afternoon, the manager's clients came in — a man and his wife. She was in black. They had recently lost their little boy. She cried at first, heart-breakingly. But, after a while, she smiled. It made me very happy when she smiled. I knew then that I had been able to express my thought.

'I was told to go on with my project and put it into white marble. . . . Quite incidentally, the people adopted the boy I had used for a model.'

At Home

October 26, 1913, 10 P.M.

It was about four o'clock when I left Randolph's house that night. I was in a grand state of mystification. I went home resolved that I would make an experiment similar to his. Before I went to bed, I tried to project my thoughts to some remote spiritual source, but was conscious of no reaction whatsoever. In the morning I decided that I had been most outrageously imposed upon by an eccentric and scowled at my own reflection in my shaving-mirror. Nobody but a visionary could do these things with any hope of success, and I was, by training and temperament, a materialist and a very cold-blooded one, at that. All that day, however, I was aware of being on a quiet, unrelenting search for some suitable clinical material to be used for an experiment in the dynamics of personality-projection. . . . The strangest feature of my mood, however, was the fact that the power I had begun, rather vaguely, to grope for — under Randolph's urging — was not the mere satisfaction of an ambition to make myself important or minister to my own vanity. . . . For the first time, my profession seemed to me not as a weapon of self-defense but a means of releasing myself!

The last thing Randolph said to me, at the door, was this caution: 'Be careful how you go into this, my friend! I do not know the penalties this energy exacts when misused. . . . I've no notion what dreadful thing might have happened to the Galilean if he had turned those stones into bread! . . . But, I warn you! . . . If you're thinking of going into this to feather your own nest, you'd better never give it another thought. . . . I'm not sure — but I think it's terribly dangerous stuff to fool with!'

My own experiences are hereinafter set forth as possible aids to whomever has had the curiosity to translate this journal. I trust I have made it quite clear why I have chosen this peculiar method of passing it along. Had I ventured to report my experiments, it would have been at the expense of my reputation for sanity. I do not know of a single friend to whom I could have told these things without putting an unpleasant constraint between us. It has been a hard secret to keep. It is equally hard, I am discovering, to confide — even with the realization that these words are unlikely to be read during my lifetime. I dislike the idea of being thought a fool — dead or alive.

You — whoever you are — may be inclined to read on; — perhaps personally interested in making an experiment; perhaps just curious. I wonder — would it be asking an unreasonable favor — if you would not consent to stop, at this point, if you are smiling? . . . You see, some of these experiences of mine have meant a great deal to me, emotionally. I don't believe I should want them laughed at. . . . If the thing hasn't gripped you a little by now, put it down, please, and think no more about it. . . . If however you seriously wish to proceed, let me counsel you, as Randolph counseled me, that you are taking hold of high tension! Once you have touched it, you will never be able to let go. . . . If you are of the temperament that demands self-indulgence to keep you happy and confident enough to do your work — and many inestimably valuable people are so built and cannot help it any more than tall men can help being tall — leave all this alone, and go your way! . . . For if you make an excursion into this, you're bound! It will plaster a mortgage on everything you think you own, and commandeer your time when you might prefer to be using it for yourself. . . . It is very expensive. . . . It took the man who discovered it to a cross at the age of thirty-three!

At Home

October 27, 1913, 2 A.M.

I was required to stop writing last night because of a summons to the hospital and now I find that I cannot go to bed without finishing what I had meant to say. This subject is not to be taken lightly and I hope to safeguard you against any misdirected experiments.

It is important that you should know how serious are the conditions to be met by any man who hopes to increase his own power by way of the technique I pursued under instructions from Randolph.

I must mention them at this juncture, because it is quite possible these words may be read by some impulsive enthusiast who, eager to avail himself of the large rewards promised, may attempt experiments from which he will receive neither pleasure nor benefit; and, dismayed by failure, find himself worse off in mind than he was before.

Indeed, this was my own experience at first, Randolph having neglected to warn me that certain conditions were imperative to success. I learned them by trial and error.

It must be borne in mind, at the outset, that no amount of altruistic endeavor — no matter how costly — can possibly benefit the donor, if he has in any manner neglected the natural and normal obligations to which he is expected to be sensitive. Not only must he be just before attempting to be generous; he must figure this particular investment of himself as a *higher altruism,* quite other than mere generosity.

Every conceivable responsibility must have had full attention before one goes in search of opportunity to perform secret services to be used for the express purpose of expanding one's personality that it may become receptive of that inexplicable energy which guarantees personal power.

My own life had been set in narrow ways. I had had but small chance to injure or defraud, even had I been of a scheming disposition. There had been a minimum of buying and selling in my program. I had lived mostly under strict supervision — in school, in college, and as an intern — with no chance to make many grave or irretrievable blunders.

Once I began to discharge my obligations, however, it was startling to note how considerably I was in the red. For example: I found that there were a good many men, scattered here and there, who had been scratched off my books. Either actually, or to all practical intents, they had been told to go to hell. In some cases, there had been enough provocation to justify my pitching them out of my life, I thought. But, more often than otherwise, they were to be remembered as persons with whom I had sustained some manner of close contact — close enough to make a disruption possible. I discovered that almost without exception the people I had pushed away from me — consigned to hell, if you like — were once intimately associated with me. . . . So far as I was concerned they had gone to hell taking along with them a very considerable part of me!

To lose a friend in whom one had invested something of one's personality was, I discovered, to have lost a certain amount of one's self.

The successful pursuit of the philosophy now before you demands that you restore whatever of your personality has been dissipated, carted off by other people. If any of its essential energy has been scattered, it must be recovered.

The original proposer of this theory, aware of the importance of insuring against such losses, advised that all misunderstandings should be settled on the spot. When an estrangement takes a friend out of your normal contacts with him, he leaves with part of you in his hand. You must gather up these fragments of yourself, by some hook or crook, so that you have at least all of the personality that rightfully belongs to you, before you attempt its larger projection.

In the next place: you may make the mistake of seeking far and wide for opportunities to build yourself into other personalities through their rehabilitation. A happy circumstance kept me from doing that. Strangely enough, the first really important service I was permitted to do, prefatory to experimenting with this mysterious dynamic, was for the daughter of the man who had shown me the way to it. . . . I risked what small repute I had, and put a mortgage on whatever I might hope to acquire, by the performance of an operation that saved her life, and, quite incidentally, brought me three pages of comment in the next edition of the *Medical Encyclopedia.*

BRIGHTWOOD HOSPITAL

Sunday Night, November ninth, 1913

That operation on Natalie Randolph's fractured skull marked the beginning of my specialization in brain surgery, and because of its importance in determining the nature of my professional activities, I feel that the events which immediately preceded it should be recorded here. If you prefer to consider them as coincidental rather than causative, you are quite at liberty to make that deduction. In my own opinion, my investment in Tim Watson and the success of my operation on Natalie Randolph were integrally related.

On Wednesdays and Saturdays, that summer, I was on duty in the Out-patient Department of our Free Clinic. This assignment was extremely distasteful. Ailing indigence, bathed and fumigated and in bed, clad in a sterilized hospital gown, was one thing; sick poverty, on its feet — with black fingernails, greasy clothes, a musty smell, and a hangdog air — was offensive to me. I was not a snob. I was born poor and brought up in a home where the most rigid economies were practiced. The first new suit of clothes I ever owned (it cost sixteen dollars) was purchased when I entered high school. But — all the same — I thoroughly detested those long, hot, midsummer afternoons in the dingy Free Clinic, and I am afraid I made very little effort to disguise my aversion to the dull and dirty patients who grimly applied for its benefits.

For the most part, it was a thankless task. Not many of them co-operated with us. They wouldn't take their medicine according to directions; complained that their treatment did them no good; the majority of them were surly, stupid, and stubborn. Many of the men stank of cheap liquor and tried to wheedle you out of a half-dollar to buy more.

Perhaps if there had been only a few patients to deal with, during an afternoon, one might have been more disposed to analyze their disgusting infirmities with more sympathy and listen to their assorted misfortunes with more interest; but they came too thick and fast for painstaking attention. In my own defense I must insist that it wasn't their poverty that exasperated me, for God knows I was having a struggle to make both ends meet, myself. My salary was small, and it was difficult to economize. Little Joyce required the attention of a full-time practical nurse, who served also as my housekeeper. Those were difficult days, and I was in a position to be sympathetic with any man whose pockets were empty.

But I hated that clinic. Our elders and betters on the hospital staff pretended to believe that it was good practice for us young fellows; but it wasn't. It was the worst training imaginable, tending to make a doctor cold-blooded and careless.

One afternoon in latter August, within a few minutes of the closing hour, a young chap was shown into my cramped cubicle with his left hand bound in a dirty rag. He was about eighteen, six feet tall, lean as a bean-pole. He had a good head, thatched with a tousled mop of the reddest hair I had ever seen. His eyes were blue and edged with premature crow's-feet which gave them a defiant hardness. If it hadn't been for the pair of boyish dimples in his tanned cheeks, he would have looked decidedly tough. He was bareheaded and badly sunburned; wore a soiled gray suit that wasn't big enough for his rangy frame, a blue shirt with a rumpled collar, and a pair of cheap and dusty sneakers.

I pointed indifferently to the other chair. He sat down and began unwrapping the hand.

'Pretty bandage,' I remarked. 'What was it, originally, a shirt-tail?'

He drew a sardonic grin, dropped the rag on the floor, and extended his injured hand.

It was badly swollen and there were deep abrasions across the knuckles.

'Looks as if it's broken,' I guessed.

'Yeah,' he agreed, 'right there: those two metacarpals.'

'Know your bones, eh?' I glanced up and met his eyes. 'What's that called?' I revolved a finger-tip lightly on his wrist.

'Sesamoid.'

'Would you say that was a bone?'

'Umm — well — it's partly cartilage.'

'Want to tell me how you got hurt — and when? This hand has been neglected. It's in bad shape.'

'Last night. The freight was pulling out of the yards and picking up speed faster than I thought. I missed my hold, and fell on my hand.'

'You must have had something in your hand, or you would have met the gravel with your palm down.'

He liked my deduction and his eyes lighted a little.

'That's right,' he said. 'Handful of chocolate bars.'

'You swiped them,' I announced casually.

He nodded and asked me how I knew. And I told him he must have been very hungry to have hung on to the candy when he might have broken his fall more safely with his open hand.

'And if you had had the money to buy the chocolate bars,' I continued, 'you would have bought a hot dog or a hamburger instead.'

'I didn't have time to think which was the safest way to land.'

'That's true,' I agreed. 'When you are very hungry, your stomach does your thinking for you. Are you hungry now?'

He nodded, adding, 'But if you're going to set this hand, I'll need a little ether, won't I?'

'What do you know about such things?' I inquired.

He grinned.

'My father was a doctor,' he said, 'and I've read a lot of his books.' He made a self-deprecatory little gesture. 'About the only books I ever did read. I hated school.'

Having confided that much, he responded to my encouragement and told me some more. His name was Watson. His father had died when he was ten. His mother had married again. The stepfather had resented his presence in their home. After a while, his mother — unable to defend him without a constant battle — began to take sides with her husband, in the interest of peace.

'But I don't blame her,' the boy went on. 'I wasn't very easy to get along with. I played hooky pretty often. And once I operated on a cat. I got licked almost to death for that.'

'How about the cat?' I couldn't help asking.

'He got well. I didn't hurt him. Doped him with chloroform.'

'You'll have to tell me about the operation when we've finished with yours,' I said, rising. 'Come on. I'll fix you up. What's your first name, Watson?'

'Timothy. Tim.'

'All right, Tim. Follow me. No — don't put that rag on again. You're in enough trouble without that.'

As I led him into the operating chamber, he was interested in everything but his injury. I think he would have been willing to undergo an amputation rather than miss the experience of seeing our preparations to reduce his fractures and clean up his cuts. The last thing he said before the anaesthetist put the cone over his lean face was, 'Gee — it must be great to be a doctor!'

They renovated him and put him to bed. I was under no obligation to look at him again that evening; but I went over to the hospital about nine. He was awake — and smiled.

'How does it feel, Tim?' I inquired.

'About the way it ought to, I think.'

'In the morning you may have some ham and eggs for breakfast.'

'And then — I'll be discharged?' he asked, a bit anxiously.

'No — I think we will keep you here for a few days; make sure those scratches heal safely. You hadn't any other plans, had you?'

Tim chuckled.

'Plans!' he echoed. 'Hell — no.'

I surprised myself by saying, 'Well — maybe we can make some. We'll see. I'll drop in again in the morning.'

He reached out his good hand and I took it. At the door, I paused to say, 'Good night.' But his face was turned away, and he did not reply.

BRIGHTWOOD HOSPITAL

November 14, 1913, 8:30 P.M.

The lacerations on young Watson's knuckles showed no signs of infection when I examined him the next morning, and the fractures would take care of themselves. He could have been safely discharged at once. Under ordinary procedure we would have sent him packing without delay. But I couldn't bear to turn him out into the street.

My own early experiences in Detroit had much to do with my interest in this chap. At his age I had wanted to study medicine; an absurd aspiration, for I had no resources at all. My chance came through what seemed at the time to have been a lucky accident. In recent years I have had reasons for changing my mind about 'accidents.' I do not mean that there are no accidents: I mean that many unexpected events, classified as accidents, deserve to be called something else.

My thoughts on this subject are still in a fluid state, but I shall share them with you, my friend, and you may make of them whatever you like.

I am not inviting you to believe (or to believe I believe) that everything occurs by design and decree. Such a theory — if pursued to its logical end — would destroy human freedom and make mere puppets of us all. But I do think that if a man is suddenly interrupted by some unheralded event — not of his own contriving — and is thereby deflected for a time from the course he had been pursuing, he would be well advised to keep his eyes open for some new and valuable opportunity which this circumstance may provide. Even if the so-called accident involves a great deal of pain and hardship, the victim may have a right to suspect that he has been very far off the track leading to the full development and expression of his powers; that severe discipline may be necessary to recondition his mind for a discovery of his unrecognized talents and capacities.

Every day, here at Brightwood, where so many victims of accidents put in for repairs, I see patients who haven't the slightest notion that their experience might be turned to good account. They whine and growl and fret over the discomforts of a tedious convalescence; and, after a few restless weeks of uncapitalized apathy, they pull on their pants and leave, with nothing to show for their time but a receipted hospital bill.

Once in a blue moon, somebody gets the idea that he may have been laid up for a purpose, like a ship in dry-dock getting her barnacles scraped off. To such as these, who have confided to me that they have found comfort in this supposition, I have lent some encouragement; but I have never taken the initiative in such a discussion. In my capacity as a surgeon, I can't go about telling people they have been whacked on the head to give them a chance to reorganize themselves and find out what they are good for. Such talk would quickly discredit a man in my position. His colleagues would crack jokes at his expense. He would soon be regarded as some sort of faith-healer; a quack, at heart; a fellow who plays around with the angels. No — if I'm serving as a surgeon I must be respected as a sound scientist; and there is no room in science — at present — for a theory of this character.

And, curiously enough, everything in me naturally revolts against such notions. Even in the face of my own experiences and observations, if some friend of mine should break down and confide to me his belief that almost nothing happens by accident; that Fate, or a busy-body Providence, or some such otherworldly Mr. Fixit trots about banging misdirected people on the topknot, or laying them low with a lumbar tumor, to the excellent end that they might have time to orient themselves in regard to their gifts, their duties, and their destinies, I should think him a little bit unhooked.

To save his face, I should probably concede that strange things do happen; that many an apparent misfortune has turned out to be a blessing. I might tell him about an eminent lawyer of my acquaintance, whose father owned a planing-mill and wanted his boy to learn the trade; and the boy collided with a saw and lost three fingers, ruining him for a career in the mill. But — all the same — I should privately rate the man an eccentric, who maintained that our seeming accidents are planned for us and our ultimate good, and it wouldn't surprise me if he turned up, some day, with the confidential report that he had just lunched with some prominent member of the Heavenly Host.

You see, my friend, I am trying to be honest with you about all this. It is a dangerous subject to talk about, and surely no man dares be dogmatic when he expresses an opinion on it.

In the laboratory, many an experiment that is utterly bewildering to the layman is clear enough to the chemist. If you pour water into sulphuric acid the effect is far different than if you had poured sulphuric acid into water — a startling phenomenon that baffles the uninformed, though the chemist knows the secret.

But this thing that we have been talking about — you may experiment with it as long as you like, and not know much more about it than when you began. In this field, nobody is an expert; everyone is a layman. And when any man sets out to prove, by his own experience, that we are all in the grip of spiritual forces, he will demonstrate nothing but his mental untidiness.

Doubtless there are plenty of real accidents which shouldn't have happened; involve no hidden purpose; hold no possibilities for good. Almost anybody could compile a few cases in which painful events opened a way to happiness — if not to greatness. I know a woman who broke her leg and wrote a highly successful novel while she was convalescing, but I have seen many women with broken legs who did not write novels or discover any other opportunity to make capital of their enforced leisure. I once amputated an infected arm that had got into trouble with a rusty fish-hook. The fellow was a loafer, with no interest in anything but fish and fishing. It was all he could talk about. We had him with us for weeks, and to entertain him we ransacked the libraries for books about fish. He went out, at length, and found a good job in a government fish-hatchery; and, to the amazement of everybody, distinguished himself as an expert in the disabilities of salmon, or something like that. But I have cared for many a loafer who never amounted to anything afterward.

You can't afford to be doctrinal when you consider accidents as the work of Providence. One man accidentally burns some rubber on the kitchen stove and discovers vulcanization; another fellow has much the same sort of accident and merely sets the house on fire. One man accidentally spills some camphor into a pan of collodion and gets celluloid; another man accidentally upsets a bottle of something into a pan of something else, and goes out through the skylight. One redoubtable reformer gets tossed into jail, and whiles away the time by writing *Pilgrim's Progress*. Another equally good and zealous martyr goes to jail and merely gets lousy.

But the ways of Providence are well worth thinking about, if one can do it in a spirit of inquiry rather than with a determination to organize a cult and enlist disciples. This thing will not stand the strain of being woven into a creed: I am sure of that.

Something tells me, though, that all persons in trouble should be exposed to a consideration of this subject, even if it doesn't obey a formula.

I have often wondered if it might not be an interesting experiment, in a hospital, to hand each patient — on arrival, or as soon as he is able to read anything — a little manual of advice.

As the matter stands, it's nobody's business to offer counsel on this subject. A few stark injunctions are tacked to the wall. Don't clog the plumbing. Don't throw banana-skins out of the window. And so forth. All the advice the patient gets presupposes that he is a destructive fool whose previous experience in public institutions has been limited to the calaboose and the poorhouse.

There is a wide-open market here for some friendly talk to these unhappy guests. The little booklet might run something like this:

We are honestly sorry for people who, through no fault of their own, are obliged to undergo discomfort, pain, and boredom, in this hospital. But it is not our fault, either, that you encountered the illness or accident that brought you here.

This is not a hotel. Hotels must pay their

own way or close up. Hospitals do not pay their way, but they do not close up; for, at the end of the year, the deficit is absorbed by a company of kind-hearted people who believe that we are trying to do our best. We hope you will share in this belief; for it is important to your comfort — and perhaps also to the promptness of your recovery — if you consider this place as a friendly refuge; not a mere money-making repair-shop.

Our nurses are well-trained. Part of this training is in the control of their personal feelings. If they do not seem very much upset over your gas-pains, that does not mean they are indifferent: it means only that they are disciplined. They have many distasteful tasks to perform, and they do them without showing how they feel on the subject; but that does not mean they are insensitive. They are just as human as anyone else; have their own little frets and forebodings; their days of disappointment and depression. Sometimes a patient's cheerfulness will help a nurse to a fresh grip on herself.

Your doctor wants you to get well as rapidly as possible. In this matter, you and he share the same wish. He will appreciate your full co-operation. Some morning when you are feeling unusually well, you may offer him a little witticism, and be dismayed to note that he fails to respond to it. But that isn't because he is indifferent. More likely it is because he has just put in an hour and a half of tense and trying service in the operating-room; and he doesn't feel jocular. If he can sense your sympathetic understanding of his mood, your attitude will be of much benefit to him.

In short — if you want to get the largest degree of satisfaction out of your experience in this hospital, join hands with us, almost as if you were a member of the organization. If you believe in the hospital, and in the skill and sincerity of the doctors and nurses, you will not be troubled by the little vexations and irritations which menace the peace of many patients.

Perhaps we, who are devoting our energies to the care of the sick and injured, should be contented if we were able to dismiss you fully restored and sound as you were before.

But we have an ambition still higher than that. It would gratify us immensely if — when you leave us to resume your activities — you might go out not only repaired physically but reinvigorated in mind and heart.

In the normal ways of an uneventful life, people do not often have a chance to find out how much pain they can endure, or how long they can wait. Here they can take their own measure, and discover their strengths. Many a man, in peace-time, has wondered how stalwart he might be on a battle-field, facing danger, risking agonies. Circumstances may provide him a chance to learn, in the hospital, whether he has what it takes to be a good soldier. We do not conduct these examinations. The patient examines himself, and marks his own grade. Ever afterward he will be pleased and proud if he passes with credit. No matter what may happen to him, in the future, he will always know exactly how much disappointment, anxiety, inconvenience, and pain he can stand. It's worth something to a man to find that out. So — if you have been informed that the doctor is taking out your stitches tomorrow, you can do yourself a good turn — that will last you all your life — if you face up to this in the morning without flinching. You have always wondered, when you saw others in trouble, whether you could take it. Now you know. It's a very gratifying thing: almost everybody finds out that he is braver than he thought he was. It's worth going through a lot of perplexity and pain — just to be assured on that matter.

Sometimes people who hadn't succeeded in making anything very important of themselves — either inside or outside of themselves — have discovered, during the enforced leisure of a convalescence, certain neglected gifts which they have thereafter exercised to their immeasurable satisfaction.

In many instances, this self-discovery has resulted in such a marked expansion of interest and success in after-life, that the beneficiary has wondered whether Destiny had not shunted him off his course in order to let him take stock of his resources.

We suggest, therefore, that you give a little thought to this subject while you are with us. Was it an accident? Was it a misfortune? Was it a mishap that brought you here? Think this over. We think about it a great deal.

Young Watson's case vividly recalled my own first acquaintance with Detroit. It was in mid-August. We had threshed the wheat, the day before, and my father and my uncle were starting, that morning, on a few days' fishing trip. I had strongly hinted that I should like to go along, but there seemed no room for me.

Barnum and Bailey's big show was to be in Detroit that day. I knew better than to ask if I might go. I had saved something like six dollars, which would be ample to cover expenses; but I knew I should be reproached if I squandered my money in this manner. But, having been left out of the fishing excursion, after a hard summer's work, I felt that I was badly treated and would be quite justified if I helped myself to a day's outing.

Father and Uncle Jim were to start at five. I quietly sneaked out of the house at four, walked three miles to the little station at Wimple, and waited for the milk-train to come along. Arriving in Detroit at noon, I took a street-car to the circus grounds where I spent one of the most exciting days of my life. I saw it all; the menagerie, the demobilization of the garish parade, the circus and spectacular pageant 'The Burning of Rome.' I also patronized several units of the side-show. It was six-thirty before I left the grounds and boarded a crowded street-car for the business district. My train did not leave until nine-thirty.

After a long ride, we were clanging through brighter lights and heavier traffic, so I got off and sauntered along the edges of the crowd on the broad pavement, staring into the shop-windows. Besides my return ticket, I had a little money left, and decided to look for a cheap restaurant. There didn't seem to be one on this street, so I turned the corner and walked a couple of blocks, looking for an eating-place that might fit my resources.

Presently I came to a café that had a very imposing front. Several very elegant turnouts were drawn up along the curb, the drivers lounging near their horses' heads. I ambled past, inspecting them with admiration. A tall, handsome man with a flushed face lurched out of the café and walked unsteadily down the street, pausing before a pair of beautiful roans harnessed to an open stanhope. One of the drivers called to his neighbor, 'Doc's pretty well oiled.'

I followed along slowly, though it wasn't much like me to take a curious interest in anyone's humiliation. The near horse, tied to the hitching-post, had tugged his bridle off and seemed about to bolt. 'Doc' was making an unsuccessful effort to put the bridle on.

'Let me do it,' I said.

'All right,' he said, thickly, 'if you think you can.'

It wasn't easy to do, for the horse was nervous, but I managed.

'You know how to drive?' asked Doc. 'I'll give you two dollars if you drive me home.'

I told him I had to take a train at nine-thirty, but if he thought I could drive him home and get back in time, I would do it — adding that I didn't want to be paid for it. My attitude seemed to please him; for, shortly after we started, he professed an interest in me. I told him where I lived; that I had come to the circus; that this was the first time I had ever been in the city alone; that I wished I could stay in the city; that I didn't like to work on the farm; that I wouldn't stay on the farm if there was any chance to get away. All this was in reply to questions, for I was not naturally garrulous.

Then it was 'Doc's' turn. He told me he was Doctor Cummings. My heart gave a hard bump. We often read of Doctor Cummings in the papers. He was said to be one of the finest surgeons in the country. It was hard to believe that I was sitting by his side, driving him home. And he was talking to me as if I really was somebody. He told me that his hostler had been away for two days on a spree; couldn't depend on the fellow any more; wondered if I could stay and look after the horses until he could find another man.

I did not pause to consider what my father might think of this, nor how much my mother might worry if I failed to show up at home. All I could think of was the fact that I should be working for a doctor — one of the greatest doctors! I said I would stay.

'And so you don't like the farm,' remarked Doctor Cummings. 'Anything else in mind?'

'I'm afraid you'd laugh, sir,' I confessed, adding, 'I have never told anybody.'

'But me,' encouraged Doctor Cummings, 'and I won't tell.'

'I want to be a doctor,' I confided, 'but I'm afraid it's no good. We haven't the money. I'm not even sure my father can afford to send me to high school.'

He didn't say anything for a while. Then he asked me my name and I told him. Then there was another long silence.

'So — you are not interested in anything but medicine; is that right?' he said, rousing from what must have been a little nap.

'That — and swimming,' I replied.

'You like to swim?'

'Yes, sir.'

'Then I suppose you must swim pretty well.'

'Like a water spaniel,' I boasted. 'If I can't be a doctor, I'll have to be a professional swimmer.'

There was another long pause.

'Well — you stay here for a while, Wayne, and look after my horses,' said Doctor Cummings, 'and we will see what we can do. I don't think there's much of a future in swimming.'

So — that was how I got my chance to study medicine. I began it by being Doctor Cummings' shadow. I was his hostler, errand boy, and diplomatic agent. Drunk or sober, he was always kind to me. And he gave me my opportunity to go to school. If it had not been for my meeting him, that night, when he needed someone to look after him, my whole life might have been set in a different key.

Perhaps that circumstance was accidental; but I don't think so.

AT HOME

November twentieth, 1913, 9 P.M.

During that summer I frequently spent Sunday evenings with Randolph. On these occasions I would finish at the hospital about four and drive home in the primitive but expensive Cadillac that Joyce had bought before we went to Arizona — an extravagance we could not afford, but it was her money. And I didn't have the heart to tell her how low we were in funds. She was not to be here long, and it was no time to be economical.

After making sure that my little girl was being properly cared for (it would presently be her bedtime), I would drive out to Randolph's sequestered home on the north side, where there would be a light supper and some good talk, with my host usually initiating the conversation. I think it was these serious but stimulating chats with Randolph that sustained my spirit through that perplexing period. But for him I fear I might have found my professional duties too irksome to be borne. I had very little work to do that presented any challenge. The nearest approach to it had been an emergency case — a pretty bad concussion — that had come in, late one night, when the only ranking surgeon available was Doctor Pyle, who, though a very able abdominal man, never tackled a head if there was anybody else at hand competent to do it. This operation wouldn't wait; and Pyle, remembering that I had been much attracted to brain surgery while in school, summoned me in. It was not a difficult operation — as such things go — and the patient made a prompt recovery, as he should have done. I lived on the thrill of that experience for many days. But events calculated to stir my interest and professional pride were few and far between. It was Randolph who held me up.

Looking back from this distance, I think Randolph was wise in not pressing me too urgently with his strange theory. After the first few days' enchanted wistfulness, following the night when Randolph confided his secret for more important living, the sheen faded perceptibly from this promising prospect. This was, of course, inevitable. It is very difficult to endure an unabating emotional storm, even if that were desirable. And I want to call your attention to this fact, before it is overlooked.

If you, my friend, are moved to a deep interest in this subject, keep it in mind that your resolve to pursue it does not insure you against the inescapable sag that follows an unaccustomed emotional exaltation. If this thing really lays hold upon you, it is likely that you will feel — for a few days, at least — as if you had come into the possession of some magic, good for all weathers; and, when you find the same old rain dampening your spirit as usual, you are very apt to say, 'Oh — what the hell!' Let me assure you that this witchery does not guarantee against any further experience of boredom; neither does it pledge that from henceforth you will enjoy all your routine tasks and smile steadily at your disappointments.

In other words — don't consider this thing as a Pullman car in which you have engaged a berth, with the understanding that it will carry you forward — waking or sleeping — toward your desired destination.

Randolph made no effort to fan the flame he had lighted in me. To the contrary, he counseled an exercise of cool common-sense in accepting the theory that had literally transformed his life.

'Some day,' he would remark placidly, 'you will find a project, and then you can attempt an experiment. But don't go feverishly sniffing about for a beneficiary. That would certainly put you into the wrong state of mind. It would mean that you wanted to do someone a service with the expectation of material reward.'

And I needed this counsel, too; for that's what I had been doing. For example: there was an old orderly at the hospital who had been there for a long time, and couldn't keep up with his job. They let him out, and I promptly nosed into his affairs to see if I could do him some little kindness. I was emphatically snubbed by the family, for they considered me a part of the heartless hospital organization that had tossed the old man out onto the scrap-pile for the relatives to gather up. He was a surly old codger, and before I had finished my proffered ministration I realized that I had picked the wrong fellow for clinical material. I told Randolph about it and he grinned.

'Better let the family attend to such matters,' he advised. 'It is their responsibility and it will be good for them to accept it. It is quite possible, though,' he added, with a twinkle, 'that the family's haughty repudiation of your interest in papa will require them to take much better care of him than they might have if you hadn't welded them together with their own outraged pride. So — perhaps it isn't a total loss — what you did.'

And we had a middle-aged nurse who was worried over the truancy of her twelve-year-old boy. This problem had provided the woman with so many alibis that I decided to look into the case. The boy was indeed a problem. While I was trying to think of something to do about it, I observed that the incorrigible's silly mother — utterly mistaking my motives — coyly conceived the idea that I was interested in her. When it became clear that she was even more eager to help me than I was to help her obnoxious son, we both dropped the matter by mutual consent.

Randolph was amused. 'Don't grow impatient for an opportunity,' he said. 'Doubtless you will recognize it when it comes.'

Young Watson had been in the hospital since Wednesday afternoon's clinic. I think he knew I should have discharged him, for he was bright and uncommonly well versed — for a youngster and a layman — in medical procedure.

On the Sunday of which I am writing now, he had said, when I called in the morning to see him, 'You have been very good to me, Doctor Hudson. But I shouldn't stay much longer.'

'Want to go?' I asked.

'It isn't that,' he replied, 'but I am well now.'

'Have you any place — in particular — to go?'

'N — no,' he confessed, 'but it doesn't matter much — does it — whether I go out bumming it today — or Tuesday?'

'We'll make it Tuesday,' I said, reproaching myself for implying that there might be a solution to his problem in a day or two. There was nothing I could do for him. I might have tried to find him some menial job, but even that would have been impossible with his broken hand. It would be five or six weeks before he would have any practical use of it. I couldn't support him until he was able to work at starvation wages. I had no room for him in my apartment. No — it was quite out of the question.

That evening, Randolph and young Natalie and I had supper under the big maple on their secluded rear lawn; and, after the girl had excused herself, we sat smoking our pipes. Randolph wanted to know, after a considerable pause in the conversation, whether anything interesting had happened in the hospital. It had been a fairly typical, fairly tiresome week, I said. The clinics had been about as drab and dirty as ever.

'Just one enlivening, and rather perplexing incident,' I went on. 'A young fellow came in the other day with a broken hand; hurt it falling off a freight-car; quite an unusual chap, for a tramp; very likable boy; left home on account of family trouble; the old stock story of a beastly stepfather and a mother who is badgered into being a stepmother; deceased father a doctor; the boy had access to his medical library; pretty well posted on Physiology. I could have discharged him, almost at once, but I didn't like to turn him loose.'

Randolph blew several smoke-rings, but made no comment.

'I'll have to let him go, in a couple of days,' I continued. 'He can't work with a broken hand; and, in any case, he has no training for a city job. Eventually — after he is sick of tramping and riding on freight trains — he'll have to stop somewhere and work on a farm. Might amount to something, I think, if he were taken in hand. But I can't see it as my job.' I paused to give my host a chance to make some rejoinder. Randolph, with his eyes half closed and his head tipped back, continued to blow smoke-rings.

'He's probably a bum — at heart,' I went on. 'Probably couldn't settle down to anything requiring perseverance.' I puffed meditatively on my pipe for a while, and asked, 'What do you think?'

Some moments elapsed before he gave any sign that he had heard what I had been saying;

just sat there blowing rings and staring into the darkening sky and the arriving stars. Then he slowly turned toward me, drew a short sigh, smiled apologetically, and said, 'Forgive me, Hudson. I'm afraid I was wool-gathering. It's such a glorious night! Shall we go in? The dew is falling. Besides — I want to beat you at chess.'

I felt rebuffed. It was not at all like Randolph to be so inattentive. We rose and walked toward the house, his hand in the crook of my arm, as if to reassure me of his comradeship. On the doorstep he paused, detaining me, and said — just above a whisper, 'I didn't mean to be so rude.'

It miffed me a bit to have Randolph binding up my babyish bruises, and blotting my tears and blowing my little nose for me; and I replied, crisply, 'I didn't mean to be so uninteresting.'

He refused to be annoyed; chuckled a little; gave me a friendly slap on the shoulder, and said, 'You were not uninteresting, Hudson; you were just unimpressed.'

'By the sky — you mean?'

'Well — the sky is impressive, tonight; that's a fact.'

We played chess until eleven. Randolph came along out with me to the gate. As I climbed into my car, he said, 'Be careful now,

Hudson. Good night. God bless you!'

It was an odd thing for Randolph to say. Be careful. God bless you. Almost as if he was giving me farewell advice. In the guarded, urgent tone of one sending another forth on some sort of hazardous mission. Be careful now. God bless you. The words resounded in my ears.

That night I went through my modest wardrobe, remembering that Watson was about my height, though lacking fifteen pounds of my weight, and selected a suit of clothes for him. And a couple of shirts and some collars.

There was a small room in the apartment which had been used as a 'den.' I had my books in there, a desk, a couple of chairs; but the room could be spared. I dragged everything into my bedroom. Next morning, on the way to the hospital, I stopped at a furniture store and bought an inexpensive cot.

I wasn't sure that Watson would be willing to avail himself of my hospitality, but I had decided to put it up to him. He was up in the solarium when I called on him at ten.

'Tim,' I said, 'I am going to let you go now.'

'Yes, sir,' said Tim. 'I'm ready.'

'But — I should like to have you stay with me, at my home, for a few days. You are well enough to be out of the hospital, but not quite well enough to be on the road. Will you do that?'

Tim shook his head.

'It wouldn't be fair,' he said. 'I'm not going to impose on you. You don't owe me anything. You've done enough.'

'But I'm afraid I should fret about you — and you don't want me losing sleep on your account. Better do as I say. You will be at liberty to go — any time you like.'

He drew a quizzical face and did not reply for some moments.

'All right,' he agreed, reluctantly. 'But I don't want to be a panhandler. Maybe there's something I could do to help myself.'

'We'll see,' I said.

I drove him home at noon.

'I can wash your car,' said Tim.

'That's good,' I said. 'It needs it.'

When I got up, the next morning, I found Tim running a dry mop around the edge of the rugs, holding the end of the handle under his left arm, and making a very satisfactory job of it, too.

I had a notion to tell him he needn't try to do any work under such conditions, but fortunately thought better of it. If he wanted to make an effort to show his gratitude, he had a right to do it.

I have had many occasions to meditate on this subject. Anyone who has had experience in giving — and getting — knows that it is much easier to be generous than grateful. Generosity expands you; builds you up; stiffens your spine. But if you are on the receiving end of this philanthropy, you either have to do something to earn it and demonstrate your gratitude, or the gift is likely to tear you down. It is indeed more blessed to give than to receive.

And I think that what passes sometimes for ingratitude is an insurmountable feeling of chagrin. It should be kept in mind that any gift — no matter how much it may seem to be to a man's immediate advantage — can do him a permanent injury if it has the effect of damaging his pride. Persons who find delight in helping others should exercise the greatest of tactfulness.

Of course any sensible person will agree to this, for it is so obvious; but it is not easy to practice. One time I gave a fairly good suit of clothes to a fellow; and, because he looked hungry, I put a dollar into one of the pockets. He had no opportunity to find the money, in my presence. I had found a box, so that the chap wouldn't have to go down the street with his new possessions over his arm. Early the next morning, he showed up at my door with the dollar, and I told him to keep it, which he did with honest reluctance. Afterward it occurred to me that I had made a serious mistake. The man thought it quite possible that I had overlooked the dollar. He wanted to demonstrate his integrity. If I had permitted him to do this gracious thing for me, it would doubtless have gone a long way toward repairing his self-esteem which had suffered when he accepted the clothing.

My proper move in this affair was to receive the dollar — and without making too much fuss about it, which would have been equivalent to saying that I was amazed to find such nobility in a man who looked so crooked. Had I merely thanked him respectfully for the money, in the same way I might have thanked my neighbor for restoring something I had lost, my dealings with him would have been perfect. He would have had the clothes, and the consciousness that he had also my esteem, which might have meant a great deal more to him — at that stage of his unfortunate experiences — than the clothes. There's a lot of very careless, thoughtless, injurious charity. It takes more brains to give something away than to sell it.

I let Tim Watson do anything he wanted to try to do, about the apartment. He dusted all of my books, he cleaned and refilled my pens, he answered the telephone with all the dignity of an experienced butler. You would have thought he was in the employ of some very important person. This may sound silly, but I think Tim did me and my professional standing a great deal of good on the telephone — even if my young colleagues at the hospital did tease me about it.

'This is Doctor Wayne Hudson's residence.' . . . 'May I ask who is speaking, please?' . . . 'Thank you. I shall see if the doctor is at liberty to come to the telephone.'

I know that Tim's technique was ever so much better than mine. I had been in the habit of scurrying to the telephone and saying, 'Hullo.' Tim cured me permanently of that careless, self-damaging method of answering a telephone call. It seemed to please him greatly when I thanked him for the favor. I think he grew a couple of inches. He replied, tactfully, that 'a scientific man, with lots of important things on his mind, couldn't pay much attention to such small matters.' It did Tim a vast amount of good to contrive an apology for me that would save my face.

Soon I discovered that it was one of the most fascinating games I had ever played — this casting about for occasions which might build

Tim up. And I think that his gratifying response to my constructive efforts in his behalf assured me that any sacrifice I might have to make for him would be justified.

It delighted me to see that what I was doing for Tim had not only done his personality no damage, but was rapidly calling out good talents which he had never been given a chance to exercise.

Little Joyce helped, too. She immediately became devoted to him. If she needed any spoiling, at that early period of her life — which I can't believe possible — Tim slavishly attended to it; and the undisguised affection she showered upon him must have made him feel exalted. Sometimes a man will get much the same quality of spiritual uplift from his dog. Dogs make good evangelists because they overlook so many obvious imperfections. One can't say as much for cats, who seem to have no capacity for concealing their contempt.

BRIGHTWOOD HOSPITAL

November twenty-fifth, 1913, 10:30 P.M.

Nancy Ashford and I have been holding an informal conference in my office for the past hour. Sometimes I wonder how I could get along without her uncommonly wise counsel. I'm afraid I have come to take Nancy too much for granted. If anything were to happen to her, I might find out how heavily I had depended on her business efficiency and loyal comradeship.

The past few days have been exceptionally trying. I should not have thought it possible for a nine-year-old child to stir up so much excitement. It seems clear enough now that a public school is no place for Joyce; at least, not yet. So we have gone back to the nurse-governess idea. Nancy found the new teacher — a Miss Wingate — who gives promise of being a good choice. She is considerate but she will be firm. She is well-balanced and has the instincts of a lady. Joyce likes her — so far. One has to make allowances for my child's willfulness and instability. We have had too many different types of people working on this job. But I couldn't be both father and mother.

It has often struck me as a peculiar thing that so many people, who have been able to redirect and improve the lives of comparative strangers, are helpless when they try to do something beneficial for their own flesh and blood.

I raised this question with Nancy tonight, and she offered an explanation. Persons living restless, unhappy, undisciplined lives are so because they are in a battle with themselves. Their conscience gets after them for their misdemeanors, and shames them until they resent any counsel from their 'censor mind.' Nancy thinks it a fallacy to believe that conscience is always a wise counselor. She holds that a conscience is just as likely to be defective as a thyroid gland. That is to say, an over-active thyroid can throw one's whole emotional machinery out of balance; and an over-zealous conscience can be so brutally intolerant and tactless that it destroys what little self-esteem you have left, after committing some indiscretion.

I couldn't help showing my amusement over this fantastic theory, but Nancy stood by her guns.

'That's why some children resent parental advice,' she continued. 'They are constantly besieged by an abnormally energetic conscience; and they are so integrally blood-related to their parents, and have so many quirks and kinks in common, that father's admonition is just another annoying harangue of the sort that the conscience delivers.'

'I gather, then,' said I, 'that a child's unwillingness to heed her father's advice is not because she lacks a conscience — but has too much of it'; and then added, 'Nancy, sometimes you have the foolest ideas — but I'll admit they satisfy, even when they haven't a leg to stand on.'

'I'd rather hold on to a legless idea that had the makings of consolation in it,' she replied, 'than a sound idea that makes you unhappy.'

'But you have given up Santa Claus,' I drawled.

'Yes — and that was a mistake. I was much happier when I believed in Santa Claus,' she said, pensively, '— and better, too.'

'You couldn't be any better than you are, Nancy,' I said. 'I never knew anyone with a sweeter soul.'

She shook her head a little, smiled, rose, said 'Good night,' and closed the door softly behind her. That's the way it always is when I express some appreciation: Nancy thinks of an errand she has to do without delay.

I wish I could obey the dictates of my own

heart. Maybe Nancy shares that wish. We have never discussed it. She is absolutely indispensable to this hospital. She is its brain and soul. She has an important ministry here. Everybody leans on her; the staff, the nurses, the patients. I have no right to disrupt this relationship. Sometimes I have almost permitted my desire to get the better of me in this matter. I think I know how she feels. Perhaps I could break her down and override her convictions about her clearly appointed duty. If I told Nancy that I needed her more than Brightwood, she might agree; but she would never be happy about it — and neither would I.

Once, a couple of years ago — we were still down in the old building in Cadillac Square — she came into my office with an open telegram in her hand and the tears running down her cheeks. Her father was dead. I impulsively drew her into my arms and she pressed her forehead hard against my white coat; then laid her cheek against my heart and clung to me tightly for a long moment. I was much moved. Presently she released herself, glanced up, dabbed at the corners of my eyes with her handkerchief — an act very like the one she had performed almost every day in the operating-room when she was a surgical nurse and would wipe the perspiration from my face — and said, softly, 'Thanks — for the tears.' But there has never been a repetition of such mutual affection, and it has not always been easy to be restrained.

On several occasions I have observed that it has been comparatively easy to finance an investment in somebody else, when it would have been difficult to do as much for myself. I do not pretend to understand this; much less explain it. I simply state it as a fact, and you may appraise it for whatever it seems to be worth.

On the tenth day of September, 1905, I was so hard up that it was doubtful whether I could pay the month's current bills in full; yet, on that day, I decided to make arrangements for Tim Watson to enter the university at my expense.

I sold the Cadillac for seven hundred dollars, a good price. The car had cost a great deal more, but that was all it was worth now, and I was lucky to get that much. It would be a long haul to sponsor Watson through college and the medical school. And I wouldn't have a car to fetch to market every September. But I was ready to take the risk, and see what came of it.

I asked for the next day off, and went to Ann Arbor. Everybody was gracious and co-operative. I engaged a room for Tim, and found a place where he could work for his board; had a conference with the Registrar; even had the audacity to call on President Angell, and came away feeling that I amounted to something. It was a great day for me. When I walked down to the station to take the train home, I wore a broad smile. People whom I passed gave me a second look, and sometimes they grinned. I remembered what Randolph had said about his own sensations. He had declared that the grass was greener, the sky bluer. It was a fact! One became acutely conscious of the birds. All colors were more vivid. The people on the street seemed more friendly, more alive. I had done something to myself: there was no doubt of that.

I had not told anyone where I was going. During the day, several calls had come in at the house inquiring for me, and were informed that I was at the hospital, and called back to say I was not there. Tim was getting anxious. I found him pacing the pavement in front of the apartment house when I arrived at seven.

'Hope I haven't worried you,' I said. 'I have been to Ann Arbor, arranging for you to enter college, a week from Wednesday. It's all settled — your pre-medic course.'

Tim said nothing. He seemed stunned. He held his red head on one side, quizzically, staring at me with a stupefied incredulity that made me laugh. I led the way in, and he followed me like a sleep-walker. We went up to the apartment where the middle-aged maid met us saying that dinner was ready and drying up.

'If you'll excuse me,' mumbled Tim, 'I don't want any.' He went to his little room and shut the door.

'What's the matter with him?' asked Lizzie, grimly.

'He'll be all right,' I said. 'Keep something warm for him.'

About nine o'clock he came into our small living-room and sat down close beside me.

'Doctor Hudson —' he began, nervously.

'Don't try to make a speech, Tim,' I interposed. 'You're going to be a doctor; and doctors aren't often very good speech-makers. I know how you feel. You are very happy — and so am I. I have never been this happy before.'

'I'll do my best,' gulped Tim.

'I know you will,' I declared. 'Now — I want you to promise me that you will never tell this to a living soul. It is nobody's business but ours how you got a chance to go to the university. It is our secret. I have a reason — and a very good one — for wanting this to remain private. Will you promise?'

Tim promised — and we shook hands on it.

Two Sundays elapsed before I went out to see Randolph again. I had phoned what time I would be there and he was waiting for me at the gate. I had gone out on a street-car, getting off at the nearest point, two blocks away.

'I see you're afoot,' said Randolph, extending his hand. 'Car laid up?'

'Sold it,' I said, casually. 'Hadn't much use for it. Street-cars go everywhere and are less expensive.'

It was too chilly to have supper on the lawn. A table had been set up in the living-room near the fireplace. The maid was off duty and Natalie served us. I had not noticed before how rapidly the girl was blossoming into a young woman. She was becoming very pretty.

Ordinarily, when Natalie had supper with us, she made no effort to participate in the conversation and excused herself promptly when the coffee came on. Tonight she was willing to talk. Randolph seemed surprised and pleased. I drew her out, and she chattered about her school, her teachers, and the thrill she was having — every afternoon — at a riding academy. It was her first close acquaintance with horses, and she was having the time of her young life. Natalie seemed a different person. She had never before paid me the compliment of showing the slightest interest in me. Now she looked me squarely in the eyes and talked animatedly, as if we were long-time comrades and contemporaries.

When she left us, for a moment, to bring on the salad, Randolph chuckled a little, and said, 'I don't know what you've done to Natalie.'

'She's a charming girl,' I said. 'I'm glad she wanted to talk.'

'I think,' said Randolph, slowly, 'she has just discovered something in you that she had not recognized before; a high capacity for friendship, maybe.'

It was a delightful evening. Natalie went to her own room, about ten, shaking hands with me before she left and saying, very prettily, that I must come again soon. I was much stirred and a little bewildered, too, over this unaccustomed attention.

Randolph and I discussed almost everything of current interest. I surprised myself by taking the lead in most of our conversation. When I rose to go, he said, 'You're in uncommonly high spirits tonight, Hudson. Perhaps your work at the hospital is growing more pleasant.'

'Yes,' I replied. 'I have really enjoyed it, lately.'

Randolph looked me steadily in the eyes and drew a sly smile, accompanied by a slow wink.

I grinned, in spite of my effort to be poker-faced. He reached out his hand and I took it. He laid his other hand on our warm clasp and affectionately patted my fingers.

'I am very happy for you, my friend,' he said, softly. 'It is easy to see that life has taken on a new meaning for you.'

And that was true. I had begun to live!

Perhaps I have been tedious in my presentation of the circumstances which preceded my operation on Natalie Randolph's head; but, to an understanding of my state of mind in that event, it is important that you shall have had the whole situation laid before you.

The investment I had made in Tim Watson might or might not be the making of him: but it had already begun to appear that it was going to be the making of me.

My relation to the hospital changed, almost overnight. The new vigor I felt within myself must have shown through, for not only did I approach my tasks with an entirely different attitude but it was easy to see that the personnel of the hospital had noted the change in me. These observations were, for the most part, inarticulate, but they were certified to in various ways. By some I was regarded with wide-eyed curiosity; by others with unusual displays of personal interest and friendship.

On the following Wednesday morning, Doctor Shafter, who was then considered the best brain surgeon in town, asked me if I would assist him in an operation that afternoon. I replied that I should like to, but that I was on duty in the Free Clinic. Within a half hour, Doctor Means — our superintendent — sent word that I was to be relieved at the Clinic so that I might be with Doctor Shafter. I felt very proud of this assignment. Incidentally, I was never sent to the Free Clinic again.

It would be difficult for me to explain what were the outward manifestations of my new relation to life and work. Perhaps my recognition of this new and vital force had found immediate expression in my manner and behavior. The old indifference was gone. I had acquired — without conscious effort — a confident stride, a more erect carriage, a capacity for making every motion count. The thing — whatever it was — had actually deepened my voice and given it a new resonance. When I gave an order, people hustled; not as if they were scared, but anxious to serve.

However much my colleagues and the nurses may have been bewildered over my strange metamorphosis, they weren't any more bewildered than I was. Crusty old Pyle came the nearest to voicing what must have been the general consensus about my case when he stopped me in the corridor long enough to remark, dryly, 'They say that even a blind pig will find an acorn once in a while. Congratulations!'

Natalie Randolph was brought into the hospital at four-thirty in the afternoon of November twenty-seventh. She had been thrown from a horse, striking her head on the hard asphalt pavement. The nearest available physician — a Doctor Juniper (since deceased) — had made a hasty examination and prompt arrangements with the hospital. The ambulance made a quick trip. Doctor Means, locating me by telephone in the Men's Surgical, told me of the accident and said that Mr. Randolph wished me to be on hand when Natalie arrived.

She was quite a pathetic little figure in her trim riding habit. Her face was scratched and already purplish; her corn-yellow curls were matted and stained with blood. Frequently, in such cases, there is a brief revival of consciousness before the coma settles in; but Natalie had not roused. Her respiration was irrhythmic, almost undetectable in its declensions. The injury was a compound parietal fracture, the deepest one I had ever seen.

My afflicted friend Randolph hovered close to the table. His face was ghastly white but he had himself well in hand.

'How about it?' he whispered. I shook my head, and told him it looked very bad. 'But you'll do something; won't you?' he asked, desperately.

'Perhaps not immediately,' I replied. It was going to be hard to tell Randolph the truth.

Doctor Means, assuming that Doctor Shafter would be called in, had telephoned his house immediately upon hearing of the accident, only to learn that the surgeon was on a train enroute for Chicago where he was to spend the next day — Thanksgiving — with his daughter.

But after a brief consultation it was agreed that an operation was impractical.

'I don't think Shafter would touch it,' muttered Pyle. Then he turned to Randolph and said, 'I'm afraid there is very little to be done here, sir.'

Randolph clutched at my sleeve and tugged me a little way apart.

'Hudson,' he whispered, 'will you try? I know that some life-giving energy has come to you, lately. Perhaps you will be able to accomplish a great act here. I trust you completely. May I tell them that you will operate, at my request?'

It was a terrific responsibility, and for a moment I was at a loss for words. I wondered what my elders and betters would think of my audacity if I consented to attempt something that even the experienced Shafter — in Pyle's opinion — would not venture upon. While I debated this serious problem, Randolph stepped back into the group about the table and announced, in a firm voice, 'Gentlemen, I have asked Doctor Hudson to operate.' Nobody looked up. I could feel their reaction.

Doubtless if Natalie had been less gravely hurt, there might have been further deliberation; perhaps a suggestion that we had better wait until Shafter could be returned; perhaps a protest from Pyle that it wouldn't be fair to commit so difficult a task to a young surgeon with no more experience than I had had in the repair of head injuries. But no one protested. In this case it really made very little difference what was done or by whom.

Pyle's only comment to me was, 'It's too bad, my boy, that you are expected to do this. But we all know the circumstances, and we'll see to it that it does you no damage. Mr. Randolph thinks you can do it, and his wishes should be served. You haven't the ghost of a chance, but Randolph will have the satisfaction of knowing that an attempt was made.'

I consented to try, but decided to wait a few hours until we had suppressed the hemorrhage by introducing a hypertonic solution. It was almost three o'clock in the morning before I felt that the surgery might be attempted.

Curiously enough, my hope began to mount from the moment I started the operation. Perhaps it was Randolph's amazing faith that I could do it; perhaps my awareness of the new strength I had lately found gave me confidence. It surprised and delighted me to find myself working with steady hands, and not a trace of nervousness. And when, at last, I made the final suture, I had a feeling that Natalie might recover. I went to Randolph, as soon as I had washed up. He was keenly anxious, but bright with hope.

'You have saved her — I think,' he said, questing my eyes for assurance.

'We must wait — and see,' I replied, prudently; but Randolph knew, by my tone, that I was not disheartened. He wrung my hand, and murmured, 'God bless you!'

If you are interested in the history of this case, from a professional standpoint, you will find it fully documented in the *Medical Encyclopedia* (edition of 1907). You will note that this was the first occasion when depressed fragments of bone were approached by a rongeur through a burr-hole opening in the adjacent normal skull. This technique is quite common practice now, but it had never been tried before. And it wouldn't have been attempted then if the case had been less desperate.

It was indeed a very close thing — our saving Natalie. And the operation was by no means the end of our dilemma. We had a post-traumatic hematoma on our hands that required the most vigilant watching and care for the next three weeks. But Natalie slowly recovered. Her appreciation of my solicitude was very sweet, and our friendship became one of the most precious experiences of my life.

One night in early February — we had taken her home that day — Randolph said, 'You remember, Wayne, my telling you of my earliest experiment in sculpture, and my earnest request — to Somebody or Something Outside — for a chance to do just one creditable piece of statuary?'

I remembered — and thought I knew what he was leading up to.

'Now you have had your big chance,' he continued, 'to do a monumental thing in brain surgery. It has already directed attention to you. You will have many opportunities, in the future, to test your faith as well as your skill.

Never forget how you came by it. Don't ever let yourself believe, when you have become eminent as a brain surgeon, that this new technique you hit upon in Natalie's case was something that *you* invented in a time of emergency. *I say it was handed to you — from the Outside!'*

'I believe that,' I said, sincerely. 'I don't understand it; but I believe it.'

And I still believe it.

At Home

February eighth, 1914, 9 P.M

You will observe, my friend, that some time has elapsed since the last entry was made in this journal. The interruption has not been due to negligence, but indecision whether to continue.

As I stated, at the outset, the purpose of these memoirs was to give my reader — whoever he might be — a glimpse of the cause-and-effect relationship between private investments in other people's upbuilding, and the rewards of such investments accruing to the donor and empowering him to accomplish things otherwise impossible.

I wanted to go on record with my belief, arrived at by experience, that if an act of human rehabilitation is secretly wrought, the development is manifest not only in the life of the beneficiary but the benefactor. In other words, if I do something for you that builds you up for increased usefulness, my own capacity is augmented by that much. I do not mean that if I do something of value for you on Thursday I may expect to exercise some new power by Saturday at the latest; for this thing doesn't always operate on a cash-and-carry basis. But I do insist — and I have consistently demonstrated this to my own satisfaction — that you cannot add to another's personal power without increasing your own.

Having finished my narration of the peculiar experiences of 1905 when, under the direction of Clive Randolph, I tested this theory and found a new and promising way of life, it occurred to me that either I had made my case — in the opinion of my reader — or would be unable to do so, no matter how much additional evidence were piled up. I debated whether it would serve any good purpose to offer more testimony of the same sort.

But something has happened lately which throws light on this subject from another angle. I think you should have your attention called to it.

In my previous entries, I have tried to give you a brief but fairly comprehensive account of my own adventures in this strange field. I want now to tell you what little I know — knowledge achieved mostly by deduction and guessing — concerning another person's experience in self-investment. You will note, as you proceed, that there are a couple of open gaps in this story of Dorothy Wickes which will never be filled in. At these intervals you are at liberty to exercise your own imagination as I have exercised mine.

And now that I have decided to resume work on this journal, perhaps it will be well if I carry on a little farther with some of my experiences subsequent to the operation on Natalie Randolph, an event that promptly gave me a new rating in my profession and set me going toward a larger success than I had dreamed of.

It may interest you to learn something more about Tim Watson and his reaction to college life. It is quite possible that you may be acquainted with Watson. Indeed it is possible that Tim may be reading these words himself. If so, he will suffer no chagrin in perusing my report of him; for, from the very first, it was evident that this loyal young fellow meant business. His marks were exceptionally good — better, on the whole, than my own grades in college — and his conduct, so far as I know, was above reproach. I was never given one minute's anxiety about him.

At the close of his freshman year, he returned to Detroit, found a job in the Olds Motor Works, where he was quick to learn, made good wages, and saved his money like a miser. When it was time for him to go back to school in September, while he did not have quite enough cash to see him through the entire year, it was unnecessary for me to do very much for him; though by that time I was able to aid him without making any sacrifice. I had discontinued work in the field of general surgery, and was giving full attention to diseases and injuries of the brain. Patients, in increasing numbers, were being referred to me from considerable distances. Sometimes they were brought into the hospital; sometimes I made long trips. Brain surgery is not the most pleasant vocation in the world. You do very well if you can hold your mortality down to fifty per cent. Most of the cases that recover have a long and tedious convalescence, the patient growing more crotchety and fretful every day. I mention this only because the burden rested heavily on me, and I was very thankful to sense the increasing devotion of Tim Watson.

I had not altered my habits of living, to any appreciable extent. We had moved to a more commodious apartment, had found more efficient household help, and I had bought another car. Otherwise, our manner of life had not been affected by the improvement in my income. It would have been impossible for Tim not to observe that I was now in a position to make things easier for him, but there never was the slightest hint that he would lean on me. Quite to the contrary, he began mothering me in a manner that was a bit embarrassing at times. He was so solicitous of my comfort that I began to feel quite elderly in his company, though there were but fifteen years between us. One evening, in summer, when he had dragged a big chair across the room for me, so that I might read under what he thought was a better light, I said, rather testily, I fear, 'Damn it; you don't have to fag for me as if I were a hundred!'

'I like to do little favors for you,' said Tim. 'It isn't that I think you're old. Certainly I wouldn't think that after yesterday.'

The day before, I had come off with some kudos in an aquatic tournament — my chief recreation was had in the water — and Tim had been much impressed.

His affectionate comment made me feel quite contrite; and, if anything, a bit older.

I had occasion to be very proud of him. In 1908, he graduated with a *cum laude*. His courses, during the Junior and Senior years, were definitely pre-medic, leaving him only two more years to do in the Medical College after achieving his A.B. I took Joyce along with me to the Commencement exercises. He led the child about, afterward, showing her off to his friends. She was very pretty. I was proud of them both. Tim deferentially asked permission to take Joyce with him to luncheon when he learned I had been invited to lunch with a half dozen of my professional colleagues. He did this in the presence of my learned friends, and his filial attitude — plus the fact that when he left with Joyce he addressed her as 'sister' — evoked a natural curiosity which I ventured to appease by remarking, dryly, 'This young man is not my son, gentlemen. He is my grandson.'

Of course I have always felt sure that it was my investment in Tim — at a time when the expense of it was considerable — that put me in a state of mind to work at my job with the highest possible efficiency. The investment had been amply justified. It had paid out handsomely. Now that it was reasonably clear that Tim was going to be a success, my satisfaction was complete.

He wanted me to get him a job, that vacation, as an orderly in the hospital, or an ambulance driver, or almost any sort of labor that would keep him in the hospital atmosphere with which he had become somewhat familiar; but I wouldn't consent to it.

'You will probably be back here as an interne after you have finished with the Medical School,' I said, 'and it will be much better for you if the nurses haven't made your previous acquaintance by ordering you to empty the slop.'

'But I shouldn't mind that,' he replied. 'If

an orderly does his job efficiently and obediently, he ought to be respected.'

'Yes, yes,' I agreed, impatiently, 'and so he is. But the orderly defines his position, in relation to other natural objects, and he mustn't try to come back later as a doctor.'

Tim nodded, not very enthusiastically, and said he supposed I was right. But I could see there was something on his mind that needed release, so I said, 'Well — what's the rest of it? Go on.'

'It's about this caste idea,' said Tim, feeling his way. 'I don't like it. From what I hear and see, there's too much of it in the medical profession; experienced nurses doing the wrong thing, and knowing they're doing the wrong thing, simply to obey a bad order that some doctor has issued through ignorance or mistake; and aware that it's doing the patient harm. Everybody afraid of everybody else, all the way up the line, from the man with the mop to the man with the scalpel, including the student nurses, who are afraid of the graduate nurses, and the graduate nurses, who are afraid of the superintendent of nurses, who is afraid of the internes, who are afraid of the older doctors. It's the bunk! It's a crime!' Tim's long speech had grown a bit shrill toward the end.

I tried to explain that while there were probably occasional unfortunate occurrences connected with hospital discipline, in the long run it was better for everybody to understand the limits of his own authority and initiative. Otherwise, everything would be on the loose, with nobody in particular responsible for what happened.

'Oh, I see that,' agreed Tim. 'But I also see a lot of red tape that doesn't do anybody a service. I'd like to see a hospital proceed on the theory that it's there to accommodate the patients rather than the doctors and the nurses. I've been looking into this thing a little, and asking questions. In most of the hospitals, the business office is entirely too fussy. A patient comes in sick as a dog and deserving every consideration, but the business office has to devil the life out of the fellow with questions that have no immediate bearing on his case and could be asked, just as well, a week later; and all this cruel nonsense practiced to accommodate some brittle little clerk who wants to keep his index-card system in order.'

'I don't believe they do much of that in our hospital,' I protested. 'I'd look into it — if it was any of my business. I'm not on that end of the machine.'

Tim stood up and waved a long arm, energetically.

'There you are!' he shouted. 'That's what I mean!'

I couldn't help being amused over the youngster's indignation. It wasn't like Tim to pop off like that; so I knew the matter went pretty deep with him. I told him I thought he was on the right track, to have the patient's welfare at heart. I also promised to ask a few questions, quietly, in our hospital.

As a result of that investigation, which I pursued deliberately for a month or more — considerably to my dismay — I began to nourish the idea of a private hospital in which commonsense discipline would take precedence over a growing tendency to mechanize the healing arts. It was for this reason that we organized Brightwood, and I have Tim to thank for unwittingly launching a project that has been a great satisfaction to us all. I realize that the disciplinary measures which are required in a very large hospital have to be more exacting than in a small one. But when I discovered that patients were roused at five A.M., from a deep sleep, to give some student nurse a chance to practice reading her clinical thermometer, I resolved to lay plans for the establishment of Brightwood.

Tim again spent the summer working in the automobile factory where he had been employed before. He must have been rather good at it, for his wages were excellent. I often wondered, through those days, whether he wasn't tempted a little to carry on in that game; for it was the coming profession, if a man wanted to make money; incomparably more promising, in that respect, than the practice of medicine.

It gratified me that he wanted to be with me as much as possible, week-ends. I found him increasingly companionable. A couple of times I took him with me on Sunday evenings at the Randolphs. He and Natalie were immensely congenial. I rather thought — and hoped — that he would make an effort to cultivate that friendship, for it was easy to see that the girl had attracted him. So far as I know, he made no attempt to enlist her interest in him. But I nourished the hope that something might come of it later.

One of my earliest cases at Brightwood was a brain tumor operation on a Mr. James Wickes. They were poor people, Wickes having been out of employment for more than a year in consequence of his illness. There was a twenty-two-year-old son, also unemployed, for some unspecified reason. Accompanying the sick man to the hospital was his wife, a discouraged, taciturn little mouse, and a daughter Dorothy who was eighteen, bright, and uncommonly attractive. Her clothes were of inexpensive stuff but modishly cut and she wore them with confidence.

They made no bones about their poverty. 'My daughter is the only one working now,' explained Mrs. Wickes, nervously. 'Fifteen dollars a week — in a store. And I must say she is a good girl. She gives us all of it, she does.' My glance wandered over Dorothy's stylishly made ensemble, and Mrs. Wickes defensively added, 'She makes all her own clothes.'

I reassured them about the financial problem, told them there was a fund available for hospitalization; that there would be no charge for surgery, if an operation were required. After a few days' observation, it was evident that the patient had a very slim chance. The case was operable, but practically hopeless. Dorothy had come alone, that Sunday afternoon. I took her into my office and told her that while I intended to operate, the next morning, I seriously doubted whether I could save him. She was grieved, but not surprised. I drew a little diagram for her, outlining the appallingly large area involved. She drew her chair closer to my desk and seemed avidly interested in the pencil-sketch.

'Can you draw?' she inquired. Her blue eyes were wet, but they lighted as she asked the irrelevant question.

'That much,' I admitted, with a shrug. 'Can you?'

She nodded, confidently.

'I have had no chance to take lessons,' she said, 'but I can draw.'

It seemed to me that the conversation had taken rather an odd turn, in view of the fact that I had been doing a rough sketch to show the girl how little hope I could offer that her father might survive. And then it occurred to me that Dorothy had been casting about for something she might do to earn the money required by her father's hospitalization. If that was it, I reflected, her attitude deserved encouragement.

'What sort of things do you draw?' I asked.

'Boats,' she answered, decisively.

'Just boats?'

'Boats and docks — and that's the trouble. I can't draw boats well enough to hope ever to sell a picture. Maybe, if I knew the principles of drawing, I could get a job as a dress designer. I have ideas for dresses, and I believe I could make some money that way.'

'I should like to see your sketches sometime,' I said, non-committally. 'You tell your mother what I have told you. Don't upset her with a report that this is definitely hopeless, but give her warning.' I rose, and Dorothy considered herself dismissed. That was about three-thirty. At five, she was back at the hospital. The girl at the information desk, remembering that she had called earlier, told her to go into my office and sit down. I found her there, waiting for me.

'You said you wanted to see some of my drawings,' explained Dorothy, laying a portfolio before me.

'But I didn't mean to cause you a special trip,' I protested.

She drew out a marine sketch and held it up. I had seen wetter water in pictures, but it was obvious that the girl was a keen observer and had talent. The shadows of the ropes and spars rippled in rhythm with the choppy swells of the breeze-swept harbor. It wasn't a great picture, but it held out great promise.

'Did you draw that?' I inquired. She nodded. 'Didn't copy it?' I asked. 'Sketched it from life?'

'Yes, Doctor. Is it any good?'

'Good? Of course it's good!'

Well — we had to let James Wickes go from the hospital to a mortuary, as I had ruefully anticipated; though, had he lived, I suspect that his survival would have been of small satisfaction to himself and his family. The next few days were so heavily weighted with serious duties that I had but little time to think about the Wickes family. On the next Sunday afternoon at five, when I was about through with the day's work, I found Dorothy waiting for me, just outside my office door. I invited her to come in. She sat down on the edge of her chair and tugged nervously at her gloves.

'It's about one of my girl friends in the store,' she began, without preamble. 'I'm so dreadfully sorry for her. She is almost crazy with worry. I want to ask your advice.'

'Is this what I'm afraid it is?' I asked.

Dorothy nodded, and flushed a little.

'But she's a very nice girl — just the same,' she declared loyally.

'Not you — by any chance,' I suggested, looking her squarely in the eyes. But the eyes did not flinch. She shook her head. 'That's good,' I said. 'I believe you. Well — go on. Tell me anything you want me to know; though I hope you're not going to ask me to think of a quick way out of this for your friend, because I am quite definitely not in that line of business.'

'N-no — I wasn't going to ask that, exactly,'

said Dorothy reluctantly, 'though of course it would be just awfully sweet of you.' *

I couldn't help grinning, though I suppose I should have been indignant. She was as transparent as glass, with no more realization of her unpleasant implications than a six-year-old.

'No,' I reiterated, firmly. 'Sometimes these cases are very sad, indeed; but — there's nothing we can do about them.'

'It's too bad,' sighed Dorothy. 'I read a story once about the older sister of Jairus' daughter; you know, the little girl that Jesus raised from the dead?'

I remembered the narrative, but said I

* Among Doctor Hudson's papers I found the notes of an address he had delivered before the State Medical Association on March 9, 1914, the subject of which, may have been inspired by this conversation. In his address, Doctor Hudson states it as his belief that many young persons, confronted by this problem, do not always realize the gravity of their efforts to escape from their desperate predicament. They cannot see farther than the immediate threat of disgrace. Doctor Hudson advised that when a medical man is approached on this matter by people half-insane with worry, instead of treating them with cold anger, it would be to his credit if he viewed the circumstances in a spirit of sympathetic understanding, and tried to suggest some ethical procedure which would not only safeguard the life of an unborn child but shield the mother from a ruinous collapse of personality. This is, I think, an interesting side-light on the man's nobility; and on his courage also, for this is a ticklish subject. (R. M.)

hadn't recalled that the child had an older sister.

'Not in the Bible, she didn't,' agreed Dorothy, 'but in this story that I read. Shall I tell you — or haven't you time?'

'Tell me — if it isn't too long.'

'Well — after Jesus had brought back the little girl to life, he left the house and was on his way up the road and pretty soon a beautiful young woman stepped out of the shrubbery and asked if she could speak to him. So — they sat down, and she told him that she loved a young Roman centurion, but her people would not consent to their friendship — much less their marriage. And now she was in trouble. And she would be disgraced; likely driven from home.

' "You gave my little sister her life back," she said. "Can't you speak a word that will save mine?" ' Dorothy paused.

'So — what did he do?' I inquired, with sincere interest.

'The author of the story didn't say. He just stopped there — and left you guessing — like in *The Lady or the Tiger*.'

I observed that it was a prudent way to finish the piece, even if it did leave you a bit curious over the outcome. She nodded agreement, and remarked that the problem must have put the Master in an embarrassing position. 'For he was always so kind and helpful to everyone,' she murmured, meditatively. Then, after a little pause, she searched my eyes, and asked, 'What do *you* think he would have done?'

I glanced at my watch — an ignoble trick — and replied that I shouldn't be impudent enough to make a decision for the Lord; adding that perhaps we'd better proceed now with the main story.

'Millie — that's my friend —' said Dorothy, settling to her task, '— can't stay in the store very much longer. And she can't stay at home much longer, either.'

It was a fairly long narrative of a selfish aunt's too exigent attentions. After Millie's mother had died and their home was broken up, she had been taken in, at the age of twelve, by her mother's sister Susan, a half-psychopathic woman of forty, with a bare subsistence income, a lame foot, and a weak heart.

She was too sensitive about her lameness to venture out of the house, except on short errands to the near-by grocery, and her erratic heart was much on her mind. One of the first things Millie had learned, upon coming to live with her, was that Aunt Susan mustn't be upset.

Shy, reticent, and self-conscious, Aunt Susan lived the life of a hermit, unsparing in

130

her stifling affection for the unhappy child, but dreading the intrusions of Millie's young friends. So — Millie gave up trying to entertain any of her girl companions; and, when she was invited to parties, Aunt Susan was distressed over what might happen to her ward. As Millie grew older, this cruelly strict supervision became more and more galling. If she was five minutes late in getting home from school, full explanations were in order. Aunt Susan, sitting at a front window, gnawing her thumbnail, would meet Millie at the door, shrill and shaky and scared.

'And that's the way it went,' continued Dorothy, 'all through her high-school days. She never had any fun. Sometimes we said, "Come on! Let your old lady worry a little, if she wants to." But Millie couldn't risk a heart attack; and, anyhow, she wouldn't have a good time, knowing that her Aunt Susan was hobbling about through the house, half crazy with anxiety.'

I nodded my understanding, and said, 'Too much devotion.'

'That has been the hard part of it,' Dorothy agreed. 'The good old lady has simply strangled Millie with her love and kisses; never lets her alone for a minute; fusses with her hair, pats her on the check, stuffs her with homemade chocolates, insists on reading aloud, in the evenings, the sappiest, sloppiest, goody-goodiest stories, out of funny old books, about sweet and obedient girls who took care of grandpa until he died of it. And —'

'And so — Millie finally broke through the fence,' I suggested, feeling that I now had the picture fairly well in hand. 'Any chance of a marriage? That might help quite a bit.'

'I don't believe he could stand it,' doubted Dorothy. 'He would have to live there. Auntie's heart would go back on her if Millie tried to make a home elsewhere.'

'Yes — I know about those hearts,' I said, 'the kind that cave in whenever their custodians can't have their own way about everything. There's an awful lot of heart disease that's just one way of putting on a tantrum.'

'They're really worse than tantrums,' declared Dorothy.

'That's right,' I agreed. 'You can spank a tantrum — but you're afraid to paddle a defective heart.' We sat there in silence, for a minute; then I said, 'I'm afraid Millie will have to figure this out, herself. Perhaps her best course is for her to make a clean breast of it to her Auntie.'

'I suppose so,' said Dorothy, regretfully, 'but Aunt Susan will have a fit.'

'Well,' I said, not very helpfully, 'people have had fits — and got over them. By the way — have you been drawing any more pictures?'

She shook her head.

'I think I should like to make a little investment in you,' I said. 'Your boats are pretty good, and they would be ever so much better if you had some lessons. And perhaps you would be able to do one for me. I, too, am very fond of the water.'

Her blue eyes widened and her pretty lips parted.

'Do you think I could — really?' she said, just above a whisper.

'It's worth trying. I know a man who is well posted on local art schools. I want you to go and see him. He will give you good advice. I shall tell him to expect you.'

'Now?' asked Dorothy.

'When you get anything on your mind, you certainly don't waste much time; do you?' I teased.

'But this is so important,' she replied soberly.

'Very well. I'll call him up. Perhaps he will be free to talk to you this evening.'

I stepped back into my private office, closed the door and telephoned to Randolph, finding him at home as I had expected. I told him

133

I had been talking with a young woman who thought of taking a course in drawing. Would he give her some counsel? Might she come out tonight? I omitted to say that I had any further interest than that in this art course.

'He will see you this evening,' I announced to Dorothy, writing Randolph's address on a card. 'And now I have an urgent request to make of you. You are not to tell Mr. Randolph that I am having anything to do with this matter. I don't care what else you tell him about yourself; but you're not to tell him that.'

'But — I'd *like* to tell him,' insisted Dorothy. 'If he is your good friend, wouldn't he be glad to know that you were being kind to me? And what you did for us — about father, too.'

'Well — maybe — but that's not the point. The point is that I do not want this told. I don't want it told about your father, either. I'm very particular about this. Tell your mother never to talk about any of this — not even to her closest friend.'

'That's funny,' said Dorothy, bewilderedly.

'It isn't funny, at all!' I replied, bluntly. 'It is an investment. And investments aren't funny. They may be foolish, but they're never funny.'

Dorothy blinked her long eyelashes a few times, and shook her head a little, dizzily; then she said, 'I hope you won't lose too much by — by investing in me; but what about father?'

'Now don't worry me,' I commanded, rising. 'You're too young to understand. I couldn't explain this to you, if I tried. You wouldn't know what I was talking about.'

'Maybe I'm not as dumb as I look,' she said, smiling.

I was anxious for her to go now. I had had a long day, and needed some relaxation. I opened the door for her.

'Of course you are!' I declared.

'I hope,' she said, gently, extending her hand, 'that I can pay it all back, sometime, Doctor Hudson.'

'That's all right.' I waved a large overhand dismissal. 'I don't want any of it back; not a nickel of it; do you understand? I'm expecting to make use of it.'

'Well — good-bye!' she said, dazedly, fingering her cheap beads. Then she backed out through the door, regarding me with an odd expression such as one sees sometimes on the faces of people visiting a zoo.

Pyle came in, a few seconds later, and wanted to know what was so funny.

I said, 'You wouldn't think it was funny if I told you.'

'Maybe not,' he growled. 'You aren't — may I venture to inquire — losing your mind?'

135

AT HOME

February twelfth, 1914, 11 P.M.

I have just returned from the annual banquet of the Lincoln Club where the commemorative speeches were, I thought, a little better than usual; perhaps because they were briefer.

One journeyman soothsayer predicted the early outlawry of war, on the ground that with modern weapons available to all nations, no one of them could resort to arms without ruining itself.

The nations, he deposed, had proved 'again and again' that war is a futile waste of men and property. I couldn't help feeling that the good man's spirit was ever so much better than his logic. Anything that has been proved 'again and again' might have to be proved yet again — and again. I sincerely hope that his forecast is more sound than his reasoning.

Pyle arrived home from Munich yesterday. We have been taking considerable interest at Brightwood in the rapid improvement of X-ray apparatus; and Pyle was sent over — financed chiefly (and not very enthusiastically) by Nick Merrick — to investigate Lilienfeld's new adaptation of the hot cathode ray tube. Strangely enough, while Pyle was abroad, Doctor Coolidge of Schenectady perfected a tube that implements the ray much more effectively. This amuses Merrick, who is intensely patriotic and hoots at the idea that we have to inquire of Germany for the latest tricks in applied science.

Pyle seems more than a little disturbed over what he thinks is a dangerous interest in militarism over there. Of course, we have had some inkling of this in the press, but Pyle says it has a more sinister appearance in Berlin than it has when we read about it over here. He thinks England is apprehensive.

But if our wiseacres, who talked at the dinner tonight, have any notion of the seriousness of the situation in Europe, they kept their frets nicely concealed. The general consensus seemed to indicate that the world had beaten its spears into pruning-hooks, and that lions and lambs may now frolic together in a state of amity.

You will recall that I had sent the Wickes girl to Randolph for advice about lessons in drawing. I had volunteered, without giving the matter any deliberation, to finance this undertaking. It couldn't cost very much. The lessons would probably be taken after

Dorothy's working hours; in the evening, perhaps. I was to learn more about that, presently.

At half past ten, that Sunday night, Randolph called up to say that my young friend had spent the evening there, and thanked me for the privilege of her acquaintance. I chuckled a little over this odd remark and assured him the thanks were all mine to offer, adding, 'Bright girl; don't you think?'

'Better than bright,' declared Randolph. 'She's got something.'

I waited a few seconds for him to add a few decorations to this cryptic comment; and, when he didn't avail himself of the opportunity, I inquired whether she had shown him her sketches.

'Yes,' he replied, '— and a few glimpses of her soul.'

'Sounds as if you might have had a fairly serious conversation,' I remarked, with mounting curiosity.

'Same sort of conversation that you and I had, the first time we met. Remember?'

'Of course. But this is quite interesting. I should have supposed she would be too full of art talk to take much stock in your personal investment theory.'

'The two subjects,' said Randolph, tutorially, 'aren't so very far apart. I told her how

I happened to do the piece of memorial statuary that gave me standing as a sculptor.'

'And Miss Wickes wondered whether a brave experiment in secret philanthropy might make a painter of her,' I surmised. 'Is that it?'

'Well — she was mightily impressed. It seemed to me that she caught the idea with remarkable promptness, almost as if she had heard about it somewhere else.' Randolph paused a moment, and then asked, 'You haven't been talking to her about it?'

'No. But Dorothy is a very intelligent young woman, and you probably did a neat job of expounding your theory. She needn't have heard it before. At least, she did not get it from me. Well — did you arrive at any conclusions about the sort of instruction she should have?'

'Tentatively — yes. There's nobody here who could do much for her. The girl has an instinctive flair for movement, composition, perspective. I shouldn't like to see her in the hands of some schoolmasterish artist who might recommend a change of technique. There's an authentic talent here that's far too valuable to be fooled with. What she needs, above everything else, is release from her job; a change of atmosphere; association with gifted young people in some art colony, perhaps; and the guidance of a teacher who will offer her inspiration and encouragement rather than the mere bare bones of planes and contours and —'

'Hi! Wait a minute! Hold everything!' I pleaded. 'I'm in over my head.'

'So you are,' agreed Randolph, apologetically. 'I hadn't meant to inflict so much trade-lingo on you. What it all boils down to is that your friend needs emancipation, for a while, from everything that distracts her mind. If she can raise the money — we didn't talk about that — I think she should go to one of the coasts and pursue her special interest, which seems to be ships and wharves. She might go to California. A couple of months might be sufficient to demonstrate what further study she should do, and under what type of master.'

'Thanks,' I said, 'for the attention you have given her. I hope she can find some way to follow your advice.'

I refilled my pipe, and walked about through the house, trying to accommodate myself to this project. I got out my pencil and added up a row of figures. The thing had sounded a little more formidable than it really was. Say three months in California. That's the travel expense and modest living costs. Then, there's the equivalent of her wages at the store, which the family will require. That isn't very much. The whole job might run to six hundred and fifty dollars. Doubtless worth doing.

Dorothy called me up, the next evening, at dinner-time, to inquire when she might see me. I told her to come at once to my house.

She was somewhat flustered, when I showed her to a big chair in my library, and her excitement accented her vitality. I had thought her a very pretty girl, but had not credited her with as much character as I now saw in her face. It was more mature than I had thought.

For a while we discussed the suggestions Randolph had offered.

'I'm afraid,' she said, 'that this must seem to you more like financing a nice vacation than a project to make a real artist of me. It's so different from the plan you had in mind for me that I shall not blame you if you don't think well of it.'

I assured her that Mr. Randolph's opinion on such a matter as this should have precedence over anything I might think, and added that it seemed entirely reasonable to me.

She seemed very reluctant about accepting my proposal to cover her wages at the store while she was gone, but consented when it was pointed out that the whole proposition was otherwise impracticable.

'Mr. Randolph's belief is,' I reminded her, 'that what you need now is a period without drudgery and without care. But you couldn't have a free mind if you had left your mother without support.'

Then I asked her if she had given any thought to the place she might go to, and she shook her head. I thought this very odd. It seemed to me that if somebody had made me a proposition of this sort, I should have made haste to investigate travel literature, consult maps, and secure data about the best locations for the purpose.

'But you are decided on Southern California?' I said. She smiled a little, nodded — but not very convincingly, I thought. Then I began to put two and two together and thought I would add them up and see what they totaled. 'I suppose you will be too much absorbed by your work, out there, to write to me,' I said, casually.

Her eyes brightened, quickly, as I went on.

'I don't think you should have any distracting obligations on your mind — not even letter-writing. So — I shall not feel bad if I do not hear from you until you are back home again.'

Dorothy was radiant. She said I was very considerate. She hoped she could prove her gratitude, some day.

So — then I knew she wasn't going to California. She was going to use this money for something else — and I thought I knew what this something else was. Very well; if that's the way it is, it is still a fine investment, I thought; a finer investment than the other.

I moved over to my desk and wrote her a check for the full amount I had felt would cover the project, and as I handed it to her I said, 'Now, I think this will do it. You need not make an accounting to me. I don't care to have a detailed report. What we are trying to do is to give you a chance to improve as an artist. You are to spend this money as you like; whatever will contribute to our hope for your success — that's what we want.'

She drew a quick little sigh of combined relief and gratitude, and said, softly, 'Oh, thank you! I am so hopeful!'

At the door, I said, 'I'll expect to see you, then, in May.'

'And I'll be thinking about you — and your wonderful kindness,' said Dorothy, holding on to my hand. 'And I'll give you the first important picture that I paint.'

And she did. I can see it from where I sit, as I write these words. It won a prize in an art exhibition put on by the Architectural League of New York.

But she didn't paint it in California.

Of course I never asked her, and she never told me, how she invested that money. I do know that she didn't leave town. One day, Nancy Ashford remarked, 'By the way, I saw that lovely Wickes girl, this afternoon, when I was shopping. What a charming young woman she is getting to be!'

'That's nice,' I replied, trying to make it sound casual. 'Did you talk to her?'

'No — she was busy. I don't think she saw me.'

I had a notion to say, 'That, also, is nice,' but checked myself in time.

One Sunday afternoon in May Dorothy showed up at the hospital. She was carrying the picture. It was indeed a lovely thing — and so was she.

'Well —' I said, 'you've done it! Have you shown it to Mr. Randolph?'

'Of course not,' she declared, coyly. 'Think I'd show it to anybody until you had seen it?'

'I'll tell you what we will do,' I said. 'I had expected to go out to the Randolphs' tonight for dinner. I'll call him up and tell him I am bringing you along — you and the picture.'

She was delighted. On the way, I ventured to ask how California was — in a vague sort of way — so she wouldn't suspect, by my silence on that subject, that I had discovered her secret. She replied, with equal indefinite-ness, that California was very nice indeed, and added that Detroit was very nice, too. I could find no fault with either of these remarks, and pursued my inquiries no further.

Randolph was excited! Of course, I thought the picture was a magnificent piece of work; but I was no artist. Randolph knew what he was talking about — and he didn't talk about anything else that night. Natalie was sober, as she looked at the painting. Then she said, quietly, 'Now you can do anything you want to do; can't she, father?'

I did not see Dorothy again for a month. It was at the hospital, Sunday afternoon. She was aware of my usual schedule of work on Sundays, and I found her waiting for me. I was sincerely glad to see the girl. She had ma-tured, surprisingly. She was now at work on another marine sketch, she said, and felt sure she could sell it. It was most gratifying to see the firmness of her self-confidence.

She was on the point of leaving when I said, 'Oh — by the way; you never told me how your friend Millie made out with her little problem.'

Dorothy was tugging on her gloves. Her eyes drifted to the window and she replied, slowly, 'She went to a sanitarium somewhere, away up in the Adirondacks. Her lungs weren't very strong. Her Aunt Susan consented to her going, when Millie told her that the money was provided for people with that trouble.' Dorothy paused, but did not meet my eyes. Then, cautiously, she proceeded. 'It must have been only a slight touch of T.B. She is well again — and back in the store, with a little better position.'

Perhaps I should not have pressed this inquiry any farther, but I was too sorely tempted.

'Well — as I recall the story,' I rejoined, 'Millie also had a slight touch of something else. Did she get over that, too?'

Dorothy's lips tightened in a reluctant little grin, but she did not risk facing me.

'Yes,' she replied, after some hesitation, 'and it was adopted, by very nice people. It will have a good home.'

'I am glad,' I said. 'Very glad.'

Dorothy's face lighted and she looked me squarely in the eyes. She gave me her hand.

'Well — good-bye — for this time,' she said, sweetly. 'And — thanks — for — for everything. You've given me such a wonderful chance to be what I want to be.'

I held her hand for a moment, debating a reply. It would have been very pleasant to me if I could have risked saying I had guessed the secret, and was proud of her. But I felt that any such comment might damage the joy she had found. These are things you can't talk about.

I simply smiled into her eyes and said good-bye. She waved a hand as she went through the door, and her lips were parted in a radiant smile. I know that she knows that I know — and she is glad that I wouldn't venture a word about it.

Dorothy and I now belong to a strange little fraternity that makes no signs, speaks no passwords; but has a mutual understanding that is rich and deep and full.

These are crowded days. We are having an increasing number of emergency cases. More people are driving automobiles. The roads are being improved. Everybody is driving faster. Last year there were *sixty-six* persons killed outright in this country; double the number for the preceding twelve months. I wonder how this reckless destruction of life is to be checked. No one seems to be doing anything about it. Perhaps the lawmakers would be more alert to this problem if they could spend a day in our hospital and see the mangled people brought in for repairs.

At Home

Watson and his young protégé Leslie Sherman were here for dinner tonight and have just left for the hospital where Tim had a postoperative case to see. Sherman was keen on going along, for he begins his internship with us next week and is bursting with curiosity over his new duties.

Yesterday morning, Tim and I drove over to Ann Arbor to see Sherman get his M.D. I was much amused over Tim's motherly concern and undisguised pride. You would have thought him an elderly relative. There are, I believe, four years between their ages.

I have been suspecting, for some time, that Tim was helping this handsome young fellow through his medical course; and now I feel sure of it. Perhaps this accounts, in no small measure, for the amazing progress that Watson has made in his work at Brightwood.

I have forgotten whether I reported, in this journal, that Watson received his medical degree in June of 1910. One of the difficulties of keeping a journal in code is that once the entry is made, and a few weeks have passed, the author himself can't find what it contains unless he goes to an enormous amount of bother. If my reader thinks this is funny, he is welcome to his amusement.

If I did not mention Tim's graduation from the Medical School, I should have done so; for it was an event of much importance to both of us. Of course, even if I had not provided a way for him to attend college, he might have contrived to do it by some other means; but it has been of immense satisfaction to me to have had a part in this brilliant chap's unfolding. It has been my privilege to witness this evolution — almost hour by hour — since that midsummer afternoon, ten years ago, when a rangy, red-headed, penniless young tramp showed up at the dirty old Free Clinic on Fort Street with a broken hand and an astonishing fund of medical patter.

Immediately after graduation from the Medical School, he came to Brightwood for his internship, but I am not sure that he ever was an interne. Nobody on the staff blamed me for the preference I showed him. They all knew I was deeply interested in his future, and I think they felt it was justified. Had he been my son, Watson could not have received more attention. He not only stood in at my most interesting operations but was as welcome to watch Pyle at work and McDermott and Harper.

Nancy Ashford, who has had an unusual capacity for attaching herself to promising people, flattering and cajoling and badgering them so that they work like dogs rather than disappoint her, pretended from the first that she was Tim's aunt — a relationship he has always played up to with effortless skill.

Had he been but one-half as intelligent and industrious, he could hardly have avoided success; for all the ways were greased, and everybody gave him a push. No one — not even Tim, himself — knew exactly when his 'internship' was over and his work as a junior on the staff began. He certainly had an early start. To the best of my knowledge, he was the youngest surgeon of my generation ever to have full responsibility for a major operation.

You will credit me, I hope, with a fair attempt to explain Watson's youthful arrival at a high rating in his profession, on the ground of his exceptional opportunities — plus his alert mind and indefatigable diligence. My own belief is, however, that all these fortunate factors in combination could not have made Watson what he is, today, without the additional inspiration of some personal investment in another's upbuilding. Tim unquestionably has the inner glow — or whatever this peculiar radiance may be called — that is to be had by one means only.

This strange motivation began to show up in him about a year ago last September. He never confided anything about it to me, but I think he knew that I knew that he knew, judging from chance remarks that tumbled accidentally into our intimate conversations. That he was making sacrifices on somebody's behalf was apparent. His modest stipend from the hospital was going somewhere; for he never had any money, never went any place, had no social life at all; yet seemed smugly satisfied to live on nothing, and could stand any amount of chaffing about his parsimony.

Through his college days, Tim had a very small part in my own social life — such as it was. Naturally we saw but little of him while he was in Ann Arbor, and during vacations he worked hard at jobs which made a considerable demand on his physical energy. He saw very little of the Randolphs. After he came to Brightwood, I suggested occasionally that it might be pleasant for him to renew this acquaintance, but he was prompt with excuses: appreciated my thought, but had something else to do.

One Sunday evening, about a year ago, I prevailed on him to accompany me to their home. I knew he was having a good time. I knew also that he had been more than pleasantly stirred by Natalie's fresh young beauty and grace. This delighted me. It was what I had secretly hoped for. I have never sought any prizes as a matchmaker, but I thought it would be interesting if Tim and Natalie should find each other as attractive as I had found them both to be.

It seemed to me that Natalie was at her very best, that night, and I couldn't help feeling that they were congenial.

On the way back, I clumsily remarked, with a pretense at playfulness, 'I'm afraid I have started something, Tim, by letting you and Natalie see each other again.'

'You must never be afraid of anything,' drawled Tim, tossing back one of my pet clichés.

Perhaps I should explain, at this juncture, that I had latterly become convinced that fear plays a very conspicuous rôle in most of the diseases of a psycho-physiological character; and I have been saying — perhaps too frequently — that many people would be able to build up their resistance to disease and increase their vitality if they identified their various phobias and went bravely to the mat with them. I have been contending that any sort of fear — no matter how apparently inconsequential — filters through all of a man's thought processes. He had better grapple with his pet fear, whatever it is.

Take insomnia, for example: here we find, very frequently, that the difficulty isn't rooted in a physical disability, but can be accounted for by a little phobia. The victim goes to bed wondering whether he will be able to sleep tonight. He is afraid he can't. He lies there fretting over the possibility that he may have this thing to contend with, all the rest of his life.

My counsel is that the man should turn on the light, open a book, and assume that he doesn't need any sleep at this time or Nature would be attending to it. He doesn't get scared if it happens that he isn't very hungry, some day at noon; nor is he so silly as to force food down his throat simply because he has been accustomed to eat at this time of the day.

Let him talk himself out of his fear of insomnia, on this common-sense basis. I have done it, myself. Plenty of nights, after I have spent a crowded day of perplexing duties — involving life-and-death decisions — I have gone to bed fairly sure that I should mentally reconstruct the whole string of dilemmas, hour after hour. I learned to handle that problem by going forth to meet my insomnia, more than halfway. And I have conquered this fear.

I believe I have done a fairly good job of conquering *all* of my fears. The only thing I am really afraid of now is fear. Perhaps I talk about it too much. I didn't blame Tim for teasing me with it, especially when I had invited such a retort by my facetious comment concerning him and Natalie.

'She is a lovely girl,' I declared, fervently.

Tim agreed to this, in such a forthright manner that there was but little left for me to say on the subject unless I wanted to be impudent enough to ask him whether he was likely to be seeing more of her.

After a studious silence, he said, 'I think you would like to see me try to get Natalie interested in me; isn't that so?'

'I had not realized that my hope had been quite so transparent,' I replied.

'If a high school boy,' said Tim, irrelevantly, 'likes a girl, but has only ten cents in his pocket, he can buy a bag of peanuts for her entertainment, and they can sit on the steps of the library and swear that they belong to each other. And no harm is done. They both know that it would be a half dozen years before this decision could lay a real obligation on either of them. My own attitude toward heart affairs,' he continued, deliberately, as if he had thought it all out and composed his speech with care, 'is conditioned by the fact that I shall be twenty-nine years old, on my next birthday. I am not in the fortunate position of the youngster who can — without any impudence — offer a girl everything when he has nothing to offer. Any man of my age, who encourages a young woman to believe that he has an interest in her, is something of a cad, I think, if he has no means of seeing it through to an honest conclusion.'

'Naturally — I agree to all that,' I broke in. 'But — young women have been willing to wait patiently until their men have accumulated something — especially in the case of professional men, whose early income is small.'

'Yes, yes, I daresay,' responded Tim, half-impatiently, 'but — well — let's suppose a case. So long as you have been thinking about Natalie Randolph, let us talk about her. I imagine that she is about twenty-three. She enjoys an active social life. Her friends are pairing off. They go to the theaters, and down town to dinner, and for drives in the country. They play golf and ride. Now — I cannot do any of these things. My work is exacting and my funds are meager. But I have some pride. And I shouldn't accept the gift of Natalie Randolph's time — not an hour of it! — in my present situation.'

'Well — if it's money, Tim —' I ventured.

'No; thank you, sir,' said Tim, promptly. 'I'm getting all the money I'm worth.'

We thought it better to change the conversation then, and we have never renewed it. But I think that Watson is in love with Natalie Randolph. And I think also that if he had the use of his income, he would be seeing something of her. Of course, that makes his investment infinitely more valuable. I hope young Sherman turns out to be something. His chance has been well paid for.

Yesterday noon, after the Commencement, Tim and Leslie invited me to have lunch with them and I gladly consented. We found my car, parked several blocks from the auditorium, and Tim drove. Before we had gone very far, I began to be a bit nervous. We were headed toward the Michigan Central station, and I knew there was only one restaurant in that vicinity worth patronizing. I should have been glad enough to go to Tony's by myself, and had done so many times; but I did not like the idea of going with anyone else.

It would have been very awkward, however, for me to have raised an objection, now that we were almost there.

'Tony's will probably be crowded,' said Tim, as we got out of the car, 'but it's the best place in town to eat.'

At that point, I should have said I knew that. I should have added that I had been here. It would have been much better, too, if I had said I knew Tony. There was no reason why I couldn't have admitted that much; but — I didn't want to discuss Tony with anybody. Tony and I had a secret that was several years old.

The restaurant was full, as Tim had threatened; full of students, alumni, young faculty men, tobacco smoke, miscellaneous noise, and the tempting aroma of broiled steaks and chops. Tony, himself — rotund, deliberate, and unrattled — was moving ponderously about, making room for his clients.

Sherman remarked that Tony was becoming a snob; wearing a white coat; just because it was Commencement, and there were out-of-town guests.

'Doesn't he generally wear a white coat?' I was hypocrite enough to ask, feeling that I ought to contribute something to the conversation.

'Doesn't wear *any* color of coat,' obliged Tim. 'Polo shirt; no sleeves; big white apron. I don't think it improves him to put on style.'

Presently Tony ambled our way and caught sight of us. His enigmatic old face lighted as he approached. He extended two big fat hands, palms up, fingers spread, grasped me

157

warmly, and said, 'Doc! Eet ees too long since you come!' He shrugged a massive shoulder and gave a despairing glance around the room. 'Now what shall Tony do with you?'

I told him we were quite willing to wait until there was an available table.

'Aren't we?' I said to my hosts, whose faces registered about as much inquisitiveness as they could hold. Tony, noting my company, bobbed a little bow to each of them, and said, considerably to my embarrassment, and doubtless to their further mystification, 'You are dam' lucky yawng fellows!'

A table was cleared, presently, and we sat down. Tony asked if we would let him arrange for our luncheon, and we were glad enough to trust his expert judgment. After the old chap had paddled away, Tim drawled, 'I take it that you and Tony have met before.' It was quite funny, and we all laughed. I was glad something had been said to ease the tension.

'It's a rather long story,' I remarked, after a while.

'Whenever he says a story is long,' said Tim, pretending to offer a confidence to Leslie, 'he just means it's a story you couldn't blast out of him with dynamite.'

I recognized a former classmate at an adjoining table, and went over to shake hands. When I returned, it was taken by consent that we wouldn't be talking any more about my acquaintance with Tony. And I observed that when the good old chap came with our incomparable steaks — which he insisted on serving, himself — he seemed to have sensed that it wasn't the right time for him to make any more allusions to our friendship. He was standing behind the cash register when we came up to settle our account.

'I'm afraid you didn't give us a check,' said Tim. 'How much is it, please?'

Tony's face grew very stern.

'Doc Hudson — he settle hees bill! Goodabye, Doc. Come again. You come — too,' said Tony, slowly wagging his head to my young companions.

We thanked him, and when we were outside, Tim — who is a fairly competent mimic — said, ostensibly for Sherman's benefit, 'Doc Hudson — he settle hees bill. Dam' lucky yawng fellows — to be with Doc Hudson!' And then he added, 'Any other place, Doctor, you'd like to visit? You don't happen to have a secret with a good tailor, do you?'

But we dropped the matter there, and Tim has never referred to it since.

It is growing late and I am tired. Perhaps I shall tell you the story about Tony, some other time.

BRIGHTWOOD HOSPITAL

October fifth, 1914, 10:30 P.M.

Nancy Ashford has been spending the past hour in my office. There is only one thing to talk about now, so we talked about that.

For two months the war has driven every other current topic into total eclipse — and no wonder. You pick up the morning paper and distrust your own eyesight, though Goodness knows the type is big and black enough to be read by the born blind. Every hour more people are being swept into this thing; and, once in, they can't get out.

Without asking for them you can get cocksure opinions, in any club lounge or Pullman smoker, on the scope, duration, and outcome of this incredible affair; and the editorials — quite indiscreetly, it seems to me — are already defining our national sympathies and antipathies. Surely, if our attitude as a nation really has to be documented, it should be expressed by the State Department. It is certainly not a job for the journalists.

I find myself growing more and more dissatisfied with the manners and morals of the public press. It has become the most potent influence on the thought of our people; and, fully conscious of its power, it has about left off appealing to the reader's calm common-sense, apparently feeling that it can do a more flourishing business by pandering to prejudice and fear.

I shocked Nancy by remarking that general literacy is a dangerous accomplishment.

'What a silly thing to say!' hooted Nancy, who takes much stock in modern progress and grows dewy-eyed when she talks about the recent inventions.

Forced to defend my statement, I maintained that it is a good thing for people to know how to read if what they read is good for them to know. If their reading inflames their aversions and fans their slumbering hatreds; or, by insidious propaganda, teaches them aversions they had not previously held, their ability to read does them damage and makes them a menace to the public peace.

I had never thought this through carefully, and in any other company than Nancy's I might have hesitated to air my unconsidered views. I admitted as much to her, and she drawled, 'Go right ahead, Doctor, and see how far you can wade before you get mired.'

With this encouragement, I began to expound. And I am recording our conversation here because I want you to think about this matter earnestly. Of course it may be that when these words are read, there will have come a complete change of conduct — if not of character — on the part of the papers. As the matter stands, the very large majority of them are definitely on the side of degradation. When sternly queried, they reply that they are giving the public what it demands. My own opinion is that they developed the public taste. And bad taste it is, too.

I reminded Nancy that the people of the world — until recent times — believed what they were told to believe, without much independent thinking.

'They lived on their prejudices,' she assisted, slyly.

'Yes — but that word needs to be examined. It has come to mean stupidity and stubbornness, but a prejudice isn't necessarily a bad idea. For example: nobody ever tried to murder me and I have never tried to murder anyone else. I never saw a murder committed; never knew anybody who had committed a murder. Neither by experience nor observation do I have direct knowledge on this subject; but I am uncompromisingly against it. I have a prejudice.'

'You and me both,' laughed Nancy. 'But where do we go from here?'

'Before printing was invented,' I continued, undistracted, 'back in the benighted old days when people lived almost exclusively on their prejudices —'

'And boiled turnips — and polluted water —' interposed Nancy, who is standing firm for our modern civilization.

'That's irrelevant,' I complained, crisply. 'They lived on their prejudices; but these prejudices were authorized by established institutions. They had dignity. You weren't yelled at, from every corner, by discordant voices. The prejudices weren't peddled around on the street. The Church handed you a creed. It may have contained some statements that a contentious individualist might disavow; but this creed was a respectable product of earnest thinking by many wise and sincere men. It may have had its imperfections, but it had solidity, maturity, sanction. At least, it wasn't something that an unlicensed hawker served, smoking hot, for a penny! It wasn't something that a newspaper man had pounded out on his typewriter, between nine-thirty and ten, with a boy at his elbow waiting to grab each article of faith as it climbed out of the machine.

'The State,' I went on, gathering momentum, 'provided the unlettered public with a pattern for patriotism. This patriotism was a prejudice, if you like; but it had roots. It had stability. You didn't have to be told — by some paragrapher or free-lance columnist — what patriotism was, and how it worked, and what it expected you to do. The State taught you your loyalties. You didn't derive them from the yipping and snarling of the scribes.'

'Well — that's a pretty long speech,' observed Nancy, when I had run down. She struck a match to indicate that I might be benefited by a cigar. I regarded her gesture with reproach, but drew out a cigar and she lighted it for me. 'Has some particular newspaper man made you mad?' she asked.

I shook my head. As individuals, they were fine fellows. I had had the most pleasant relations with them. They were bright, congenial, obliging. I couldn't remember ever having asked a favor that they hadn't granted. No — it wasn't personal.

But the papers were a bad influence. To begin with, they had a mighty low regard for the people's intelligence, imputing to them a sort of brutishness that isn't a normal characteristic of the average citizen. They assumed that the people had no respect whatever for private griefs; no sensitiveness about pushing themselves in to gaze upon another man's misfortunes. The press would risk its very life and limbs to take photographs of mourners weeping at the grave of an accident victim. It would force its way into a hospital to torture an interview out of the next of kin, in some sad circumstance. Only half-witted and mentally diseased persons would have the morbid curiosity to flatten their noses against the windows of homes afflicted by tragedy; but the newspapers did it, on the assumption that the public is psychopathic. Their arrogant impudence knew no limits. They had utter contempt for the dignity of the courts, and taught the public to share their rude defiance.

All that being true, what could you expect of the press at a moment when the public needed to be kept steady and dispassionate in their attitude toward a world-cataclysm crowded with menace?

Nancy reminded me that we believed in free speech. But I think it is to the people's serious disadvantage that they are able to buy, for two cents, a stimulant to hatred, morbidity, savagery, and scorn for the elementary decencies.

If it is illegal to peddle heroin, cyanide, and nitroglycerine on the street, what excuse is there for the general distribution of printed matter that debases the mind? If a manufacturer is required by law to state on the ketchup bottle that it contains benzoate of soda, the newspaper should be made to say — at the top of page one — 'This edition contains stuff that whets the appetite for ghoulishness, sadism, and similar psychoses.'

Nancy said I was getting excited again, so we agreed to wheel out the newspapers, and discuss a few other agencies dealing with the public's thought. According to report, some inspired ass on the local Board of Education had inquired, yesterday, whether it wasn't about time to discontinue the teaching of German literature in the high schools. I wonder if we are going to allow our prejudices to unbuckle our reason. Here pops up a glowing patriot, who — only thirty days after a European war begins — wants his children sheltered from the sinister influence of Goethe and Schiller. I suppose the next thing to expect will be a frantic attack on Mozart. Perhaps they'll ban the performance of *Parsifal*.

'Maybe I'll have to go to the calaboose,' I growled, 'for using a Zeiss microscope.'

'You'd better be careful where you make such remarks,' advised Nancy. 'They'll say you're pro-German.'

'Well — I'm not,' I muttered. 'Far from it!'

Nancy bade me good-night at that point, sweetly suggesting that I go home and sleep it off, which I mean to do presently. But I want to add a reflection or two before I stop writing.

I wonder what manner of influence, if any, the churches may exert in this bewildered time. If they were able to unite on a policy calculated to steady the public mind, it might produce good results. I do not know much about the churches. I do not attend their services. Sometimes, on Saturdays, I have glanced over the sermon topics announced for the next day. I regret to say that I do this largely for entertainment, and it does me no credit to be amused by these irreverences. For the most part, the topics imply a gift of omniscience, on the part of the clergyman, which reflects sadly on his mental housekeeping. The out-and-out lunatic always has a disturbance of the ego. In some instances, his ego atrophies, and he develops an inferiority complex. In many more cases, his ego becomes inflamed and distended, resulting in 'hallucinatory omnipotence.' Sometimes he thinks he is Napoleon. Sometimes he is Moses. Not long ago I saw a sermon-topic, 'What God Thinks of Detroit.' I wonder just what is the difference between the mental condition of the cracked old man who says he is Moses, and the up-and-coming prophet at the Holiness Tabernacle who knows what God thinks of Detroit. Very sad business, this. And the saddest feature of this humorless state of mind is the assumption that people will come to listen.

I presume that in the dignified old churches a more reasonable policy is pursued. I know that my good friend Dean Marquis, of the Episcopal Cathedral, isn't going to get off any such balderdash; nor is Doctor Spence likely to make himself ridiculous in the presence of a churchful of conservative Presbyterians. I dare-say there are a dozen or more who wouldn't countenance the sort of thing that obviously goes on in the big wooden tabernacle.

But — that's exactly where the trouble is, you see. Reverends Marquis and Spence and Rossman and the other intellectuals are dealing with a clientèle largely composed of privileged people, who — it may be assumed — have learned how to think calmly. They cannot be easily stampeded.

The enormous crowds that gather in the big tent, where 'Buster' Beecham, the saxophone-playing evangelist, holds forth, and in the wooden tabernacle, where 'Bob' Somebody thinks for God, are not people of privilege. They are excitable and more reliant upon their emotions than their intelligence. It is absurd to hope that the Gospel of Peace — as interpreted in these places — will have a steadying effect upon people's minds. That's where the trouble is: the very people who are most in need of steadiness are the least likely to have it offered to them.

Last Saturday I noted that one howling sensationalist was going to preach on 'When a Christian Should Fight.' Doubtless he is getting ready to rattle the saber.

As I understand the original message of Galilee, it was distinctly pacifistic, whatever may have been the shocking history of Christianity as a militant force. In peace-time, the churches are for peace. In time of war, they join the army. Indeed, they mobilize a little ahead of the army!

I wonder whether there is, today, any powerful influence at work in this country that may keep the public on an even keel. I doubt it; and I am very unhappy about it.

The papers say, today, that three hundred and fifty thousand people jammed the churches of Detroit yesterday to pray for peace, in response to the President's nationwide appeal. I wonder how much good such prayers accomplish. It has been my experience that before a prayer for a great favor can be offered with any hope of success, one has to put up some security; some valuable collateral, to attest one's sincerity and willingness to toss into it everything one can assemble. I expect our people would have to bring forward a mighty fine record for internal and privately possessed peace, before they could hope to do much with their petition for Europe.

Brightwood Hospital

May sixth, 1915, 4:30 P.M.

It has been a long time since I wrote anything in this journal. Many events, which in less tempestuous times might have been worth mentioning here, have seemed utterly insignificant in the face of the general stress.

To be quite honest, I had almost forgotten about this little book. And I doubt if I should be writing in it now had it not been for the fact that I stumbled upon it, a little while ago, while searching in my office safe for a deed to some country property.

Of course I might have set down in this journal a day-by-day commentary on the appalling things that are happening overseas and their repercussions on this side; but this project was not conceived as a history of contemporary movements in the world. It had but one motive: to record my own experiences in self-investment and the rewards accruing from such adventures into the lives of other people.

When you read these words, the Great War will undoubtedly be over; for it will reach its end by sheer exhaustion, one of these days, if not by a decisive victory. You will have more information than you want on this subject. You may be bored by any reference to it here. But it is a live issue, I beg you to believe; and one can't think or talk or write about anything that doesn't swing on this one pivot.

The President has had an unenviable job; trying, on the one hand, to serve the wishes of the majority who want us to be kept out of it, at almost any cost of national dignity, and the passionate patriots who strongly counsel him to put an end to the temporizing with something that we will have to do, pretty soon, whether we like it or not.

Most of the men with whom I associate are feeling that the President's diplomatic notes of protest to Germany have now reached a point of futility where they are beginning to seem a bit ridiculous.

Last Wednesday night, at a Chamber of Commerce dinner, one militant speaker satirized this situation rather cleverly. I doubted whether it was in very good taste to do it, but it was undeniably amusing. He illustrated by taking off an exasperated mother issuing requests, entreaties, and commands to her incorrigible nine-year-old brat. The monologue began in a comradely mood, and moved on through dulcet cooing to indignation and hysteria.

'Johnny — please be mother's fine little friend — and don't do that: that's a good boy.'

'Johnny — mama is going to be offended.'

'Mama doesn't want to scold her little boy.'

'Must mama tell papa?'

'Johnny! Now you listen to me!'

'Now — you do that once more, young man, and you'll see what happens to you.'

'*Johnny!* Stop that — this minute! This is the last time I am going to speak to you!'

'*Johnny!*'

It sounded funny, at the moment; but it isn't really very funny. The President is in an awkward position. He is probably as anxious as anyone else to preserve the national honor, and it must be a bitter dose to have oneself reviled for spineless cowardice when one's big hope is to save our people from avoidable bloodshed. And there's another question, too. Far as I can learn, we haven't much of an army to send over there, even if we should decide that our patience is exhausted. One hears all manner of conflicting opinions on how long it would take to mobilize, equip, and train an army strong enough to be effective.

The typical speech, urging a declaration of war, is amusingly illogical. The harangue usually begins on a highly altruistic note, demanding that we plunge into this mess 'to save civilization,' and ends by threatening that if we don't the Germans will come over here and lick the pants off of us, after they have finished with France and England. So — we have two excellent reasons for going in. We can help save civilization; and, incidentally, save our own skins. I feel that these two appeals — so divergent in motive — instead of being placed in the custody of a single orator, should be handled by specialists. One man could present the idealistic appeal, accenting our selfless interest in humanity at large; and another man could present the more practical aspects of our case in particular.

I have a lot of sympathy for the President. Many people think — and I find myself sharing this view — that Mr. Wilson would ease his own strain somewhat if he took advantage of the statesmanly counsel to which he has access. He seems to be trying to do it all himself. I said that to Pyle, the other day, and he replied, 'Well — Lincoln didn't have any very valuable advisors; did he? And there was a time when George Washington seemed to be playing a lone hand.'

I had to admit that these things were true;

but, all the same, I think a lot of the responsibility, that now seems concentrated in one man, might be shared. After all — the President does have a Cabinet.

But it is easy to criticize. I know that if I were placed in such a perplexing position as that of the President, I should find the gravity of it insupportable. Even without any such crushing cares, I am naturally fagged by this long-continued tension. Perhaps it might not afflict me so much if I were in a less depressing occupation. More and more I am confronted with brain surgery in which half of the cases are potential funerals before I see them. Maybe, in normal times, my task would not weigh on me so heavily. Maybe, if my job were not so dreadfully serious, I could view the world's predicament — and our own national perplexity — with less fretting. The combination of the two is very wearing.

When the news broke, today, about the sinking of the Lusitania, yesterday afternoon, I felt that we had turned a sharp corner on the road that inevitably leads to war. In the event that we go into it, I may be needed; and, if so, I shall go, of course, and 'do my bit,' as the saying goes, these days.

But, in the meantime, I realize that I must try to find some quiet retreat where I may spend a day, occasionally, apart from the racket and strain. I asked Carter to give me a going over, the other day, and he thinks there is a slight aneurism; advised me to take it easy. How can I take it easy? He might as well suggest to the Fire Department to take it easy! The cases I deal with won't wait until the surgeon has himself a two months' vacation.

A couple of years ago I inadvertently acquired a little ten-acre tract of untamed scrub-oak and briars on the rocky east shore of Lake Saginack. There was a decent old chap named Baldwin, who had brought his wife into the hospital for an abdominal operation that revealed a malignant condition. It was Pyle's case. He advised them not to go back to the country; to remain in town, if possible, close to medical attention. Baldwin got into conversation with me about his problem. It developed that he had very little to go on. There was this unpromising tract on Lake Saginack (the wrong side) which he could put up as security for a loan. I knew he needed the money in a good cause, so I let him have it, and took a deed to the land. His wife died, and he followed her, not long afterward. One of these days, I shall build a little cottage up there, and sneak away from town, weekends. Meantime — I think I shall pitch a good tent, and try camping out. I have never done

176

anything of the sort and I daresay it will be deucedly uncomfortable.

Perhaps I forgot to say that I built a commodious home, on the north side of town, two years ago. Joyce spends most of her time in a girls' school, but she entertains her friends at home during vacations, and she needed something better than an apartment. The money was well spent, I think, though I can't see that Joyce is any the less restless in our more attractive quarters.

Of course I cannot expect to get her interested in going out with me to the lake. She would be bored to death. I am not sure what the solitude may do for me, if I attempt this. But if I don't arrange for something of the sort, I may get into trouble. At least, that's what Carter said; and he is a very good heart man.

I have just come from another wearisome interview with Maxine Merrick — Cliff's widow — who has been under observation here for a week; thinks she is going crazy; and so do I. Far as I can determine, the only thing that ails her is self-pity and too much concentration on the bad treatment she has had. It is true that Cliff treated her like a dog, and broke her spirit; but now that he is out of the picture there seems no reason why she should not brace up. There is nothing physiologically wrong with Maxine's head. Her trouble is emotional instability. I feel sorry for her, and sorrier for good old Nick, who has been trying to compensate for Cliff's neglect. It is a pity that Nick couldn't have had a son for whom he might feel some pride. He has built a huge country house — a costly mansion — on the west shore of Saginack, and is living there alone with a battery of servants. I doubt if he gets much pleasure out of it. If I were in his place, I should travel. But Nick wouldn't know what he was looking at, if he did travel, unless it had something to do with machinery; and he can see more machinery here in Detroit than anywhere else in the world.

Maxine has now developed into a typical hypo. She has pains. She has pains in her inner ear. She has a pain in her neck. Watson, who has examined her, says she *is* a pain in the neck. She also has much discomfort in her left shoulder, in her lower abdomen, and in her heels. Not that she hasn't been diligent in trying to find relief. She has been to Carlsbad and Aix-les-Bains; she has been to Lourdes. Every so often, in the past three or four years, she has packed her trunks and a maid or two and her badly spoiled son, Bobby, and has galloped away for another sort of treatment. She has had violet rays, mud packs, and Hindu philosophy. She has tried Battle Creek, Theosophy, Arizona, Christian Science, White Sulphur Springs, the Wisdom of the East, and enough calonics to sap the vitality of an army mule.

At present, her anxiety over her own disabilities is somewhat distracted by the untimely arrival of Bobby from the Culver Military Academy where, she said, he had been getting along so nicely. Bobby came to see her yesterday, carrying a huge armful of red roses. You can't help liking him; neither can you help feeling that he must have missed a large number of spankings to which he was justly entitled.

Maxine sent for me to come to her room and meet Bobby, whom I had not seen for a long time. He conversed, without reticence, about his recent retirement from Culver. I rather expected he would try to throw the blame for his expulsion onto the school, but he didn't; was entirely unabashed in reporting that they had 'put up with a lot,' and declared that the Colonel was a mighty fine man. Bobby was very tender in his attitude toward his mother, but I don't see how he can have very much respect for her, in her unbalanced condition. I sympathize with the boy. His father was no good, and his mother is a damn fool. I wonder what will become of him. He's bright enough to be anything he wants to be.

When I dropped in to see Maxine, this afternoon, she was sitting up in bed, attractively jacketed in something made of pink satin and white feathers, and intent upon a little book. Without preliminaries, she asked me what month I was born in; and informed me — after a good deal of leafing back and forth — that I was very firm, very strong, and very stubborn, as indicated by my astral control which, she had discovered, is Alpha of the Nebulae Andromeda. I thanked her for assigning to me such of these attributes as might be considered complimentary, and asked her if her bowels had moved well, today, which she seemed to feel was irrelevant.

'Right while I'm telling you,' she complained, 'about your horoscope, you ask me a rude question that shows you weren't paying the slightest attention.'

I assured her that the two topics were not so incongruous as they seemed; that her defective elimination and her interest in Astrology might be more closely related than she thought. Maxine laughed a little, which I considered a good sign. It has been a long time since she has exhibited any appreciation of humor.

But it was only a fleeting promise. Pretty soon she was back on one of her pet subjects:

what to do next in the great cause of her health and what she calls 'mental rearmament.' Most of our current clichés have a military flavor.

What Maxine really needs is something constructive to do, but I hesitate to suggest a philanthropy. I am sure she would be an insufferable nuisance on the board of a charity, and she would unquestionably make a mess of any attempt to befriend an individual.

Before I left, she showed me some literature she had received from a goofy colony in Southern California where you study what Maxine says is an eclectic derived from Rosicrucianism, Bahaism, and Buddhism, in combination with a vital diet, cosmic breathing, and systematic meditation. I told her it was just the place for her, and I hope she goes. I don't like to see the hospital taking her money. I should like to have given her a stern lecture about her amazing silliness, but it wouldn't have done the slightest bit of good. *

* Had Doctor Hudson foreseen that it would fall to the lot of Maxine Merrick's son to transcribe this journal (a most unlikely circumstance when viewed from the date of this entry), his comments on her eccentricities might have been less severe. I suppose he was sorely tried by my mother's hypochondria and general instability. At this period of her life she was indeed difficult and pitiably unhappy. (R. M.)

***

As I was in the act of locking the safe, there was a tap on the door, and to my surprise and delight Natalie Randolph breezed in. It has been a long time since I have seen anything so pretty. Natalie certainly knows how to dress.

She was very animated, very much on tiptoe.

It was the first time she had ever honored me with a voluntary call, and I was curious to know what her errand might be.

'It's easy to see,' I remarked, 'that you haven't come to consult me professionally. You never looked healthier in your life.'

'I had a few minutes to wait,' she explained, 'and I thought I'd run in and say Hello — if you weren't too busy.'

I assured her that I would never be too busy to talk to her; inquired about her father; answered questions about Joyce; asked whether she had come to see one of our patients.

She flushed a little, most becomingly, and said, 'I have driven over to carry off one of your doctors for dinner. Do you mind?'

I tried not to seem too foolishly pleased, and had sense enough not to press any questions. Mind? Of course, I didn't mind!

'It's going to do Brightwood Hospital a lot of good,' I said, 'if one of our doctors is seen in the company of such a charming young woman. What we need over here is a little more class.'

She made a puckery little mouth at me, told me to be careful what I said to impressionable young women, offered her hand, and dashed away.

I hope this thing comes off. Tim deserves a girl like Natalie. He has been pretty sly — keeping this a secret from me.

Brightwood Hospital

May tenth, 1915, 9:30 P.M.

Late Friday afternoon I had a telephone call from my friend Doctor Russell in Chicago asking if I could run up and attend a consultation the next day. I asked him what it was about and he said it was a glioma. I might have suspected as much, for whenever I am called to a medical center as well equipped as Chicago the case is almost sure to be one of the forty-nine gliomas.

If it should happen that you do not know anything about this, it may be sufficient to tell you that a glioma is an intracranial cyst — and it is no picnic, either for the patient or the surgeon.

If you do know anything about it — and it is indeed quite probable that the person who comes into possession of these memoirs is well informed on medical matters — it may have come to your attention that it has been my good fortune to have experienced a considerable success with these gliomas. Until nearly six years ago, I tried to content myself with the usual procedure.

The customary technique was to empty the cystic cavity, and let it go at that. I assume that every surgeon suspected there was a localized tumor nodule responsible for the secretion of the fluid that caused the pressure and set up the general derangement and degeneration of the brain; but it is very serious business to go exploring in a cystic cavity, in a blind search for something practically indistinguishable from the convolutions of normal brain tissue.

My own practice was to drain the cavity, and hope for the best; and I think that almost every other neurologist believed in the same procedure.

On the first Saturday of July, 1909, I operated on a young woman who, three years earlier, had been hospitalized elsewhere with a cerebellar cyst. The surgeon had done what I should have done in that instance. He had emptied the cystic fluid. There was nothing unusual about the history of the case, after that. The patient made a fairly satisfactory recovery. That is what one might expect. Customarily, a gratifying convalescence promptly ensued. In the course of a year — possibly up to two years — you would begin to find the same old symptoms showing up again; early morning headaches, nausea, faulty vision, and an ataxic gait.

This erratic and violent nausea, by the way, frequently misled medical men, formerly, who were disposed to look for the trouble in the gastro-intestinal tract. But I suppose you know that.

On the occasion to which I am referring, my patient had all the stock symptoms that had been exhibited immediately prior to her previous operation. I did the only thing that was indicated; drained the cavity; and would have stopped with that.

But I was having a few peculiar symptoms that day, myself. I'm afraid I can't describe this sensation very well, but I felt something that might almost be defined as prescience. I don't mean prescience in relation to a divining of future events, but something like prescience in respect to a sensitivity a little beyond one's reach. Am I making myself clear, at all? Well — it was as if the nerves in my fingers extended to the end of the probe; as if the probe were an integral part of my hand, alert as the antennae of a bee.

Of course, if you want to think that one acquires this faculty by constant exercise, backed by the utmost concentration, you are taking a very commonsense view of the matter. You have a good deal of testimony on your side. Blind persons, who read Braille, offer an excellent example of what diligent training will do to make a fingertip cognitive. I hope you will not object to this word cognitive. The intelligent blind man will tell you that he can read Braille with the tip of his right index finger, almost as rapidly as you can read a newspaper by sight. If he uses the tip of the second finger of his right hand, he has to spell the words — letter by letter. If he runs the tip of his little finger over the raised letters, he can't read Braille any better than you can. It might — by accommodation — be said that this blind man's little finger, in respect to literacy, is still an infant. His second finger, in respect to literacy, is five years old. His index finger is adult. Does that help any to illustrate what I am trying to say about this 'cognitive' quality that came into my hand? I believe that I could read, with the tip of my probe, where the tumor nodule was located!

Let me repeat — if you want to think this had come about through practice, all very well; but the fact is that I had never been so acutely conscious of that faculty before, or so confident that I could exercise it with any hope of success. So — I went after that nodule. Hunting for a needle in a haystack, compared to this quest, is merely child's play.

I was very fortunate, that day. After the removal of the tumor, my patient's recovery was rapid and decisive. She regained her health and there has been no recurrence of her trouble. Since then, I have approached these cases with a great deal of confidence. They are still serious enough, but we have cut down our operative mortality from fourteen per cent to four, which is a nice gain.

There are a few other men, in my specialty, who have had much the same success. How they came by their faculty of prescience (if you can endure that not very adequate word in this connection), I do not know. But I know how I came by mine. And I'm not ashamed to admit it, no matter how crazy it sounds.

I performed that epochal operation on a Saturday afternoon in July. On the Tuesday before, I spent six hours with Tony Bontempini, shopping for a kitchen range, assorted pots and pans, stone dishes and steel cutlery, so that he could open up a little restaurant. There is no doubt in my mind but I found there were nerves in my probe, in my lancet, in my scalpel, because I made something important of Tony.

Tony Bontempini had been a patient of mine. A railroad surgeon had brought him in, one afternoon in April, with about the sorriest-looking head I ever saw, which is saying quite a bit. The railroad doctor hadn't the slightest notion that Tony would survive any attempted repairs, and neither had I. It was one of those cases that make a cold shudder run down your spine, no matter how accustomed you may be to compound fractures. Nancy lost her lunch.

I asked the doctor why he had gone to the bother to bring this man away out to Brightwood, and he said he wanted Tony to die in some institution where, it might be conjectured, everything had been done for him. The doctor didn't even wait to consult; said we could phone him when it was all over, and he would attend to the rest of the job.

In other words, Tony Bontempini was a pretty sick man. I wouldn't have bet ten cents on him.

Before leaving the hospital, the railroad doctor — a very good fellow, but quite inured to the sight of bad accidents — remarked that it was rather a pity, for the affair was no fault of Tony's. Tony hadn't been careless. There was an old chap in the section-gang who was very hard of hearing. Tony saw him about to be mowed down by a shunted freight-car; had grabbed him to drag him to safety; and was himself struck a crushing blow by the protruding end of a coupling-rod.

When the doctor was gone, I went up to have another peep at Tony. He was breathing stertorously, but with fairly steady rhythm. Watson drifted in, and after watching for a while, remarked that Tony must have some good stuff packed away. At nine, Tony was still pumping along at the old stand.

'He seems to be practically indestructible,' I said to Tim. 'I'm going to get in there and see if anything can be done.'

I have seen people die, who might have been saved if they had been a little bit sicker. So long as there is a ray of hope, a surgeon is likely to be prudent; sometimes too prudent. If the patient is going to die, anyhow, and it doesn't matter what you do to him, you are likely to be audacious. Once in a while that audacity will do the trick. I've seen it happen. It happened to Tony. He must have had the constitution of a horse, or he couldn't possibly have survived what we had to do to him. Tim muttered, 'I've never seen this much of the inside of a head since I studied Anatomy.'

Little by little, Tony came plodding back from wherever he'd been, and I wondered whether we had really done him a service. All he was good for was a pick-and-shovel job. It was obvious that he could never do anything like that again. And he seemed to realize that the outlook was most unpromising. You couldn't get a rise out of him. He was glum, torpid, incommunicative. I think he understood English much better than he pretended; responding to questions concerning his appetite, his discomforts, his physical wants, but becoming dumb as a moron if you tried to interest him in anything that might distract his mind and lift his depression.

The railroad doctor began to call up, with increasing frequency, to learn how Tony was getting along and when he might be discharged. I do not think that the doctor was positively annoyed by Tony's recovery, but it would have been a much less complicated situation if Tony had confirmed the early forecast.

Every afternoon, the nurse would wheel Tony up to the solarium where he sat staring at the sunshine, taking no stock of his fellow convalescents, and pretending not to understand them when they tried to be pleasant. Finally I got an order to discharge Tony as soon as he was able to be released. I couldn't keep him any longer. I went to his room and told him; expressed my hope that he would find something to do. The railroad was going to arrange some sort of compensation, no doubt. They were always quite decent about such things, I had found. But Tony didn't want to be kept in idleness. The prospect of a pension was merely another cross to bear.

After a protracted silence, he made a weary, despairing little gesture with his bony hand, and said, in a dull monotone, 'Eet ees no good, Doc. You are a dam' fine feller. Fix Tony's head. But Tony ees no good — no more — no good.'

'Perhaps there is something else you can do, Tony,' I said, not very hopefully. 'You mustn't work with a shovel, any more, and you mustn't work in the hot sun. But there are indoor jobs. Is there anything you know how to do?'

'I cook — mebbe. Aw — not so good,' he shrugged, self-deprecatingly, ' — just — what you call plain cook. But — nobody want poor, seeck wop for cook.'

I grabbed at this straw as we were going down for the last time.

'Cook!' I exclaimed, happily. 'Now we've got something.'

'Aw — no, Doc,' protested Tony. 'Mebbe — in soma poor leetle dump — by myself — but not to work all day.'

I had an inspiration.

'Tony,' I said, brightly, 'over in Ann Arbor there is a big college. You know what I mean?'

Tony nodded, comprehendingly, and muttered 'Footaball,' which made me grin a little, so accurately had he hit the thing smack on the button.

'Many hungry boys,' I went on. 'Eat all day; eat all night; eat anything, everything; eat on stools, eat standing up; eat out-of-doors — in the rain — in the snow —' Could I believe my eyes? Tony was pulling a reluctant grin. It was the first one he had ever put on in my society. I continued, with enthusiasm. 'Good place for little restaurant. I want you to go there and start one. I am going with you! We are going tomorrow! I shall set you up in business. It won't cost very much. We will find a little room somewhere and buy you a skillet.'

Tony grinned, and rubbed his jaw hard with the palm of his hand, like an embarrassed child. Then he rubbed both fists in his eyes; and, after a good deal of swallowing, muttered that I was a damn fine feller. I couldn't take any more of that, at the moment, so I went away.

Next day, I went head over heels into an adventure that I knew nothing about; but Tony seemed to know what we wanted. You wouldn't have recognized him for the same fellow, as we drove to Ann Arbor; chattered like a magpie; understood everything I said to him — all but my earnest request that he must never, never tell.

He couldn't get this through his head, but he consented. He warmed genially to my suggestion that if — sometime — some cold night, maybe — a hungry chap came in, looking pretty hollow, perhaps it would be well to feed him — and forget the loss. I wasn't quite sure how Tony would feel about that proposal, but he nodded, emphatically, and said, 'Alla right, Doc. Tony will turn no one away hawngry.'

He proved to be a good bargainer. I was doubtful of his wisdom when he selected his location. It was a long-abandoned, shabby storeroom, about a block from the railroad station.

'You won't be able to catch a very profitable class of trade down here, Tony,' I protested. 'This is off the beat. The students won't come into a place like this — so close to the racket and dirt of the railroad.'

Tony grinned, superiorly.

'College fellers,' he declared, 'same as any other yawng fellers. Lika de railroad, lika de noise, lika de dirt. Home-seeck — come down to seea de railroad. Tony feed 'em. Gooda place.'

I gave in, and we rented the storeroom from an old codger who let us have it at our own figures and almost kissed us when we made an advance payment. Then we bought the range, and the rest of the stuff. I took Tony to the bank I knew best and introduced him, placing some money at his disposal.

'Gooda-bye, Doc,' said Tony, when I was ready to go. 'I paya you back — soma day.'

'I don't want it back. I have other plans for that money. Do you understand, Tony?'

'Hella, no!' said Tony, scratching his head, and regarding me anxiously.

'No matter,' I called after him. 'Good-bye, Tony!'

'Gooda-bye, Doc,' he said, waving his hat.

That was Tuesday.

On Saturday I did the first of that long string of gliomas, with which I have had such gratifying success. Maybe these two matters have no relation. Maybe they occurred coincidentally. My own opinion is that my investment in Tony Bontempini made me aware of what I had in my cognitive hand. Sometimes my friendliest colleagues have pleasantly remarked that I am 'a good guesser.' But I am not a guesser. I wouldn't say this anywhere else than in a private journal that will not be read while I am living: I have what might be called a prescient hand.

And I know how I got it!

It was pleasant to hobnob with Clark Russell again. We were classmates in the Medical School. I always considered him a brighter and more responsive student than myself, and admired him greatly. We meet frequently. He was very fortunate in marriage. Clara Russell has an excellent mind, shrewd wit, and an amazing capacity for developing lasting friendships. Whenever I go to Chicago on a professional errand, if I have an hour or two to spare, I see the Russells. Sometimes I go out to their home. If the time is short, we meet down-town for dinner.

I arrived in Chicago Saturday morning. We went into consultation over Russell's glioma at nine. I said, 'I can't see why you called me in. You knew what it was.' And Russell replied, amusingly like a small boy caught in the jam-pot, 'I thought perhaps you'd like to take it out.' So — I operated, though it isn't going to do very much good, for the growth was a glioblastoma multiforme, which will presently reinstate itself, and fully a third of them are malignant. Our patient was a woman of fifty. She will be free of her bad headaches for a year or two. It's worth an operation. One of these days, she will die. So will Russell and I. And you. But, in the meantime, we have a right to be relieved of our aches and pains, if we can find a way. I think this sort of surgery is justified, even if it doesn't hold out much promise of permanent recovery. What *is* permanent recovery? How permanent do you think you are?

I dined that night with the Russells: and, because I had planned to take a ten o'clock train for home, we had our dinner at the Blackstone. We talked about the war. Russell is sure we are going to be in it presently, and I suppose he is right. At all events, we had no debate on the matter. I aired my recent reflections on the deplorable lack of steadying agencies at a time when the public needed reliances in which the people might place their trust. I was pretty stern about the newspapers, and I had some unflattering things to say about the churches.

Clara conceded my points, in the main, but wanted to call my attention to at least one church — the one she attends — where this matter is receiving proper attention. I inquired about it, and Clara said it was Trinity Cathedral. Then she went on to quote generously from some of the recent remarks of the preacher there, Dean Harcourt. I had occasionally seen his name in the papers.

As I have said, I have a great deal of respect for Clara Russell's intelligence. Anything that she thinks is sound is likely to be worth consideration. I listened attentively to what she had to say. She believes that if the people at large had access to Harcourt's august philosophy it would brace them up.

'The intellectuals, you mean,' I remarked.

'Not exclusively,' she said. 'That is the triumphant thing about Dean Harcourt's sermons. They appeal to the intellectuals, but are understood by people who have never learned how to think straight. They learn it there. I wish you could hear him.'

The Russells went home at nine-thirty. I went up to pack my tackle, expecting to go to my train, only a ten minutes' taxi-drive. Then I decided, impulsively and to my own surprise, that I would stay over and hear this man Harcourt in the morning. For I needed some bucking up myself.

Nancy Ashford, whom I had not seen since my return from Chicago, has just been in to tell me I have been working long enough and should go home to bed. This is good advice, and I shall defer a report of my visit to Trinity Cathedral until my next leisure hour. All I care to say about it now is that I was strangely moved by that event and I believe that if this man Harcourt could be harnessed up somehow to a wide-spread channel of communication he could do a great deal for the public.

I asked Nancy if anything interesting had happened, and she said, 'Your attractive young friend, Natalie Randolph, was here again this afternoon.'

'Came for Tim, likely,' I remarked, with

satisfaction. 'That affair gives promise. It will be good for both of them. I hope they make a go of it. Couple of thoroughbreds.'

'It isn't Tim,' said Nancy. 'It's Leslie Sherman.'

AT HOME

June twenty-fifth, 1915, 11 P.M.

Joyce is at home again for her summer vacation. I think twelve years must be a difficult age for a girl. She isn't a mere child, and has a long way to go before she is a young woman. I am not quite sure how we are going to amuse her here.

She says she doesn't want to study during vacation, and one cannot blame her for that. She has no very serious interest in the piano or any other music. Having been out of town for so many months, she seems to have lost connection with her former friends here. I asked her if she would like to invite a couple of her school companions as house guests for a while, but she thinks they are all spending their holidays with their families; many of them at the seashore. Joyce wonders why we can't go to the seashore, too; but it is quite impossible for me to get away now. I suggested a girls' camp, but she doesn't like the discipline; admits that she is too lazy to keep up with the various activities.

I am afraid I have not done a very good

job in bringing up this child. Joyce has fleeting seizures of demonstrative affection for me, interspersed with longer periods of detachment. She is restless, and I cannot contrive anything to occupy her mind. Everything will be all right when she returns to school in September. She has a good many of the erraticisms of her Grandfather Cummings; not all of them, I devoutly hope.

In my last entry in this journal I referred to the interesting experience I had, a few days ago, at Trinity Cathedral in Chicago. I was much impressed by some remarks made by the preacher, Dean Harcourt. I judge him to be a little east of fifty, though his manner is more venerable, due, no doubt, to the fact that he is a victim of infantile paralysis, seriously crippled, and bearing the deep crisscross lines about his eyes which certify to the pain he has endured. There is tracery around the mouth, too, that tells its own story; though there isn't the slightest indication of self-pity, rebellion, or despair. Quite to the contrary, it is a reposeful face. I never saw a man whose outward bearing seemed so well deserving of the word 'spiritual.' He inspires confidence. You have a feeling that nothing could shatter him or make him afraid or quench his inner glow.

I tried to analyze the whole event, that Sunday morning. I was deeply moved, yet curious to discover the predominant factors which had stirred me; whether the organ, the choir, the architecture, the solemn reverence of the place, the sermon, or the man himself. I suppose it was the perfect harmony and complete integration of all these persons and properties.

In the very first place, you had a sense of the solidarity and sureness and effortless self-confidence of the building itself. It was massive and it was sincere. The walls not only looked like stone: they were stone. I thought a little about this as I approached. Some of our churches are built of concrete blocks, in imitation of stone. And some of our wooden steeples, fussy with jigsaw ornamentation, are painted gray to resemble stone. I had never considered this matter, but it occurs to me now that a church should never be an imitation of something. If the people cannot afford to build their church of stone, let it be made of wood; but, in that case, let the wood be wood.

This may seem to be cavilling over a very small matter. The more that I think about it, the more important it grows. If the church wants to have a steadying effect upon the people, it must begin the task by being absolutely honest. The individual may not pause to ask himself why it is that the church he attends does not compose his spirit, but I think it must have a disquieting effect on him if the building itself is an architectural fraud. If he can't believe in the integrity of the structure, how is he going to believe in the soundness and sincerity of the institution?

I hope I am not making too much of this, but I think the feeling of repose, reliance; the feeling that I was, for a little while, in the custody of something substantial, enduring, and impeccably honest, had a lot to do with my mood, that day. Everything was genuine. The candles on the altar were candles; they were not electric lamps fashioned to resemble candles: they were candles.

There was something about that stately music that had the essence of permanence. It was elemental stuff.

In the village church that we attended, when I was a youngster, the minister — a kind, well-meaning man, with an obsequious smile but no dignity either of speech or bearing — would open the service with a short prayer in which Deity was verbally patted on the shoulder after the manner of a genial greeting between a couple of lodge-brothers, and then the good man would announce a song, such as — 'Only an Armor-bearer, Proudly I Stand.' Or — 'Let the Lower Lights be Burning.' The announcement of the song was always accompanied by an informal — sometimes jocular — admonition urging the congregation, whom he habitually addressed as 'folks,' to join heartily in the singing. Often he would add, playfully, 'If you can't keep on the tune, try to make a joyful noise.'

I realize that this may be an exceptional case of irreverence; or perhaps 'gaucherie' might be a less severe and more accurate designation. But from what I can learn about the prevailing habits of the majority of our churches in this country, I strongly suspect that the difference between that village church procedure and the current customs of our churches is a difference of manner rather than mood. The idea seems to be that the church is a social club; and, as such, should avoid anything like formality. Let us all loudly sing now, folks, and make whoopee for the Lord.

As I sat there in Trinity Cathedral, waiting for the service to begin, I felt conscious of an other-worldly environment. This was not a club. An usher had quietly shown me to a seat. He had not pawed me. Nor had his manner indicated that I was doing Trinity Cathedral a very good turn by honoring it with my presence. I gathered that Trinity Cathedral hadn't been fretting about the possibility of my non-attendance. The place was very quiet.

Everybody faced the thing alone.

Presently the organ began. One couldn't see the organist at work, and one couldn't see the organ. It gave the swelling music a chance. The vested choir came down the broad, stone-flagged aisle. The people stood. The choir filed slowly into the chancel, singing. Two young men in vestments supported on either side the tall, white-haired, crippled man, who came into the chancel from an adjacent door. There were prayers, chants, readings from the Bible, stately hymns. I confess I was almost suffocated with emotion when the august hymn began — 'O God Our Help in Ages Past; Our Hope for Years to Come.' I had been so dreadfully upset; so beaten down with worries; so riddled with anxieties — in my professional work — and anxieties over the stunning deeds of violence abroad. My eyes burned and flooded while that confident hymn confessed its faith in the everlastingness of the Divine Guidance. 'A thousand ages in Thy sight are like an evening gone.' Here was permanence for you. 'Time like an ever-rolling stream.' The hot tears rolled down my cheeks. It was the first time my neural tension had been relieved for a long, long time.

When I began to write this, I had it in mind only to record a few of the things that Dean

Harcourt said, that morning; but it occurred to me that you might be a little more impressed by them if you realized the mood I was in when I heard them. As I have said, I was deeply moved, that day. I suppose almost anything the man might have said would have found me wistfully receptive.

I don't think there had been a sermon topic announced, and I am not sure that the Dean began by stating his theme, but what he talked about was the insured life. It was a tribute to our spirit of co-operation, he thought, that we had been able to insure so many of our interests. Once upon a time, if a man's house burned down or his horses were stolen, he took his loss alone. We had now reached the point in our socialization where we were bearing one another's burdens.

The Dean digressed a little here to remind us of the great progress we had been making in this field. Only a little while ago, as Time is counted in terms of epochs, the social order was hardly aware of itself as an integer. The handful of kind-hearted men and women in a community did what they could to aid their neighbors and kindred in distress, but the kindness was sporadic. There was no enduring momentum to it.

'May one suggest to the dismayed,' said the Dean, 'that instead of deploring the long way we must yet go until we have reached an era of universal amity, we rejoice over the immeasurably longer way we have come from an era of universal suspicion, distrust, and fear. This is not a single day's march — from the jungle to the city of light — but we are much closer to the light than we are to the jungle. We are not there yet, but we know which way we are headed. There have been many detainments, many detours. It has not been — and may not be — a straight and steady course toward the Golden Age, but the general direction is forward; the general movement is upward. We cannot afford to be patient, if patience — in our opinion — means apathy; but we can well afford to be patient, if patience means poise. We are not indignant with our ancestors because they moved no faster, nor should we be too critical of ourselves if, in our time, we have days of plodding with leaden feet.'

All things considered, thought the Dean, we had not done so badly. One of the evidences of our increasing willingness to befriend one another was manifest by the widespread interest in insurance. If a man's house burns down, the community builds another.

'It will not build him another unless he has previously given evidence that he, himself, would help restore another man's house; but if he has declared his willingness to assist in defraying the cost of another's accident or illness or death or the care of his helpless survivors, he can expect that the age he lives in will do for him whatever he stands ready to do for others. There are many imperfections and inequities in our social order which need correction, but our present system warrants our optimism. We have a right to be hopeful — and hope, I think, is the first requisite of courage.'

Perhaps these words that I am trying to quote, and I believe I am recording at least the substance of them, may sound trite and obvious; but, in the solemn stillness of that place, they had a peculiar steadying quality. The world — in spite of its problems — wasn't galloping a tam-o'-shanter to the devil. The world was operating on a long-term schedule. Its defects were many, but they were not as many as they were a hundred years ago. We were too close to this movement to observe its progress. Did William the Conqueror come forth from his tomb, and survey the world, he would observe the course and distance we had come. Sometimes it is difficult for us to note the world's advancement — but William could see it, if he came back.

So much, then, for progress, of which insurance was a good sign. It had come to pass that we could insure almost anything; insure an outdoor pageant against the loss occasioned by rain; the pianist could insure his hands and the dancer her feet.

But there were still some possible losses which a man must bear alone; some risks he would have to carry without aid.

Here the Dean remarked that it would be indeed a great comfort if one could insure one's memories so that they would ever bless him, and never burn.

'You can insure your memories,' said the Dean, 'but you will have to do it by yourself. And they are very real property, too. Some of them are assets; some of them are liabilities. Be careful what kind of memories you store up to live on in a rainy day.'

Let me repeat: perhaps this sounds commonplace, apart from its setting. But everything was so strangely hushed. It seemed as if you were getting a direct message from Headquarters!

'Be spiritually thrifty!' advised Dean Harcourt. 'Put aside some memories that will nourish you in your declining years. Be mindful not to stock memories that will keep you awake nights. It will be too bad — too bad — if, every time there is a little cessation of the noise and confusion, you hear the sound of people sobbing — people who loved you.

It will be very good if, when the noise about you subsides a little, you can remember the words and tones of gratitude — gratitude of people who lived more abundantly — because of *you*.'

This whole affair made a profound impression on me. I do not think that I shall live long enough to forget it. I hope my reference to it may be of benefit to you.

I went out of the Cathedral feeling that I had been fitted with a new balance-wheel. I wish everybody had access to such an inspiration in these troubled times.

I am driving up to my 'estate' on Lake Saginack tomorrow. The idea of pitching a tent up there is, I feel, absurdly impractical. But perhaps I may want to build a little cottage there. It is not so very far away. I might have a good deal of satisfaction in a quiet place like that. I am taking Joyce along, but I fear she will not find it very entertaining. I do wish I could think of something that might give pleasure to this restless child.

BRIGHTWOOD HOSPITAL

December fourth, 1915, 9 P.M.

Henry Ford's peace ship sailed this afternoon from Hoboken and the papers are amused. Perhaps they cannot be blamed, for this excursion does seem a bit fantastic.

But it isn't much harder to believe that a dozen unauthorized pacifiers could hope that they might stop the war than that such a war could have been precipitated. The whole thing is an incredible nightmare!

Of course the main point of weakness in this well-meant adventure is the conspicuous absence of anyone officially empowered to represent the United States government. Assuming that this party of altruistic cruisers voices the thoughts and hopes of many millions of American citizens — and I think it does — it has no recognized standing. Governments — not private citizens — make wars. And when wars come to an end, the governments end them.

Ford's project is put on by laymen. It is very doubtful whether the governments of the countries involved will pay the slightest heed to it; except, perhaps, to sneer at it. But it is by no means an ignoble gesture, however futile. I was glad to see that none of the spoofing paragraphers has insinuated that Henry might be doing this to show off; for that wouldn't have been true. Henry does not hanker for front page publicity. He is not a vain man. Nobody can accuse him of exhibitionism. He has gone into this thing sincerely.

And in spite of all the editorial snickers, I'll bet there are a lot of people, throughout this country, who are earnestly hoping, perhaps expecting, that something may come of this expedition.

I am mentioning this event here because it is likely that when these words are deciphered the Great War will have passed into ghastly history, and I want you to realize the mental condition of our people in these closing days of 1915. If a man as bright and cold as Henry Ford will charter a ship, at the instigation of a not very thoroughly credentialled Hungarian woman, and sail for Europe with a little group of newspaper men and parsons, intending to stop the war 'and get the men out of the trenches by Christmas,' you can get a general idea of the dishevelled state of mind in which the less bright and more volatile find themselves. We've got to the point where we think that nothing short of a miracle can save civilization. And if the Ford expedition accomplishes anything, the feat will prove that our surmise has been correct.

Dorothy Wickes has sold two more pictures for excellent prices. She has stopped working in the store; has moved her family to better quarters.

Somehow I had gathered that her older brother Harry was not passionate on the subject of work. But a chance remark of Dorothy's, a few months ago, gave me a better impression of the chap, and I exercised myself a little to find out what he thought he could do.

Harry said he believed he might be useful in a shop handling art supplies. I liked this. It has been my observation that when some member of a family exhibits a special talent, the brothers and sisters are likely to be jealous. Their favorite method of showing how they feel about it is to manifest a cool indifference — if not positive contempt — toward everything related to the fortunate one's art or trade.

Harry Wickes not only didn't have a trace of this sulkiness in him: he was exultant over the honor that had come to the family; proud of his sister and intensely interested in what she was doing. He had no artistic talent himself, but it delighted him that Dorothy had it. His enthusiasm and glad surprise must have meant a very great deal to her in those days when she was trying so hard to express herself. Now he wanted a job selling drawing-boards, pencils, easels, paints, canvas, and brushes, because they were the implements of Dorothy's success.

When I learned this, I made an effort to find him a place in an art shop. He has done very nicely. I think there is a pleasant future for him in this trade. I see him frequently.

More and more I am believing in what someone has styled 'the contagion of character.' And I make a deliberate endeavor to expose myself, whenever possible, to the influence of people who possess some peculiar nobility.

I venture to call your attention to the importance of this. Of course, it would be the very supremacy of selfishness if one were to pick one's friends on a basis of what they had to give forth. There are plenty of people, in need of our attention, who have very little with which to repay us. But I feel that we are well within our rights if we cultivate the acquaintance of persons whom we have discovered to be in possession of specialized talents in the field of character-building. One such acquaintance may serve as a stimulant to us; another as a sedative. One man laughs his fears and frets away and another growls at them. It is fortunate for us if we can recognize the exact effect that other people have on us. Then we know when to seek or avoid them.

These persons may or may not be of our own social stratum. I find that I get a good deal of solid satisfaction from people who seem to live narrowly restricted lives. Some of them are like beavers. They don't know anything but how to build dams; and, if their dams are torn down, they begin immediately to build again. So — if you find you are no good at building dams, or get too easily upset when the dams you have built are torn away, you can learn much by observing the beavers; provided, of course, that you do not frighten them away.

There is, for example, an orderly at Brightwood named Blake. He has a fourteen-year-old daughter at home with the mental age of four. He is quite devoted to her and insists that she is going to be all right. I listen to him, with sincere interest, whenever he wants to talk about Dolly, whose name, I think, is singularly appropriate. No amount of persuasion has succeeded in convincing him that he should place Dolly in a school for backward children. He thinks she is better off at home, and — in the circumstances — I agree with him. It may come to pass, some years from now, that the child will be too grave a problem for Mert Blake and his wife to handle; but there is plenty of time to decide on that matter. For the present, the child may as well stay where she is.

Mert tells me that Dolly is getting on nicely with her spelling; especially with the names of animals that are not too difficult. She spelled 'mouse,' the other day.

Now I don't want you to leap to the conclusion that Mert Blake is a soft-headed sap with a mentality not much more advanced than Dolly's. Down inside himself, Mert knows that Dolly hasn't really grown an inch or gained a pound mentally since she was a mere tot, and he knows as well as I do that she is never going to know any more than she knows now. There is a constant ache in Mert's mind that never eases. It is aching when he wakes up in the morning, and it is still aching when he goes to sleep at night. He sees the neighbors' budding young girls, ready for high school.

And Mert — who is no fool — knows that I know all about Dolly; for I have gone through her with a lantern; and, if there was anything to be done for her, Mert knows that I should have had a go at it.

And — all the time that he is chattering away, with an optimistic smile, about Dolly's fine progress — and all the time that I am punctuating his lively reports with little exclamations of pleased surprise — Mert knows that we are both playing relief parts in a heartbreaking tragedy. I like Mert because he has the stuff in him that enables him to do that. Not everyone has an authentic talent for it. I wouldn't exchange a half hour's chat with Mert Blake for a dozen dinner engagements with as many brilliant intellectuals.

I have thought that this might be worth mentioning to you. It has become my practice to nourish my own character by exposing it to the influence of specially endowed personalities who, by sublimating their griefs or by inventing ingenious compensatory devices, have — unwittingly, perhaps — made themselves very important.

It's quite easy to miss chances to improve oneself in this way. I might have skipped the blessing of Mert Blake's friendship if it had not been for Tim Watson's remarks to me on the subject of caste in a hospital. Once upon a time, I should have considered it the wrong thing to do — from a standpoint of good discipline — to encourage Mert to come into my office and sit down and talk about Dolly. I have happily graduated from all such nonsense. And I strongly recommend to you the policy of establishing close and comradely connections with people who have something of spiritual fineness in them, regardless of their social rating. Don't be misled by the fact that the man may use very faulty diction, and have uncouth manners, and be in need of a thousand dollars' worth of dental attention. If he is a spiritual athlete (Can you bear this phrase?), you can afford to watch him do his tricks.

Most people of our sort pick their friends on a sheer basis of propinquity, congeniality, and social equality. If you want to build character, you must not be content to know only persons who are no stronger than yourself.

Young Wickes' range of interests is not very wide. You couldn't load what Harry doesn't know about almost everything into the largest moving-van on the road; but he has got something in him that I should like to have more of.

I do not believe that I am, by nature or habit, a jealous or envious person. That is: I do not think that whatever jealousy or envy I may have tucked away in me is virulent enough to show through in my bearing and conversation. But — not to be envious is, after all, a negative virtue. Wickes has moved over into the positive zone, in respect to this matter.

He asked me, point-blank, one Saturday night when we were at dinner together downtown, why I 'bothered' with him. And I told him, with equal candor, that he had been given a clean-cut talent for magnanimity (which I had to define for him), and that it built me up, quite a bit, to be in his company. He blinked a little, but got the idea. I daresay he later examined this gift of his, in his mirror, and decided to give it a little more air and light.

Next time I met Dorothy, she said, 'What have you done to Harry?'

'Have I done something to Harry?' I countered.

'You know you have.' Her tone was intimate. We were the same age now. She searched my eyes from under long lashes. 'Harry is a precious darling — and you are making him more precious, every day.'

'That's nice,' I replied. 'You ought to know. When a fellow's sister thinks he is a precious darling —'

'I'd like to swap a few stories with you,' broke in Dorothy. 'I don't see why we can't. If you'll tell me what you've been doing to Harry, I'll tell you what I did for —'

'Stop!' I pointed my finger directly into her pretty face, and grew very stern. *Do you want to spoil it?*'

Randolph tells me that Natalie and Leslie Sherman are engaged. I wonder if Leslie knew that Tim was interested there. I hope he did not.

If Tim has been hurt, you wouldn't know it by his manner. But he always did have himself well in hand. You could skin him alive without getting an outcry. I like this about him, though I think that in order to achieve such a distinction a man has to sacrifice a lot of emotional sensitivity which is really imperative to normal living. I can't help admiring stoicism in other people, but I think the overhead charges on its maintenance come pretty high. You bottle up too many urgent wishes and you can't be sure whether the chemical reaction is going to make a saint or a sourpuss.

Whenever a person espouses a martyrdom, he needs to be mighty careful about the mood in which he goes to the stake. I have known a lot of fried prigs.

BRIGHTWOOD HOSPITAL

June seventeenth, 1916, 10:30 P.M.

Natalie and Leslie Sherman were married this evening at the Randolph home. There were only about twenty guests, but the affair did not lack distinction, the house beautifully decorated and the excellent dinner served expertly by the best caterers in town. Natalie, who grows more winsome every day, was dazzling in white satin and orange blossoms. She had wanted a church wedding, but economy is in the air just now and such pageants are not popular.

But while this restriction may have been slightly disappointing to Natalie, I daresay Leslie was not annoyed by the fact that he assumes his new obligations at a time when frugality is fashionable; for, so far as I am aware, he has no resources beyond his small income at Brightwood.

Tim Watson was Leslie's best man. His athletic figure showed up to great advantage in his evening clothes. I observed that the bridesmaids were pleasantly impressed. Whether Tim consented to stand up with Leslie because

(a) he really doesn't care, any more; or, (b) wanted to prove there was no constraint between him and his longtime chum; or, (c) thought he would be healthier if he cauterized his wounds — nobody is going to know. Tim keeps his own counsel. Perhaps he is part Indian.

On several occasions in the past few months I have been on the point of writing something in this book, but most of the things I might have recorded will be accessible to you elsewhere.

What part we intend to take in the European war has been the one burning question that monopolizes all conversation. The controversy between the preparedness advocates and the peace-at-any-pricers grows more acrimonious; or, rather, the onslaughts of the militant group against the pacifists are becoming more savage. The latter are on the defensive; and, I think, on the decline.

Anyone who would have risked saying, a year ago, in the conservative atmosphere of St. Paul's Cathedral, that 'a pacifist is an anarchist,' might have found himself criticized; but it was said there, a month ago, and it does not appear that the statement has been challenged. Thus far have we moved toward a warlike mind.

Many solidly substantial men, whose normal

attitude toward debatable questions has testified to their sound judgment and sportsmanly tolerance, have lately given themselves to expressions of opinions so hot that they sizzle and sputter. A man can hardly believe his ears. Conservative old codgers, some of whom have never been notorious for any other extravagance, are now quoted as making wild remarks utterly foreign to their training and temperament.

There is manifest, on every hand, a pious lip-service to patriotism. The theater orchestra always plays the National Anthem now, with unprecedented vigor; standing in a row, facing the audience, and blowing itself pop-eyed and purple, perhaps to give assurance of its own loyalty, for the names and personal architecture of many of our professional musicians are unmistakably Teutonic.

With the unleashing of the brasses and tympani, everyone bounds to his feet and assumes what feels like a military posture; stiff, severe, statuesque. Out of the tail of our patriotic eye, we invoice our neighbor's behavior in regard to this solemn rite; and should he be detained by so little as a split second in displaying a zeal that matches ours — perhaps while retrieving his hat from under the seat — we furtively analyze his physiognomy to see if he is something other than pure Nordic.

We have also learned to salute the flag more ceremoniously, which is doubtless good for us. We were always a bit too casual toward the sacred emblems of our patriotism. But we have been well cured of that apathy. We now not only pay our own devout tribute to the Stars and Stripes with deep fervor; we also scrutinize the other fellow pretty carefully to make sure that his obeisance has the sanctioned form and substance.

Any man with a German name is out of luck. The fact may be that Fred Schroeder (unfortunately nicknamed Fritz) is of the fourth generation of his family since its migration to this country, and it may be that his grandfather's brave old bones rest in the National Cemetery at Gettysburg: but nobody is going to listen to Fritz while he explains that America is his native land. Fritz is regarded with suspicion. If — alarmed over his unhappy situation — he seeks to mend matters by spelling his name 'Shrader,' we conclude that he did have something to be frightened about, and a self-deputized committee of superpatriots visits his meat shop to challenge his loyalty. Children on the school playground boo and catcall at his hapless little Gretchen.

It has occurred to me that a few of these minor tragedies of the war might well be mentioned here. As for the more epochal events, you will learn them from other sources. But perhaps history will not bother to reconstruct the atmosphere in which we are living now. Here we are, riddled by factional disputes, angry and distrustful; humiliating honest people with whom we never had a quarrel and for whom we had respect, all because of a war four thousand miles away.

If we can contrive to get ourselves into such a mental state as this — before taking up arms — I wonder what may happen to our skittish brains in the event we decide to toss ourselves into it.

The American is not a very good hater, perhaps for lack of time. To be a really competent hater, you have to give yourself to it with earnest diligence. You can't hate efficiently and get much else attended to, for you have very little nervous energy left over. A man will burn less carbon while sawing wood than while maintaining a steady, glowing hatred.

Our people have always been anxious to succeed in their business undertakings. To make money, acquire property, equip for a rainy day, and have something to bequeath to the children, has been of more importance to us than the relative superiorities of races and nations. We are all comparatively recent imports from ancient lands. Most of us rejoice that it is our happy lot to have escaped from worn-out soils and age-long feuds. If we could sell a man something, at a profit, we didn't care what language he spoke; nor did we inquire into his former loyalties and inherited antipathies. It was our boast that these things were so. It was our first point of national distinction — the ability of all these polyglot, polychrome people to live together in neighborly fashion. We are now in the process of tossing this unique merit to the winds, and — whether or not there is to be war for us — we are going to regret this tragic blunder!

Now that it is popular to disparage our own citizens of German extraction, we have gone into it with a thoroughness that is no more cruel than ridiculous. We are calling sauerkraut 'liberty cabbage.' This, in my opinion, practically completes our recent struggle to achieve a finished asshood.

But no man, if he values his reputation at all, can afford to speak his mind on this matter. He mustn't laugh. Indeed — however absurd these things are — he doesn't want to laugh. It has passed the point of being ludicrous. It isn't funny any more.

The dispatches concerning the German army's inhuman atrocities continue to come, growing in volume and appalling details; mutilations, crucifixions, eyes gouged out, hands dismembered. Belgian refugees are coming over; most of them small children. It is said that some of these unfortunate little things are without hands, though it has been difficult to locate anyone who has, himself, seen these cases.

Many of our preparedness orators say that they have talked personally with people who had seen such mutilations, but I have not heard any man say that he saw such things with his own eyes.

Yet the dispatches, reporting such atrocities, come to us with what appears to be official sanction. While it is very difficult to believe that any nation in this modern world would resort to such frightfulness for the sake of terrorizing the enemy, it is absolutely inconceivable that the high officials of a nation would deliberately concoct and disseminate such stories about another nation unless there were properly attested facts to warrant it.

If Germany has actually committed these crimes, she will have to pay dearly for them. And if the other people have been maliciously lying about this, that too will have to be paid for. No cause can be worth very much that has to win its way by mutilating civilians and prisoners; nor can any cause be worth very much that has to win its way by a campaign of willful defamation of a nation's character. If it may be assumed that these premises are sound, I think it is of great importance that we find out, pretty soon, whether the atrocity stories are true or false. If true the barbarians should be crushed, no matter what it costs to do it; if false, any further talk about our side as 'a righteous and holy cause' is, of course, a lot of hypocritical nonsense; though it would ill become us to criticize anyone else for hypocrisy — much less nonsense — in our enfeebled mental condition.

My friend — if I were to hand these pages to a newspaper, tonight, I should unquestionably spend tomorrow at police headquarters, trying to give an account of myself. But I want to document my thoughts about war — as of this date — and put them away for safekeeping. I have no notion what mood our nation will be in when you read these words. If the war is over, and the public's sanity has been approximately restored, you may not find my opinions on this matter differing very much from the prevailing thought of your time. If the war is not over — or another war is in sight — you will realize how imprudent it would be for me to express my feelings publicly.

I am a very unhappy man. I have taken pride in my practice of living above fear. I have held that if a man is afraid of anything, his fear filters through everything he thinks and does. And now I know that I am afraid to stand up and say to my neighbors that I think war is a degrading thing, that war soils everything it touches, that no war can be truthfully considered 'holy.'

The American Medical Association has been in convention here since Friday. A couple of distinguished army surgeons have made speeches; but, in view of our theoretical neutrality, neither Surgeon General Rupert Blue nor Assistant Surgeon General Rucker adverted to the war, which I thought was in excellent taste and a commendable pattern of speech and behavior.

Doctor Blue said that the physician's greatest enemies are ignorance and intemperance. I couldn't help wondering, while he spoke, whether — when he referred to intemperance — he wasn't thinking of intemperate talk as well as intemperate habits.

Doctor Charles Mayo made a statement that I find difficult to understand. He was tracing the progress of the race, particularly stressing the advancement in medicine and surgery. It was a very thoughtful address. The conclusions he arrived at, however, were a bit startling.

'The Slavs,' he declared, 'will be the coming nation of the earth.'

Surely this is not the logical outcome of the scientific progress that had been laid before us in such a masterly array of facts. If the Slavs are to dominate a world that has been blest by scientific discovery and invention, one naturally gathers that these people have been and are in the vanguard of this evolution, and may be expected to rule as a reward for their superior contributions to our advancement. But I can't recall any outstanding service that the Slavs have performed in this field.

The doctor further went on to say that we ourselves are destined to be a commercial nation of the meanest type. I can't agree with this, either. Just because we have become temporarily upset mentally, and have been showing up at a disadvantage, it does not follow that we have permanently lost our souls. We have pounded ourselves pretty hard on the subject of our greed, our frantic grab-and-get ambitions; but I think it should be remembered that we have been quite soft-hearted toward other peoples in distress.

I think it was a generous act when we returned the indemnity to China that had been paid to reimburse us for our losses in their revolution, asking them to spend the money on scholarships for their boys. Whenever there has been a great catastrophe affecting the people of cities and nations thousands of miles away, we have subscribed huge sums for their relief, without any other motive than human kindness. I wonder if the Slavs are to take the lead in world philanthropy. If so, they should get themselves going in this direction. At present, they do not seem to know whether they are afoot or horseback.

As a cosmic prophet, I think that Doctor Mayo is one of the most brilliant surgeons in this country.

I had a few sketches drawn for a cottage on Lake Saginack, but the time is not propitious. I doubt if I would use it, even if it were built. Besides, it will be prudent to economize now. If we have to get into the war, it will be very costly.

HOTEL PONTCHARTRAIN, DETROIT

December second, 1917, 8:30 P.M.

I gave up housekeeping a week ago, drained the plumbing, locked the shutters, and moved to this hotel. It wasn't worth the bother to maintain my establishment, under existing conditions.

Joyce is at school in Philadelphia — or I hope she is, the management having reluctantly consented to let her remain, on probation, with the understanding that she is to be more obedient. I have had a merry time, these past few weeks, with this mischievous young lady who has a gift for getting into scrapes.

Nate Swihart — who for the past three years has been my man of all work — is at Camp Custer, marching twenty miles per day with full equipment which, he writes me, includes everything but the piano. Gladys, his wife and my cook, has been threatening to die of loneliness and worry, so I have packed her off to Owosso where she will live with her parents 'for the duration.'

My decision to retire from the irksome farce

of keeping my house going was precipitated by the alarming coal shortage. I have suspected that a good deal of the country's noisy economies, in recent months, was part of the phenomena of our patriotism; but the resolve to save coal is certainly not an affectation. The fuel situation is so grave that unless it is relieved promptly the factories will have to shut down.

We are all on a war basis now, with everything regimented. Heatless Mondays, lightless Tuesdays, meatless Fridays. Save sugar, save butter, save flour, save coal, save peach-stones, save democracy. Posters everywhere, advising, challenging, prohibiting, threatening. It is a hell of a way to live, after one has gone one's own gait for more than two score years.

And yet, if one can endure this temporary sacrifice of personal liberty, without too much irritation, it has its commendable points. There is nothing that this country has needed more than discipline. We have had plenty of laws, but very spotty enforcement. The average good citizen has fallen into the habit of obeying such laws as he finds convenient. For the present, everybody walks the chalk. Unquestionably this gives us more respect for the government, and for ourselves too.

This generation of children has had a minimum of supervision, either at home where their parents are too busy or too pleasure-loving to oversee their conduct, or at school where the new psychology encourages Junior to express himself. It is the first unspanked generation in the history of the world. Now that military mores have the right of way, even the little children are readjusting their ideas to fit the time.

One would have thought that our soldiers, suddenly tugged out of their civilian freedom to be barked at by cocky young sergeants, might have resented such treatment; but they seem to have accepted it as good sports, and when hard put upon they sing, 'We're in the army now.' And so are all the rest of us in the army now — or what comes to the same thing. Little Junior eats his oats without grousing, having been sharply informed that he should be mighty thankful he has oats to eat, seeing what the Belgian children are living on. And Junior's erstwhile bridge-playing mother works all day at Red Cross Headquarters making bandages and other hospital necessities, while Junior's father is losing his excess fat as he gallops about selling Liberty bonds. The whole family is invigorated.

I find democracy a more comfortable form of government, but there is no denying the fact that this temporary autocracy has been beneficial to most of our people. The majority of us indulged ourselves too much. We have overheated our houses in winter. We have eaten too much meat and sugar and white bread. Moreover, we have lacked a unifying motive to stimulate our herd loyalty. Many people were too individualistic for their own good, striving for some manner of uniqueness which often resulted in mere silly posing.

You might be amazed at the difference all this has made in the public health. Fully a third of the rooms at Brightwood are unoccupied. My own business has not been affected, one way or the other, diseases of the brain not seeming to discriminate much between peace-time and war-time; but Pyle's days are not so crowded, nor Carter's, nor Jennings's.

Perhaps it has not been such a bad thing for us to have had a sniff of dictatorial, militarized government, after so long an experience of an easy-going democracy. Of course, the thing is a novelty now, amply justified by an emergency. We might fret under it if it were permanent. We might even fret under it now, if we feared it might become permanent.

And it might easily become permanent, I think. The federal government has discovered how simply and promptly it can get whatever it wants. The states have largely waived their accustomed rights to exercise their individual prerogatives, willing to conform to orders from The Top, for the sake of expediency. Today, if the national government resolves upon some drastic action at ten o'clock it publishes the decree at eleven, and by noon the thing is in full operation in high gear.

This naturally pleases the government, whose power is now concentrated, and it must be of immense gratification to be able to shout an order to a hundred million people and hear an immediate 'Aye, aye, sir!' I surmise that the federal government will be very reluctant to hand this privilege back to the states, after the present emergency is over.

I do not pretend to know very much about the philosophy of history. I am not sure that anyone knows much about it, judging from the wide divergence of expert opinion on the subject. But I think it is generally agreed that democracy is not a hardy perennial. Even a temporary compromise of democracy endangers its life. It wouldn't surprise me if — when the war is ended — we never fully recover the liberties we have given up. Whether it would be a good thing to have a permanent concentration of more power in the national capital would depend, of course, upon the manner in which such power was exercised.

If the leadership was wise and just, you might get a better government than was had under the old system. There is something to be said for a benevolent despotism. The trouble is to find your benevolent despot.

I should give a good deal to know how all this is coming out. Washington is packed and jammed with government employees. When the war is over, I wonder whether these extra thousands will be willing to go back to their homes and resume their former occupations.

Shortly after war was declared, I presented myself for service as a surgeon, and was promptly rejected — as I had anticipated — on account of the faulty heart. Owens, of the Medical Examining Board, kindly attempted to condole with me over my rejection, but I assured him that I was quite contented to remain in my hospital and do my accustomed work.

I could afford to be entirely honest in making this statement, for the question of a doctor's courage in enlisting for service was not at issue. The army doctor's personal risk is negligible. He is not a combatant. He is probably as safe in the camp hospital as he is at home.

Pyle registered as willing to go, but the board put him on the reserve list, on account of his age, and he will not be called. They have plenty of doctors.

Tim Watson was promptly accepted and is at Fort Sheridan where his duties are light and not very interesting. Tim has always been very ambitious, especially in developing his surgery. At present he is mainly occupied with administering cathartics and looking at lame feet. If he is sent abroad, it will be a different story; but, until now, he is doing nothing that couldn't be done as well by a trained nurse. When he wrote me this, I requested that he be released on leave, for important work at Brightwood. It was thirty days before I had a reply, but when it came it was a most impressive document — an assembly of printed forms, duly stamped and signed by a dozen officials located in district, regional, and national headquarters. The upshot of the voluminous communication — which I did not take time to read in full — was that my request could not be granted; so Tim stays by his castor oil bottle and acknowledges the salutes of tired youngsters who have stubbed a toe.

Leslie Sherman is at Camp Custer. I don't think the war has discommoded him seriously. Natalie is living at the Post Tavern in Battle Creek, and Leslie sees her every day or two. Randolph has closed up his house and is living in New York.

★ ★ ★

It is of much interest to me, in these days, to note what the sudden imputation of military authority is doing to different types of men.

For many years I have preserved a delightful friendship with a man named Zimmerman, who lives in Ann Arbor. We were quite comradely during our freshman and sophomore years. Dan got into the manufacturing business and became very well-to-do. He was a fine executive.

He has always taken a vital interest in military affairs, and has ranked high in the National Guard. When the Officers' Training School was opened at Plattsburg, Dan was early on the ground. Then he was sent to Texas, during our difficulty with Mexico. Now he is at Camp Custer, a major.

I was called over there a few weeks ago on a professional errand which concerned a young non-com in Dan's outfit, and learned that his men were sincerely devoted to the major and proud to be under his command. He came into the room, while I was in the camp hospital, and exhibited the same concern for the young patient that he might have shown toward a nephew. Everybody had stood at attention when Dan strode in, tall, bronzed, physically fit. I liked the gentle tone with which he said, 'Please be at ease.' I don't think he lost a mite of prestige.

Now — Dan Zimmerman, I happen to know, is not much of a back-slapper. He is essentially an aristocrat, lives in a palatial home, moves in an exclusive social set, and has the general bearing of an English squire. At a hasty glance, you might have guessed that there would be a pretty wide gap between this major and the rookies. But Dan, without the sacrifice of his authority or any negligence in discipline, had his men welded into one solid chunk — and all of them ready to follow him anywhere.

It is going to be good for these chaps to have this sort of association with aristocracy at its best. They can't help being finer men after having observed the effortless sportsmanship of Dan Zimmerman. He wore his uniform as if he had been born in it; and, because it came naturally to him to obey and command, he inspires not only confidence and loyalty, but affection.

A few blocks from Brightwood Hospital there is a tony food store. The manager is an amiable and hard-working fellow named Brink. Jim Brink has grown up with the business, and knows all about it. His clientele is composed mostly of wealthy people who know exactly what they like in the way of delicacies and are able to pay for them; or, at least to order them and consume them, though I suspect that Jim carries on his books a good many assets which would make a banker laugh.

I shouldn't think of envying Jim his job. All day long, for years, he could be found saying — to customers quite too valuable to be handled by a mere sales-person — 'Yes, indeed, Mrs. Northby, if we haven't got it, we will find it for you.' — 'Yes, yes, Mrs. Highwall, we will make a special delivery, of course. Thank you! Thank you — very, very much!'

It was difficult to imagine Jim in any other setting than his snobbish shop; but, to the amazement of everybody, he decided that the government needed him badly. He went to Grayling to train. He is at Camp Custer, now, with the rank of second lieutenant.

Not very long ago, a private in his company, on leave for a day to visit a sick relative, got into a trolley accident a few miles from here and was seriously hurt. Because it was thought he had a skull fracture, they brought him to Brightwood. The head injury did not amount to much, so Pyle put him together again, a tedious job, for the young fellow was broken in a half dozen places.

Yesterday, Lieutenant Brink showed up at the hospital. Announcing at the desk that he had come for the private, whose name I have forgotten, he was referred to Doctor Pyle, who at the moment was with me in an operation. Informed that he would have to wait a little while, the lieutenant became very much annoyed; came up to the operating-room, pushed the nurse out of the way who told him he must not come in, and stalked — booted, belted, spurred, and bright-buttoned — to the side of the table.

Pyle, half-stunned over this amazing impudence, glanced up and said, 'Why — Good morning, Jim.'

'Lieutenant Brink, sir, if you please,' snapped Jim. 'I have come for Private — (whatever-his-name was).'

'You had better leave him for another week or ten days,' advised Pyle, swallowing his indignation. 'He isn't able to travel yet.'

'I shall be the judge of that,' growled Jim. 'Where is he?'

This was too much for Pyle, who is not accustomed to this kind of talk, and he exploded.

'You get out of here, Brink! You know better than to invade an operating-room in street clothes. Just because you've harnessed yourself up in leather —'

'That will do!' broke in Jim, shrilly. 'I want my man — and if you don't take me to him I shall put you under arrest.'

'Very well,' said Pyle, breathing hard, 'you arrest me — and we'll see what comes of it.'

Jim stiffly consented to wait until the operation was over, but insisted on taking his cripple away with him in a taxi; had to have him lifted in, though he himself did not assist. Pyle thought he might have to go to Battle Creek and make explanations, but heard no more about it.

So — here we have a pretty nice little problem in psychology. It doesn't require very shrewd deduction. Jim Brink is compensating for years and years of bootlicking. A few months ago, he was the most obsequious little yes-yesser in this town; a grinning, fawning, stickily sweet toadier who always seemed to be saying, 'No bother at all. Glad to do it, I assure you. And you may kick me if you want to.' Now he is a disgusting type of the *brute in buttons!* I suppose it is one of the hazards of war that impressionable young men have to be exposed to close-up contacts with freshly hatched officers who are trying to mend their damaged personalities after long and bitter experience in some relationship where they have played expertly the rôle of whipping-boy.

I am told that cases of this sort, while far from being in the majority — thank God! — are frequent enough to constitute a menace to the efficiency of the army; for a contempt-ible fellow like that couldn't hope to enlist the honest loyalty of his subordinates, and wouldn't dare lead the way for his men in battle where so many accidents have been known to happen to officers who had earned the hatred and contempt of their troops.

It has been interesting to note the predic-tions of our local prophets in respect to the ultimate good that is to result from the World War. They seem generally agreed that civi-lization will take a fresh grip on itself and march forward into a new day.

I haven't been to any of the churches, but I read reports of the sermons in the papers. They are very heartening; perhaps a bit too optimistic. I have clipped a few of these pulpit observations, and am going to record them briefly here. When you read this, you will note that we are fairly hopeful of the future, and justify the savage means by the noble end to be achieved.

One prominent minister said, not long ago, 'There are signs now which indicate that every autocracy will be driven from the earth through the agency of this war, and that gov-ernment of the people, for the people, and by the people will be established everywhere. At the close of the war there will be a greater brotherhood of individuals and nations than the world has ever known.' Perhaps this is a pretty tall order, but it seems to meet with general approval. Everybody thinks the war should do us all a lot of good. I hope so.

Another preacher declared, 'This great conflict is hastening the coming of Jesus in his reign over mankind. It will end in his crowning as King of Kings and Lord of Lords.' This strikes me as being a bit hysterical, to say nothing about its being illogical. I can't think that a world-wide acceptance of the Galilean teacher would be the natural outcome of a general war. War doesn't seem to be the right build-up for it. Of course it is conceivable that everybody will be so weary and hurt and remorseful, when it is done with, that we will all resolve to follow a different program in the future. But it is certainly a hope that has little encouragement from history.

All sorts of special interests are banking on the war to solve their assorted problems. One preacher sees the complete abrogation of class distinctions, another forecasts the end of disputes between capital and labor. Life in the trenches, where rich and poor have mingled their blood in a common cause, will bring about an enduring brotherhood. Maybe there is some sound sense to this. At all events, we are taking much comfort in the thought.

I see that a Mrs. Kohut — a prominent leader in Jewish education — speaking at the Temple Beth El, said, 'The war will develop an international psychology which will end forever the persecution of our race.' This, I feel, is worth looking forward to; for the Jew has surely taken an awful lot of beating, in the past dozen centuries, and I expect he will be right thankful to get some sound insurance against any more of it in the future.

There are a good many howls for revenge and punishment which, it seems to me, would be more fitly spoken in camp than in church. One parson is quoted as saying, 'The war must go on until Germany is on her knees begging for mercy and the militarists are punished in their persons for their hellish wrongs.' This chap is probably not a bad fellow when things are normal, but his value as a leader of people's thinking — in a time of excitement — is questionable. I surmise that he is the sort of chap who, when the house is on fire, would throw the baby out the window and carry its cradle downstairs in his arms. As a spokesman for Christ, who said to his enemies, 'Father, forgive them for they know not what they do,' this brother seems to be slightly off the old reservation.

New York papers quote one of their eminent clergymen as shouting in his pulpit, 'To hell with the Kaiser!' I have often wondered whether, with all the accumulated inhibitions of speech and conduct laid upon him, a preacher might not sometimes wish that an occasion would arise permitting him to let himself out a little. Doubtless it was the irksomeness of a steady devotion to piety that led the medieval sculptors — at work on stone angels, apostles, martyrs, and such things, for the great cathedrals — to have each his own pet rock, out in the back yard, on which he operated for amusement, off hours. These sculptors probably got so damn sick of the uprolled eyes and penitential smirks of the saints that they had to do a grotesque and sinister gargoyle to restore their emotional balance. This war has given the preachers a chance to yell 'hell,' 'damnation,' and 'filthy swine!' It is in questionable taste, but probably provides a sort of much needed neural laxative, human nature being such as it is.

I do not possess a monopoly of this thought. Last week I attended a luncheon in Ann Arbor, of doctors and University executives. In the course of general talk about the table, somebody referred to the wild intemperance of speech in the pulpits, and President Hutchins dignifiedly observed, 'Yes — the war has been a Godsend to the preachers.'

I should have liked to hear him express his

opinions on the subject a little more fully. Hutchins is one of the wisest men I know. The University has been very fortunate in her choice of presidents. Everyone feared, when Doctor Angell retired, that it would be difficult to find anyone who could so widely command the love and esteem that he had earned. Hutchins has it. It does me good to be in his presence. This man has ballast! It is a great blessing that a person of his august mind directs the University in these trying days.

BRIGHTWOOD HOSPITAL

October sixteenth, 1918, 2 A.M.

I have not been outside for three days. This hospital is a pesthouse. Every available inch is filled with influenza victims.

It may seem odd to you that I am taking time, in this distressing situation, to make an entry in my long neglected journal; but, utterly fagged as I am, I cannot sleep. Neither can I think about anything else but this catastrophe. So I shall briefly record what is going on here — and everywhere — all over the country.

This is by far the worst scourge that our people have ever known. We have had sporadic epidemics of 'flu' for many years, but not this type. Usually the disease, in its primary stages, has been hardly distinguishable from a stubborn cold. It would drag along for weeks, leaving the patient a depleted prey to whatever he was naturally vulnerable; arthritis, sinus and mastoid troubles — or, indeed, almost anything; heart, sometimes. Now and then a pneumonia developed. It was a tedious thing; particularly hard on elderly people and others with low vitality.

The influenza we have now is swift and savage. One of its peculiarities is the high rate of mortality among young people. The better equipped they are with physical resources, the more promptly it consumes them. It is mowing down the young doctors and nurses in appalling numbers. You may use your imagination on what is happening in these big cantonments where — even at their best — the camp hospital is more or less makeshift and not rigged to care for a large-scale pestilence.

The disease gives very brief warning. It strikes a hard blow. The patient melts like wax under high temperatures, while you stand there helpless. Nothing does any good. If it was smallpox, we would know what to do.

In any other circumstance, I should have gone to Battle Creek today — yesterday — to be present when they shipped Leslie Sherman's body back to his family home in Bay City. He was sick, in the crowded camp hospital, only four days. I couldn't leave Brightwood. There was nothing I could have done for him, anyway. The doctors over there know as much about this deadly stuff as I do; more, maybe; certainly no less. You can't subtract anything from nothing.

I have just been talking with the Battle

Creek Sanitarium. They say Natalie is holding her own; perhaps rallying a little, though you can't count much on the usual signs for encouragement. Your patient will seem to have passed a crisis; temperature begins to recede; you begin to take heart. In an hour or two your patient is sub-normal; other customary warning-signs absent; no cyanosis, no Cheyne-Stokes respiration. Now your man is alive; now he is dead. Just like that.

Randolph had just arrived from New York; quite unfit to travel. They had put him to bed. Natalie has not been told about Leslie. I shall call up again in the morning.

We are growing seriously short of help here. We have five nurses in bed. I know that McDermott was running a temperature tonight, though he denied it and got almost peevish when I accused him of it.

The papers are quoting various persons as believing that the flu germs were released in several regional centers in this country by enemy agents. I suspect that this is a precious lot of poppycock. We have been imputing to the Germans a great deal more ingenuity than they possess.

I had a comforting telegram from Joyce tonight. She has spent her first month in Capital Seminary; and, from early reports, I honestly believe we have struck the right place for her.

It is the first time she has ever seemed to be contented in school.

Recent letters extol the charm of the teachers and the comradeliness of the girls. Joyce writes that each new girl is assigned a Junior advisor, who gives her helpful hints about her studies, her manners, and her adjustment to the school's regulations. This seems a desirable arrangement, especially in our case, for we have had a difficult time in as many as three reputable schools, and if we can contrive to keep our footing now it will be a great comfort to a lot of people — including the young lady's papa.

During the past couple of weeks I have been hearing much about Joyce's beautiful mentor. My child's description of this Miss Brent involves a string of adjectives not often used except in services of worship. I hope Joyce's infatuation is not a mere passing fancy. If she will hang on to the Brent girl, and accept her counsel, for love's sake, perhaps we will have solved our problem. I hope so. It's about time!

The teachers at Capital Seminary have had the good sense to prohibit the girls from going into any public places, since the epidemic set in; and, so far, they are free of it. I am mighty glad that Joyce is fairly well insured against it. This is, at least, something to be thankful for, in my distress over conditions here with which I cannot cope.

I must resume my too great burden now. I have rested for an hour. Nancy Ashford consented to go to bed at midnight. She is completely tuckered out; but, so far, unaffected by The Thing.

HOTEL PONTCHARTRAIN

November eleventh, 1918, Midnight

The war is over. We thought so last Thursday, but the announcement was premature. This time the news seems to be authentic.

The celebration began long before daybreak and still continues with remarkable vigor. It is growing hoarse, and a bit rowdy, but it has a good deal of vitality left; enough, I think, to keep everybody in this hotel awake all night.

We are calling what has happened the 'armistice.' I'll bet there aren't forty people in Detroit who had ever used that word in a sentence until a few days ago. I'll bet also that ninety-five per cent of the population had never heard the word before. Two thirds of them don't know now what it means. All they care is that it stands for Peace. Germany has asked for an armistice, which means that the war is over. Nobody has bothered to look up the word, which means 'a truce; a temporary cessation of hostilities.'

There will be a conference of the powers to determine what manner of peace terms are to be offered to Germany, and it is expected that such terms — whatever they are — will be accepted, for Germany is not in a position to put up much of a debate on this subject. If the Allies want to, they can strip Germany clean to the hide. And I suppose a great deal of pressure will be put upon the council to do that. In their present temper, the people of the Entente will not be very magnanimous.

Personally, I think there is something to be said for the old Chinese doctrine of 'face-saving.' So often I have seen how nicely this works out in man-to-man relationships. I wonder why it might not be practicable in the settlement of difficulties between nations.

There is nothing worse that can be done to an individual than the destruction of his self-respect. Of course, if he wrongs you, it is just and right that he make amends. But I think great care should be exercised that his personal pride is not destroyed. In the heat of passion, you may get some satisfaction from seeing him down on all fours with his chin in the mud, confessing that he is a lousy scoundrel, unfit for association with decent men. But the trouble is that after you have done that to him he has nothing more to lose; and a man who has nothing to lose makes a very mean antagonist.

I think that when Grant told Lee to keep

his sword, thus implying that he had been at war with a brave man, a gentleman whom he respected, his act was of priceless value in the unprecedentedly rapid healing of the wound between the North and the South. Grant had a chance that day — and I daresay he would have had a lot of applause from short-sighted people, clamorous for a long-term vengeance — Grant had a chance to humiliate Lee by a display of cocky arrogance, and make the South sore forever and ever! I never realized how much was at stake there until I began to speculate on the present problem abroad. Grant was a great man, that day!

Then he told Lee that the Confederates could take their horses home with them, and whatever other equipment was needful on their farms, as to say that the South — far from being ruined — would now be resuming the usual activities.

Looking back on it from this safe distance, I think we have been disposed to minify the enmity generated by that war. It was a hard-fought thing, and the mutual hatred it developed was fierce, passionate, virulent. But it was not contemptuous. That was what ultimately saved the Union. People can fight and hate each other, and get over it, so long as they concede gallantry.

I hope this magnanimity may be observed

when the peace is made in Europe. Otherwise, 'armistice' — in this case — may eventually mean no more than it means in the dictionary.

The flu, which strikes fast and hard, has eased up appreciably, at Brightwood, anyhow, where the number of new cases is falling off. Things are by no means normal, but they are so much better that we are beginning to breathe more freely. Doubtless this diminution of the epidemic may be attributed to the city's strict quarantine enforcement, and the closing of theaters, churches, and other places of public assembly where the contagion operated at a deadly advantage.

Dorothy Wickes came to the hospital this afternoon to tell me that Harry, who is in France with the Rainbow Division, was well and in good spirits when she last heard from him, a letter dated October thirteenth. Naturally, she was rejoicing over the peace, and the prospect of having her brother back home in the near future.

'Of course,' she admitted, suddenly shadowed, 'some terrible things could have happened to him since that letter was written; but' — brightening quickly — 'I have a feeling that he is safe.' Then she asked, soberly, 'You believe in hunches; don't you?'

'Well,' I replied, cautiously, 'I believe in my own hunches.'

'Did a hunch ever let you down?' she asked, childishly.

'Yes,' I confessed. 'Occasionally.'

'Do you have a hunch that Harry is coming home?'

'Yes,' I said, adding that I hadn't really laid hold on any deep convictions about it; but, now that she asked me, I felt quite confident I should be seeing Harry again.

'I have that hunch too,' said Dorothy. 'Don't you think that two hunches are better than one?'

'Twice as good,' I declared, reasonably enough, I thought.

There was a little pause before Dorothy inquired, with blue eyes wide, 'Where do hunches come from?'

I toyed with my watch-chain and smiled ineffectively.

'I've noticed that whenever you're stuck,' drawled Dorothy, with the bland impudence of a five-year-old, 'you begin to wonder what time it is. Does that watch trick of yours mean that you want to get rid of me; or, do you do that when you're alone — and stuck?'

Never having examined myself on this matter before, I hesitated in replying, a chink she promptly filled with 'But maybe you're never stuck — when you're alone.' And when I failed to answer quickly she added, 'Are you?'

Now, ordinarily, I should find this sort of impertinence very annoying and would make an effort to discourage any more of it; but Dorothy Wickes and I are close friends, in spite of the disparity of our ages. I like her immensely, partly because she is such a lovely creature, and mostly because she is so sensible.

'Yes,' I said, 'I get stuck when I am alone. Just at the moment I am feeling quite jubilant over the prospect of being unstuck from a problem that accounts for much of this gray hair.'

'Hunch?' asked Dorothy.

'A little better than a hunch.'

'Want to take your hair down?' she inquired, companionably.

'Beg pardon?' I said — unfamiliar with the phrase which appears to be a recent device when inviting a confidence.

'I mean,' explained Dorothy, with a puckery-lipped grin, 'do you want to tell all? If so — I have plenty of time.'

'It's about my daughter,' I said. 'She has been away, nearly all of the time, for years, in girls' schools, because she has no mother and I could not give her the attention she needed.'

And then I proceeded to give Dorothy, who

was most attentive, a fairly comprehensive sketch of my anxieties — through the years — winding up happily with my recent assurance that things might now be much less troublesome.

'Of course,' I added, 'I cannot expect this Miss Brent to be at Joyce's elbow twenty-four hours of the day. There's the Christmas vacation, for instance. Joyce will come home. This young set that she was training with, last summer, may upset everything.'

'Perhaps this Miss Brent could come home with her as a guest through the holidays,' ventured Dorothy.

'Not very likely,' I said, doubtfully. 'All of two years difference in their ages. This girl probably has her own home and friends. But — it's well worth looking into.'

'I should think,' said Dorothy, 'that if Miss Brent has had such an unusual influence on Joyce, she might be willing to make a little sacrifice of her own holiday pleasure. Maybe it could be put up to her on that basis.'

'You are about her age,' I said. 'What would you think if somebody made such a proposal to you?'

'Well — if I was aware of all the circumstances, and believed that I might help, I think I would do it. And' — she added — 'I've a hunch that Miss Brent will do it — if she can. She must be a pretty good sort, or she couldn't have had this effect on Joyce.'

I said I would take her advice, and see what comes of it. I wrote to Joyce this evening, asking her if she would like to invite her friend here for the holidays. Joyce will undoubtedly consent. I hope it works out. I should be glad to see this interesting girl, myself.

I said as much to Dorothy, before she left, this afternoon, and she grinned impishly.

'But I suppose you haven't any hunches about that?' she teased.

'If you are implying that I might become interested in Miss Brent for any other reason than the one you know,' I said, 'it may clear the air for you if you remember that I am twice as old as this young lady.'

Dorothy poised her head on one side, wisely, and said, 'Even so — there's no —'

'No fool like an old fool,' I assisted.

'Suppose I had said that,' chided Dorothy.

'It would have been true,' I declared.

'But you wouldn't have liked it.'

'Well — no; perhaps not.'

AT HOME

January twenty-eighth, 1919, 10 P.M.

For quite too long a time my entries in this journal have been a dismal record of tragic events.

I am not by nature a morbid person and I have had no pleasure in reporting these various frights and frets, but they have bulked so large, during these past few years, that it was impossible to ignore them.

I have made sketchy notes on the war, or such aspects of it as might be remarked by a remote spectator. I have dragged you through at least the edge of our devastating pestilence. I have occasionally adverted to my personal perplexities, chief of which was my worry about my willful child.

It will gratify you to learn, after wading through this almost interminable wilderness of woe, that my mind is now more at ease than it has been for a quadrennium.

Of course the one overpowering torture that had dwarfed all other agonies was the war. We are done with that now, and a sort of peace has been arranged for. You will have been fully informed about that, so I shall add nothing farther about the nature of this peace, except to say that many thoughtful people are wondering whether it gives promise of durability.

It seemed to be taken by common consent, the world over, that our President would guide the deliberations of the Peace Conference. This seems rather strange, too, for Mr. Wilson made no bones about his hope that this parley would establish a working agreement for international amity in the future, rather than to conduct an autopsy over the late German Empire.

It must have been a serious disillusionment to this lonesome idealist when he discovered that the delegates had not assembled primarily to implement a practical peace, but to punish a beaten foe. If correctly reported, that Conference must have resembled nothing quite so much as an avaricious group of expectant brothers and sisters, cousins and second cousins, nephews and nieces, in-laws (and outlaws), convened to divide among themselves the realty and personal effects of a stricken relative who had died intestate.

Once this division of property is amicably agreed upon, and everyone has made off with his share, it may be presumed that the peace has been concluded. This arrangement, how-

263

ever, is shakily founded upon the belief that our belligerent relative is indeed deceased. Should it turn out that he is not dead but only in a deep coma from which he may emerge some day, it is not inconceivable that he may insist upon a restoration of his goods.

With customary generosity, the United States has not asked for so much as an old brass hat, for a souvenir; and, in token of their appreciation of our magnanimity, the other surviving relatives have voted us the privilege of financing a good deal of the expense incident to the last illness, until such time as our kinfolk can conveniently liquidate.

Mr. Wilson has found himself in the awkward position of having proposed to the enemy peace terms which he is now unable to confirm. I suppose the main trouble here grew out of the fact that he made this tentative offer on his own hook, without making doubly sure that his proposals would be approved at home and abroad. If this was a blunder, I can see how a man might easily make such a mistake with the very best intentions in the world. Because it was a time of great stress, everybody had been willing to confer unprecedented power upon the President. The only way you could insure a solid front and a steady drive was to let the President hold all the reins.

I surmise that almost any man, empowered with such authority, might come to feel that suggestions and queries and counsel — however well meant — were distracting annoyances which shouldn't be added to his already crushing load. Of course, his attitude — in that event — presupposes that this one man — and he alone — can provide the necessary wisdom and direction. Any practicing psychiatrist will tell you that no man can carry a burden like that very far without crumpling under it.

As for the epidemic, it has been considerably relieved. I don't think we learned much about it. I'm sure I didn't. When fatal, it almost invariably wound up in a swift pneumonia. Whether these pneumonias were all of the same type, I do not know. They were similar in their deadly effectiveness.

My most grievous personal loss, during the worst of this plague, was occasioned by the death of my valued friend Clive Randolph. He practically reorganized my life. He helped me to whatever I am and have. It is difficult to believe that he is gone. His spirit was so bright with light and energy that one can't consent to its being extinguished. Nor can one be quite contented with the thought that Randolph will continue to speak through the lives he has illumined. Perhaps this sort of immortality should suffice for any man. But — even so — it is not easy to dispose of Randolph by declaring him henceforth an inspiring memory in the minds of grateful friends. Personal survival is a baffling doctrine, hard to accept. But, for me, it is more worthy of credence than the thought that Randolph, as a person, has reached the end of his life. I have no convictions about heavenly harps, streets of gold, or any celestial properties or employments. I have no guess to offer concerning Randolph's present abode or manner of living. But I strongly suspect that — somewhere, somehow — he is alive. If this seems unscientific, and lacking in sound evidence, keep it in mind that until you have stood by the open grave of a cherished friend the testimony in favor of immortality is not yet all in.

Natalie's convalescence was naturally retarded by the shock of her bereavement. To have lost her husband and her father, within a few days, and in circumstances which made it impossible for her to be with them, was an almost insurmountable grief. It must be said for her, however, that Natalie's acceptance of this tragedy was a credit to her training and her personal character.

By the middle of December she was sufficiently recovered to leave the Sanitarium. I had visited her there several times. She had told me of her intention to go to Denver for a few weeks with an uncle and aunt who lived there. But shortly before it was time for her to start, Natalie had word that her uncle was ill. Realizing that she would be only an additional burden to her relatives at this time, she accepted my invitation to come to Detroit and remain through the holidays.

I reopened the house, sent for Gladys, found some additional help, and prepared — not without some uneasiness — to entertain three young women; Natalie, physically frail and emotionally upset; Joyce, who might or might not manage to adjust herself to the mood of a recently bereaved guest; and Miss Brent, whom I had never seen and whose reaction to this delicate situation was indeterminable, though — from what Joyce had written of her — I was willing, in advance, to give her the benefit of the doubt.

Natalie was with me for three days before the school girls arrived. I brought a lively young nurse over from Brightwood, rather for my unhappy guest's entertainment than any need of professional care. It was natural, I think, that Natalie should have talked quite freely to me, almost as if I were a relative. She seemed eager to discuss future plans. Her father had confided to her the general nature of the estate she would inherit. It was pleasant, but not surprising, to learn that Randolph had amply provided for her. There was some valuable real estate, besides their home which would be easily marketable in case Natalie decided to give it up — as she undoubtedly would; a respectable list of conservative stocks and bonds, and fifty thousand dollars worth of life insurance.

So — we didn't have that to fret about. Natalie's future, considered from an economic standpoint, was safely guaranteed. She doubted whether she could be contented to live with her uncle and aunt, even if that were agreeable with them. She had seen little of them in recent years and had very few friends in Denver. She wasn't sure that Detroit was the place for her, with its inevitable reminders of her former happiness and present desolation. New York might provide distractions, but it sounded pretty lonely without her father. As for going to live with Leslie's people, that was definitely out. 'I hardly know them,' she said. 'It wouldn't be fair to them — or me, either.

'Sometimes I have thought,' she went on, 'that foreign travel might help me; new things to see; new acquaintances who wouldn't be talking to me about my trouble. I could take a long trip; around the world, maybe; be gone a year.'

I let her prattle on, without interruption, about an extended tour. Apparently she had been thinking about it a good deal; for she seemed well posted on the subject. Only half attentive to her recitation of possible itineraries, I found myself reviewing some of the cases I had known of bereaved people who had fled from their loneliness at home to experiment with loneliness abroad.

My opportunities for observations in this field have been fairly frequent. As has often been remarked in this journal, brain surgery is not always successful. In the past dozen or more years I have been invited to counsel with many bewildered persons — women, mostly — who, having lost their husbands, wonder what to do with themselves. If they are left with meager resources, the problem is to find something profitable to do. This isn't always easy, but it is easier than to deal with the widow who has been well provided for. A typical case finds the widow possessed of more ready cash than she has ever seen before. Plenty of times — in cases where the death was the result of an accident, and I see my share of them — the life insurance carries double indemnity, which materially increases the inheritance.

I know at least a score of widows who, today, would be much happier and in better health — mentally and physically — if they hadn't been left a nickel. People do not often look for work unless they need to do so, and sometimes the only insurance they can get that will defray the emotional expense of a serious bereavement is to be found in some responsible job, a job with a lot of wear and tear to it, one that demands an alert mind and a dextrous hand.

When Natalie had disembarked at Singapore, or somewhere, to give me a chance to comment, I surprised her by saying, 'I wish I could be a little more enthusiastic over this, my dear.'

Her eyes widened inquisitively.

'Don't you want me to?' she asked.

'I'm not sure,' I replied, slowly. 'If you had been left penniless, I know that your friends would think it a great pity. They would say, "Poor Natalie! As if it wasn't enough to bear a double bereavement, she will now have to go to work!" But, however sympathetic and kind, these friends will be missing the point exactly. They would be thinking, "If Natalie had not suffered such frightful blows, it might not be so terrible for her to have to go to work." Such reasoning is incorrect. It is *because* Natalie has been dealt these exceptionally hard blows that she *should* find work to do.'

'You mean that — seriously?' she asked.

'Yes, dear; seriously. I don't believe you are going to find an anodyne for your sorrow aboard a ship, or in the Alps, or on the Riviera. I don't think it is going to help you, the least bit, to make casual acquaintances on a voyage or in foreign hotels.'

'But perhaps you do not care for travel?'

'Indeed I do, and I hope the time may come, before long, when I may be free to do it. And you, too. Some day you will travel with enjoyment. But I think you'd better reorganize your life first. You see' — I went on, encouraged a little by her show of interest — 'the chief ground of your distress at present is the loss of your motive for living. You had two important employments; loving and cherishing your husband and your father. Of course, you are dreadfully lonely without their love and care for you; but the most serious feature of your bereavement is not the loss of what they were doing for you, but of what you had been doing for them. You had a responsible job, and now you have lost it. Do you see what I mean? If you sit down now with folded hands, to brood upon your loss, you are ruined. And you're too young and sweet and capable to be wasted. We couldn't

271

afford to lose Leslie, and we couldn't afford to lose your father; but we can't solve these problems by losing You!'

'I couldn't do anything,' muttered Natalie, half to herself. 'What could I do? I ride horses, but I couldn't show anyone else how. I play the piano, but I couldn't teach it. I trained Scotty to do some clever tricks, but I don't believe we could go on the stage.'

'Yes, yes, I know,' I growled. 'And you bake nice angel food cakes. You couldn't earn enough money to keep yourself in shoelaces, doing any of these things. But — if you honestly want a job, we'll find you one.'

'Well — I certainly don't want to go through the motions of doing something, aware that I wasn't earning my wages,' said Natalie. 'It's worth thinking about. I'll be open to suggestions.'

Perhaps I have made too long a story to account for Natalie's present employment in the Winslow Art Store. It was easy enough to arrange. They were short-handed. Young Wickes, whose division is still retained with the Army of Occupation, may not be home for some time yet. Mr. Winslow was glad enough to avail himself of Natalie's services. He and Randolph were long-time friends, having so many common interests. I think he assumed that Natalie, having grown up in an atmosphere of applied arts, might come fairly well informed about the implements of these professions.

Natalie went to work on the sixteenth. She came to see me last Sunday. I was amazed at the change in her face and manner. She was positively radiant. I have often marveled at what blood transfusions will do. That's what the new job had done for our girl. Almost back to normal was Natalie. She bubbled with enthusiasm over her new interests. They were paying her twenty dollars a week and she had resolved to live on it.

'Just to show myself that I'm capable of paying my way,' she explained proudly. 'And — anyway — it will be interesting to find out how people manage on small incomes. Maybe I'll get tired of it,' she added, 'but — so far — it has been like a new game. I've never had to study the luncheon menu before, with economy as the main consideration.'

I found myself deeply interested in Natalie's adventures. It had been a long time since I had done much skimping. As she rattled along with her droll story of the joys and excitements of her self-imposed frugality, I vividly recalled the days when the new suit of clothes — albeit not made of very good stuff — brought me pride and confidence. I know I got more profit from the book that I couldn't buy in

September, and had to wait for until another check came in. One's purchases, in those days, were made with care. Natalie was valuing what she owned, for the first time in her life, she said.

'It's really amazing,' she went on, 'what very nice things you can get at the ten-cent stores. They have almost everything.' She fondly patted a glittering brooch at her throat. 'How much do you think I paid for that?' she asked, lowering her tone, confidentially.

'Well — if it's real,' I replied, judicially, 'I should think it must have cost about two million, five hundred thousand dollars.'

'A quarter!' confided Natalie.

She had taken a room in a private house on a once fairly prosperous residence street, lately grown shabby and cluttered with little one-man shops. Her neighbor on one side was a locksmith. Natalie had already got acquainted with him, through the Horner family with whom she lived.

'Jim makes keys while you wait,' she remarked, in passing.

'Do you call him Jim?' I couldn't help asking.

'Why not? That's his name.'

There was no Mr. Horner. We hadn't learned what had become of him, but we

274

guessed he wasn't dead or Mrs. Horner would have said so. There was a son, about twenty-two, who worked in a factory. His name was Ethan but everybody called him Jack.

'I can see how they might,' I said.

'But he doesn't sit in a corner,' observed Natalie. 'Soon as evening dinner — or supper, rather — is over, Jack hurries down to a bowling alley. I'm afraid he doesn't contribute much to the family's upkeep. But his mother idolizes him and is always quoting the funny things he used to say when he was little. I think he outgrew that.' Natalie was stripping her gloves onto her fingers.

'No, no, no,' I protested, 'not yet. Tell me some more about the Horners. By the way — is your room comfortable?'

'It isn't what the movies show you when they do an impressive boudoir scene,' admitted Natalie, 'but it is warm and the bed can be slept in if you're pretty tired. People who work all day don't require expensive mattresses. Same thing goes for food. Pot roast is quite tasty if you have worked hard enough to be hungry. The rest of the Horners? Well — Winnie is seventeen and in high school. She has a beau who doesn't look any too good to me; and I'm afraid the affair is rather serious, for he helps Winnie with the dishes almost every evening.'

'Sounds to me,' I put in, 'as if this boy's heart is in the right place.'

'It isn't his heart,' explained Natalie. 'His heart's all right.'

'Well' — I persisted — 'any young fellow who will wash the dishes for his gal must have something to him.'

'No, sir!' declared Natalie stubbornly. 'He is going to be doing that for Winnie, all their lives. He'll wash the dishes, and Winnie will have to go out and earn the living.'

I was amazed at the versatility of her new interests. I don't suppose Natalie knows a nickel's worth about domestic-relations problems as comprehended by the group-lingo of Social Science experts. But she has her eyes open, and it is going to be of great value to her to have discovered a few facts about the way people live who are not of her social rating. It's a new life for her. It has taken her mind off her trouble.

'Any more besides Winnie?' I wondered.

'I have been saving Sammie for the last,' said Natalie. 'Sammie is ten. He belongs to me. Very lovable little fellow.'

'Sickly?' I asked.

'Well — he isn't very strong. How did you know?'

'You said he was lovable — and ten years old.'

'What do you suppose he wants to be?' asked Natalie, mysteriously.

'I wouldn't know. Fireman, maybe?'

'Doctor!'

My thoughts were busy for a moment with several reels of reminiscences.

'We will always need doctors,' I said.

'You know —' murmured Natalie, dreamily. 'Now that Leslie's gone — and so early in his life —'

I tapped my lips significantly with my finger-tips, and shook my head.

Natalie's eyes were thoughtful and her lips presently parted in a slow smile. She nodded her head, understandingly. I wonder how much Randolph may have talked to her about such things. It is evident that she knows the principles. She gave me her hand, at parting, and said, softly, 'Funny. That's what Father would have done — if I had started to tell him what I had been thinking.' Then — after a pause — she had slipped her arm through mine, affectionately — 'You and Father had a lot of secrets; didn't you?'

'Yes, dear,' I replied, 'but we never shared them.'

'I often wondered,' she said, just above a whisper. 'I knew how devoted you were to each other. I knew Father had secrets. His life was full of little mysteries. I always thought you had some, too.' She looked up into my face and shook her head inquiringly, as she went on, 'But you never told each other — about your secrets?'

'No.'

'Did any of your secrets leak out — just a little — around the edges?'

'Just a little, I'm afraid. But we always pretended we hadn't noticed.'

'The way one does, before Christmas, when one stumbles upon a parcel — in a closet — on a high shelf?'

I thought it was time we terminated this conversation, and accomplished it by remarking that one rarely stumbled over things on high shelves.

I think Natalie is in a fair way to make her life mean something very important. How glad Randolph must be — if he knows?

It had been my intention to write something here, tonight, about the gratifying change in Joyce's disposition and behavior — all of which is to be accounted for by the quiet influence of Helen Brent. I had thought also of recording a few of my impressions of this charming girl who has so singularly stirred my heart. I am too tired to do this adequately. Indeed I am reluctant to do it at all. I have discovered that if you want to remember something, there's no better way than to write it down. Perhaps I should not write anything about this girl. It may be much better sense if I try to forget her. Did you ever try to forget anything? A tricky job, that. *

AT HOME

January twenty-ninth, 1919, 9 P.M.

We have been enroute to National Prohibition
for some time and now we have got it. Enough
states have ratified the Constitutional Amend-
ment to make it effective, and the Secretary
of State announces today that it is so ordered.

The Drys are ecstatic, as they have every
right to be, seeing how long and zealously they
have battled for this, and are in a mood to
chant, 'Rest, soldier, rest, thy warfare o'er.'

I have seen this prohibition movement in
all its phases: township option, county option,
state option. When the township was the unit,
the enforcement was nearly perfect. It was
everybody's business, and the officials had no
alternative but to be lily white. When the
county attended to the enforcement, it was
still pretty well done, though infractions of
the law were more frequent than when the
township carried the responsibility. When
whole states went dry, it didn't work quite
so well. Many of the close observers thought
the county had done a better job.

Now the whole country is dry, and Washington is going to see to it that the law is enforced. I surmise that there is trouble ahead, but I wouldn't risk saying so where anyone could hear me; for I might be considered a Wet. I am not a Wet . . . I have had plenty of opportunities to know what strong liquor has done to a great many people. It has been responsible for much poverty, illness, violence, and humiliation.

Being a surgeon, I have had no choice whether or not to drink. For many years there has not been one moment when, waking or sleeping, I might not be summoned immediately to perform some delicate, life-or-death operation requiring the utmost precision of eye and hand. So, I couldn't drink if I wanted to, and am therefore disqualified to regard my own abstinence as a virtue.

For this reason I have tried to avoid seeming self-righteous on the subject. And I shouldn't presume to regulate another man's habits.

Of course, in my professional capacity I frequently warn gluttonous patients against digging their graves with their teeth, and I advise the hard drinker that the human liver — however sturdy and obliging — is not rigged to deal happily with copper and fusel-oil. But never, as a citizen at the polls, have I had the impudence to vote that my neighbors shall not have a gin-fizz or a third helping of pickled tripe and fried onions.

Privately I wish that strong liquors could be abolished by common consent. So very many people drink who do not know how, and what a pestiferous nuisance they are when they have overdone it. Too many youngsters have had easy access to it at a period of their immaturity when surely they are lightheaded enough without seeking any artificial devices to numb their wits. Not many adolescent brains are important enough to be preserved in alcohol. I fear that my Joyce has a tendency to experiment with it. I hope she has not inherited her eminent grandfather's proclivities in this direction.

Now that enforcement is in the hands of the Federal Government, I suspect that it will be handled clumsily, with a minimum of effectiveness and a maximum of expense. The issue will probably be regarded as another political football. If I were a captain in the Dry Army, I wouldn't unlace my boots yet.

As I was writing here, last night, I briefly alluded to the satisfaction I had in Joyce's visit home, during the holiday vacation. I had not supposed it possible for so great a change of attitude and disposition in the course of a few weeks.

To be sure, Joyce is getting to be a young

lady now and she is aware that a little more dignity of decorum is expected of her. But one would think she might have been somewhat impressed by that fact a couple of years ago.

No; there is only one way to account for the new Joyce. She has been completely carried away by the charm of her student counsellor, whom she worships with full devotion.

And this I can readily understand; for Helen Brent is indeed an adorable creature. From the first moment, I felt that she belonged to us. Not to me; to us.

My sober judgment warns me against dwelling too much on my impressions of this endearing person, but I shall indulge myself, for a moment, and then avoid any further reference to my own feelings toward her.

I met them at the train. It was a bright, crisp morning. The station was crowded, because holidays were at hand and everybody was going somewhere or meeting friends. The gateman reluctantly let me go through. I did not know what car my people would be in. By the time I arrived on the platform, there was much confusion. I tramped hurriedly back and forth, trying to watch several vestibule-exits where emerging passengers were gathering about their baggage.

Presently I identified Joyce's corn-yellow head. She was pointing out their tackle to a red-cap. I began threading my way through the crowd when this lovely girl gave me both hands and a comradely smile. I have never seen such vivid contrasts of color; hair so black it was blue, with an even fringe framing a close-fitted toque on an extraordinarily white forehead; dark, long-lashed eyes, set wide apart; expressive lips — and dimples. When she spoke, her voice was of a deep contralto quality; a very unusual timbre; it makes everything she says sound like a confidence. Perhaps that helped to create the illusion that we were old friends.

'You're Helen,' I said, a bit rattled. 'So glad you've come.'

She tucked a hand under my elbow and we moved on to join Joyce.

'I knew you by your picture,' she said.

Joyce was all over me for a moment, and we three started down the platform, arm in arm. I was immensely proud of them. I couldn't help being amused by the almost startling difference between them; Joyce such a striking blonde, Helen as brunette as something Latin. I don't think they will ever be mistaken for sisters.

There was a wave of almost poignant tenderness swept through me, as we marched along; not only toward my own dear girl, who was clinging tightly to me, but toward the new one too, hugging my arm as if she belonged to me. It was quite exhilarating.

After we had gone a little way and were about to descend the steps, Helen, wanting to make sure the boy with the bags was in tow, slowed our gait and turned halfway round to look back, but she did not relax her tight hold on me. She was so close that when she turned, her face brushed my sleeve. It was almost a caress, and it warmed my heart. I hope I am not making myself ridiculous in your sight. It stirs me deeply to recover that enchanted moment.

Many persons are distrustful of themselves when standing on the edge of high precipices. The possibilities of the situation seem to exercise a sort of hypnotic urge. It isn't that they have a temptation to destroy themselves; but there is a strange infatuation here that startles persons who become suddenly aware of their unsuspected phobia.

I found myself a little bit unsure of myself in the close presence of Helen Brent. I believe and hope that she did not realize the effect she had on me. I know she did not, or she would have gone to more pains in avoiding chance contacts offering opportunities for a caressing touch.

Joyce is lazy and took advantage of her liberty to breakfast in bed. Helen had hers with me. It is my habit to glance over the telegraph news in *The Free Press*, in my library, before breakfast. On the next morning after the girls arrived, Helen sauntered into the library, came to my chair, took my hand, and said, 'Breakfast. I'm hungry. Take me to it, please.' She had on some sort of lounge costume; black velvet skirt and a high-buttoned chartreuse smock belted with a heavy cord and tassels. It was such an exquisite outfit, and so uncommonly becoming, that I told her she shouldn't ever wear anything else.

'If you feel that way about it,' she replied, in that husky voice of hers that will be always getting her into trouble, I fear, 'I'll never wear anything else. But' — she added — 'it will look funny sometimes — at the theater, and ball games.'

I liked the way she made friends with Natalie, who — to my surprise — wanted to talk with her about Leslie; his good humor, his kindness, his diligence as a doctor. I hadn't thought Natalie would open up that way to a stranger. But Helen isn't a stranger. She has some peculiar faculty of — belonging to you. I'm afraid I can't do any better than that.

286

I know this will sound silly unless it should happen that you meet this woman, some time. Then you will know what I mean. *

We three made the most of the holidays; went to see *Aïda* and *Pirates of Penzance*, put on by the Chicago Grand Opera Company, had dinner downtown at The Pontchartrain and the Statler and the Cadillac; saw Charlie Chaplin in a rollicking farce in which — attending a show — he climbs back and forth over outraged people seated in the same row and gets embroiled with the orchestra; one of the silliest, one of the most devastatingly ridiculous things I ever saw. In one of the more riotous moments, when we had all laughed until we were half hysterical, Helen pushed her forehead hard against my arm and said, 'I'm not going to look, any more. I've got a pain in my side.' I took her hand, and she held it tight, like a little child.

* I know what you mean. (R. M.)

AT HOME

February twenty-fourth, 1919, 10 P.M.

Yesterday noon Nick Merrick called up to inquire whether I could conveniently dine and spend the evening with him at his country place on Lake Saginack.

It was an unusual request. I had never been invited there except on a couple of occasions when Nick was having a large dinner party. When he wants to talk to me about anything, he suggests luncheon at one of the downtown clubs. It wasn't like him to invite me out to his home on such short notice, and when he added, 'There will be no one else,' I concluded that he wished to consult me about something of importance.

I had made other plans for the evening, but felt that I owed it to Nick to comply with his request, so I promised to go. About three he called up again to suggest that I plan to stay the night and avoid a late drive back to town. I felt sure then that Nick's confidences promised to be somewhat extensive.

I had often wondered why he wanted to build that palatial twenty-room mansion away out there in the country. Mrs. Merrick was long since dead, and Cliff, too. Maxine was an inveterate traveler, and when in the States she lived mostly in hotels and sanitaria. Nick is essentially a city man. His whole life has been spent in the clatter of big factories and the amiable buzz of the Columbia Club.

Once I tried to sound him out a little on his pastoral interests, and discovered — what I had already suspected — that he didn't know a dahlia from an aster or an azalea from an hydrangea or a hawthorn from a flowering crab.

He maintains a herd of pedigreed Guernseys and a staff of trained dairymen to look after them, but I doubt whether there is anything in this project that amuses Nick beyond the fact that his milk costs about five dollars a quart. It is good milk.

Nick also raises fancy Berkshires. One day he told me some of the distinguishing marks of a Berkshire. The under-carriage of the hog's head should be shaped like a rocker. This tilts up the snout. The forehead should overhang, leaving almost no face, at all. A really damn good Berkshire hog, said Nick, should be barely able to see out between his eyebrows and his nose. The legs should be short and slim. There had been a movement to breed for slimmer legs, Nick explained, but the thing had gone too far. The improved legs weren't strong enough to carry the hog, so they had been obliged to breed the sturdier legs back on again.

These genetic phenomena amuse Nick, but I can't believe that he gets very much entertainment out of it; for he has nothing to do with it aside from looking at his expensive pigs, occasionally, when someone visits him. I saw them, one afternoon, couple of years ago. They are clean as cats. At precise intervals, in their recreation yard, lathe-turned and rope-wrapped posts are planted for the accommodation of the hogs when they want to scratch.

There are also pens of highly bred poultry, cages of pheasants, and a green-tiled duck-pond with a little fountain in the middle.

Every morning, weather permitting, Nick takes a stroll, inspecting his livestock. Then, if the day is bright, his poker-faced Powell drives him into town where he has an office on the top floor of one of the new skyscrapers and an ancient secretary who shares alone with God the knowledge of Nick's reasons for coming in; for he is done with business and makes no pretense of keeping himself informed about the dizzying progress of the industry which he helped to inaugurate. I understand that the stock market reports, and a succinct summary

290

of the previous day's business in the Axion Motor Company are always laid on his desk, and the inkwell is kept filled.

Last night I found out why Nick built the big house he calls Windymere. It is intended for Bobby. Bobby is unlikely ever to do anything but play, and this will be just the place for him. He will undoubtedly do a great deal of traveling about. His appetite for going places was acquired early. He had made seven round-trips to Europe before he was eighteen. But Windymere is to be his permanent address, and he will be here at least every four years to vote the Republican ticket. It takes six men to keep the lawn in order that slopes a quarter-mile to the lake shore where there is a commodious boat-house containing a high-powered speed-boat, a cabin cruiser with a capacity of ten passengers, and a couple of sail-boats.

It was to talk with me about Bobby that Nick invited me out. I was so sorry for the old man I could have cried.

I arrived about half past six. The day had been quite spring-like, but after sundown it was snappy. Nick had a comforting fire in his big library and the welcome he gave me was as warm. He had been reading a new detective story, and queried me about my taste in such fiction. When I confessed that I wasn't up on the subject, he informed me — and quite soberly, too — that if a man really needed a time-killer, there was nothing equal to it. His library shelves are loaded, almost floor to ceiling, with crime and mystery tales. I daresay these shockers are diverting, but it seems a pity that Nick's range of reading is so restricted. There are so many other things in which, one would think, he might find enjoyment.

After dinner — a man's dinner, oxtail soup, superb steak, baked potato, head lettuce salad, cheese, and coffee — we returned to the crime-and-mystery museum. Our table talk had dealt mostly with the peace, which Nick thinks is impracticable, and with prohibition, in which he has even less confidence. He gets it from his men on the farm that liquor in plenty is coming across the Canadian border, and believes it will not be long until a systematic evasion of the law will develop a new industry; says we will have a bootlegging profession, same as we have wholesale fish dealers.

In the library we settled into luxurious leather chairs, before the grate, and lighted our cigars. They were good cigars; much too good for me, because I do not often set fire to anything that costs a dollar.

'I had a rather distressing letter, this morning,' began Nick, puffing industriously. 'Thought I'd like to talk to you about it.'

But first, he announced, he would have to tell me something of the circumstances which had produced it.

'My grandson, after several years of getting kicked out of one prep school into another, finally struck his stride at the University. He is a junior now. I haven't had any complaints about his conduct over there. Of course, boys will be boys, and you can't hold too tight a rein. Bobby spends a good many of his weekends over here, always brings three, four, half a dozen of his fraternity chaps along. Naturally, they are a bit noisy. They take over the house and raise hell with it. They drink and play poker and sleep late in the morning and upset the servants. But I suppose they're not any worse than other high-spirited young fellows, enjoying a couple of days away from the grind of college work.'

I nodded, comprehendingly, and remarked that such festival occasions must bore him.

'Not any more,' explained Nick. 'This is the third year of it. I used to try to play host, but I gave that up. When the racket begins, on Friday night, I pack a bag and go into town.' He paused, for a moment, and added, 'Maybe that wasn't the thing to do. They might have behaved a little better if I had been on the premises.'

'Anything special happened?' I wondered.

Nick reached into his breast pocket and produced the letter. He did not open it at once; just sat there slowly tapping his thumb with it.

'I had this by special delivery early today. It is from an old friend of mine in Grand Rapids, Knute Larson. Knute was with me in the Axion Company for many years; retired now. His family is pretty much scattered. Only one left in whom he has any particular interest: his grandnephew. This boy is one of my Bobby's closest friends. He has been over here so often that we feel quite well acquainted with him. Several times Knute has dropped me a line or two, thanking me for hospitality to his youngster. I had gathered that Knute liked to have the boy visit us.' Nick drew the letter from the envelope and adjusted his nose-glasses.

The contents of the Larson communication did not surprise me very much, after the introduction Nick had given it. Mr. Larson was more than grateful for the many kindnesses shown to young Knute at Windymere, but it was becoming more and more evident that the boy would be much better served if he could be induced to pay serious attention to his university work.

' "I have heard from the dean," ' read Nick. ' "He happens to be an alumnus of the same fraternity to which our boys belong. I hope this is not going to worry you, but the dean says your Bobby is not good for young Knute." '

'I should have thought,' I put in, 'that if the dean felt this way about Bobby, he might have hinted as much to you, and given you a chance to counsel with Bobby about it.'

Nick puffed vigorously, for a while, before replying.

'I was afraid you'd ask me that, Doc,' he growled. 'Fact is; the dean has spoken to me about it, a couple of times.'

'And how did Bobby feel about it when you talked to him?'

Nick shook his heavy mop of white hair, and made a jabbing little gesture of futility.

'Oh, he just screwed up his face, the way he has always done, ever since he was a baby, when someone tries to correct him — and said the dean was a prissy old sissy. "His trouble is," Bobby said, "that he has to live on college wages — and he's jealous. Always dragging me in to pan me for showing the other fellows a good time." '

'Maybe the dean has a case, Nick,' I suggested. 'Perhaps you might solve your problem if you reduced Bobby's allowance.'

'I would,' agreed Nick, promptly; 'I have! But this damn-fool mother of his makes it up to him. I can't forbid him the house! And I can't stand here and play policeman every week-end!'

We were both silent for some moments, and then I inquired again whether anything in particular had happened to provoke the Larson letter. Nick scowled and nodded.

'They celebrated Washington's birthday over here,' he said, glumly, 'and drove back to Ann Arbor late in the night. Seems they got into a little accident on the road; hit a farmer's market-cart.'

'Sounds as if it might have been early, rather than late,' I remarked, grinning a little.

'Yes — I guess so,' grumbled Nick. 'They were all asleep but this young Knute. He was driving. They tried to settle with the old man, but he had them arrested. Knute spent the forenoon in the calaboose.'

'And your friend Larson thinks it's time to change the program a little.'

'Exactly — and so do I. But I don't know where to begin,' admitted Nick, helplessly. 'Can't take him out of school. No use sending him somewhere else. He probably wouldn't go, anyhow. He's not dependent on me. Has plenty of money of his own.'

'Bobby has never struck me as the sort that would stand up and defy you,' I said.

Nick promptly rushed to his grandson's defense.

'No, no,' he exclaimed. 'He wouldn't be mean about it. Bobby's polite enough. Picked that up in France. He would just grin and pat me on the back — and do as he pleased.'

It occurred to me that if Bobby had had a little less money and a few more spankings his prospects would be brighter. Without taking second thought, I said that aloud. Nick shook his head.

'Bobby is a fine boy,' he said, half to himself. 'It isn't his fault that he hasn't been brought up like other boys. His father died when he was a mere child; and you know how unstable his mother is. And I never felt it was my job to be his nurse.'

'Well —' I said, 'something will have to be done.' I was glad Nick didn't take my comment for more than it was worth, and ask me what I had in mind. 'Does he ever talk as if he wanted to do anything — in particular?' I asked, to chink the long pause.

It was at this point that I could have wept for good old Nicholas Merrick. He leaned forward — sagged forward — in his chair, with his elbows on his knees and his chin in his mottled hands, silently shaking his head. *

After a long, agonizing minute, he straightened up slowly and said, 'Doc, my boy Cliff disappointed me, poor chap. I was too busy, when he was young, to give him proper direction. I have hoped that Bobby might find himself and amount to something. He has some very good traits, a fine mind, a nice disposition. Everybody likes him. He makes friends easily. Why, sometimes, when he is here alone with me, he goes to the piano and plays for me by the hour; things he knows I like. But — mostly — he's whooping it up with his rakehell friends. What would you do — if you were in my place?'

I have never been at such a complete loss for adequate words. I tried to console Nick with the empty surmise that Bobby might come to his senses; mumbled something about his being young yet; that he might tire of loafing and carousing, and give himself to a worthwhile job. But, all the time, I felt that Nick was assaying my hollow phrases at their exact value.

'If we could get him into a little different atmosphere,' mused Nick.

* This thing has nearly broken my heart. I wish I had known how deeply Grandpère had grieved about me. I am glad he has lived to see a little brighter prospect for me. (R. M.)

'Yes,' I agreed, woodenly, 'different atmosphere. That's right. That might do it.' A very silly rejoinder. Bobby carries his own atmosphere along with him. 'What he needs,' I went on, 'is the influence of some sound young friend who isn't a mere playboy.'

Then it occurred to me that I might as well give Nick a glimpse of my own problem, and its happy solution, so I told him about Joyce. And the amazing change that had come over her through her devotion to Helen. Nick was very attentive. His deep-lined face brightened.

'Now that is fine!' he said, momentarily dismissing his own perplexity to rejoice with me. 'All the girl wanted was proper direction. And there weren't any rules or regulations that would keep her in line. What she had to have was the inspiration of somebody she liked. Think it will last — when she gets out of school, and away from this other young woman?'

I could only tell him that I hoped so. Our conversation lagged a little. Perhaps that was my fault. Nick's comment about the time to come, after Joyce's school days are over, when she may be seeing little or nothing of Helen, depressed me.

For I have responded, as gratefully as Joyce, to the tenderness and radiance of this exquisite girl. She is much in my thoughts; much too much.

Nick and I played three games of Russian Bank in which I was so decisively licked that his victories could hardly have brought him any satisfaction. I'm afraid my mind wasn't on it. The good old boy dragged out his watch, about ten-thirty, and considerately observed that I had to work next day. He took me to my room with a graciousness of hospitality that would have done credit to a prime minister bedding down his king, patting the pillows to make sure they were the right ones. Poor, rich old Nick!

Ever since I was a lad, I have read and heard about the inadequacy of wealth to provide happiness. Mostly, I have let all such platitudes in at one ear and out at the other; for these reflections were usually offered by parsons and professors whose knowledge of money was limited to the fact that they didn't have any. I suppose the typical essay on 'What I Would Do with a Million' is usually written by some poor devil who hopes to sell his piece for enough to pay an overdue gas-bill.

But, last night after I went to bed, it occurred to me as a solemn and somewhat startling fact that large wealth is really about the most feeble resource anyone can lean on who is in search of happiness.

Take Nick's wealth, for example. It made a rotter of his only son. It induced Nick into an early retirement that has made him utterly wretched. It is going to ruin his grandson.

Bobby is Nick's last stand. Everything else has palled on him. Nothing left but Bobby.

And now Bobby is no good.

It is too bad.

I wish there was something I could do, but I'm sure I don't know what it would be.

This was Pyle's birthday and I invited him to dine with me at The Pontchartrain. Tim Watson and Natalie came in, and tarried a moment at our table. It pleased me to see them together. I hope something may come of this, eventually. I must try to have sense enough not to seem too much interested.

BRIGHTWOOD HOSPITAL

June twenty-sixth, 1919, 10 P.M.

Helen came home with Joyce two weeks ago, expecting to spend at least a month with us, but upon receiving a summoning letter yesterday from her uncle, left for Philadelphia this morning, greatly to our disappointment.

I have been blue and restless all day. My saner judgment tells me it is probably for my own good that Helen has been called home. More and more I have been looking to this girl for my happiness. And the fact that I find myself, today, distrait and day-dreamy and indifferent to my tasks, surely should be enough to warn me against this tug at my heart. It will not be long until there will be no occasion for Helen's present relation to Joyce, and then I shall have to give her up.

She hasn't talked very much about her home life, but one gathers that it is pretty bleak. Doubtless that accounts for her tender attitude toward me. Her uncle, with whom she has lived for years, is a taciturn, frugal, small-time lawyer, whose clientèle is limited to a group of elderly people — widows and spinsters, mostly — living on incomes derived from conservative bonds and rentals of small business houses. Mr. Brent paddles about, collecting rents, overseeing repairs, ousting undesirable tenants and haggling with the others. It is that sort of legal practice. I infer that it is not very lucrative, and I suspect that the nature of it has made the old man mean.

It seems that Helen has a little income from a trust left by her deceased father, which accounts for her ability to go to a fairly expensive school. I hope the uncle is dealing honestly with her in the handling of this money. And I have no reason to suspect that he is not, aside from my own observation that penurious people — adept at driving hard bargains and pinching pennies — sometimes find it difficult to release their grip on money that rightfully belongs to others. If this old man has worn the same derby hat for seven years, which Helen has humorously reported in mentioning Uncle Percival's eccentricities, I think it is not improbable that he would consider himself morally justified in withholding from his niece the full payment of funds to be spent on what he might consider unnecessary fripperies.

It certainly is none of my business to be making these deductions, and the very fact that I am mentally sticking my nose into their affairs means nothing more or less than that my personal interest in Helen has grown out of all proportion to my slim claim on her friendship. It's not my habit to mole into people's private lives.

But — though I suppose I should despise myself a little for these petty sleuthings — I have been thinking a great deal about Helen's probable home life, since she left here on such short notice this morning, and I have constructed a picture of old Percival Brent which certainly does not flatter him. Helen says that her Uncle Percival's patron saint is Noah, his main interest in life being preparation for a rainy day.

When I was a boy, in the country, there were stories about stingy farmers whose policy it was to eat the spotty apples first, from the barrels in the cellar. By the time some more were needed for the table or for cooking, there would be another batch of apples which had become defunct in the meantime. So — the family ate half-rotten apples all winter. I think the same psychology prevails with the inveterate rainy-day economist. It is always a rainy day. It begins to rain on such people when they are thirty, and the sun never shines again.

Not much wonder that Helen responds to a little brighter home environment. I know that is why she snuggles close to me. I have to repeat that to myself, over and over, to keep my head.

Uncle Percival's son Monty, who lives at home, is in a brokerage house. Probably posts the board. Unlike his papa, Monty is not fretting much about a rainy day. Helen seems very fond of him, probably because of her concern over his improvidence rather than in admiration of his virtues. Father and son do not have much in common, naturally, and they can eat dinner together at the family table without a syllable of conversation. I suspect that when this Monty goes broke, he wangles some money out of his cousin. When Helen refers to him, it is usually with a quick little sigh and an anxious shake of her head. 'Poor, dear Monty,' she calls him. It wouldn't surprise me if it was some scrape of poor, dear Monty's — may his tribe decrease — that rushed her off to Philadelphia today.

I realize — you needn't tell me — that I have made a dismaying self-disclosure in the things I have said here. But it frets me to know that Helen is unhappy, and I can't help mulling over the obvious causes of it. I think that between sour old Percival and slick young Monty the girl's life is deucedly unpleasant. It would be a godsend to her if she could be emancipated from such a dreary and stultifying atmosphere.

Perhaps some cold-blooded psycho-analyst

would suggest that my wish to get Helen out of that glum and frustrating home is not quite so altruistic as I have been making myself believe. He might inquire if I wasn't more concerned about rigging some good excuse to get her into *our* home. Very well, professor, I'll admit it, if that tickles your vanity. If Helen were in straitened circumstances I could propose that she come to us as Joyce's companion and counsellor, when her school days are over. As matters are, it would be an impertinence to hint at such a thing. But I cannot think of anything else that sounds the least bit plausible. I must put this enchanting creature out of my thoughts.

AT HOME

June twenty-eighth, 1919, Midnight

Joyce, lonely without Helen, went down to the Winslow Art Store this afternoon for a glimpse of Natalie. At dinner this evening she reported having met Harry Wickes, who has just arrived from France. She raved about him with shrill, boarding-school enthusiasm and accused me of having tried to conceal him from her.

'You might have told me about him,' she said, reproachfully. 'You must have seen a lot of him, from the way he talks about you.'

'Sorry,' I said. 'You're almost always away, you know. And Harry has been abroad for a long time.'

'I asked Natalie to come to dinner next Saturday evening,' said Joyce. 'And I invited Harry too. Hope you don't mind. I think he's marvelous!'

I agreed that Harry is a fine fellow, and said I was glad she was having him here, provided it would be agreeable with Natalie. Joyce felt sure about that. How could Natalie help liking him?

'Harry has an uncommonly bright and pretty sister, too,' I said. 'Perhaps you might enjoy meeting her. Would you like to ask her to come with Harry?'

'Next time,' said Joyce. 'How about asking Tim? You said he and Natalie were friendly.'

I grinned and Joyce made a nose at me.

'Of course you may ask Tim,' I said. 'He hasn't been here for months. And that will leave you free to back young Mr. Wickes into a corner and get acquainted.' I had never teased Joyce about a young man before, and apparently I hadn't done a very neat job of it, for she scowled a little as she stabbed at her salad.

'I can't see why you are saying that,' she protested. 'I'm not in the habit of making war on every good-looking boy I meet.'

'I was in fun, you know.'

She drew a conciliatory little smile and said she knew that; then added, 'But I don't like to be teased about such things — any more than you would.'

I glanced up to meet her eyes, and said, 'I?'

'Sure! You would turn a cartwheel, right out through the window, if I teased you.'

'What about?' I asked, indiscreetly.

'What about!' she echoed hollowly, and

then, in a tone of elaborate irony, mumbled, 'As if you didn't know.'

I was considerably shaken by this unexpected challenge. Surely if anybody ever made an earnest effort to sublimate his feelings, I had been doing so. And this mere child had seen through me. I told her I should like some more peas, and she rang the bell. My failure to make a rejoinder didn't help my case very much.

'It's all right with me,' said Joyce, maternally, when the maid had retired. 'I'm sure I don't care. You know how very fond I am of her.'

'Helen?' I asked, rather unnecessarily perhaps.

'Don't be silly, darling,' recommended Joyce.

'Well —' I said, not quite sure that it was well, 'I certainly hope you haven't been imprudent enough to discuss with Helen whatever ideas you may have on this subject.'

Joyce shook her head and pursed her pretty lips.

'No,' she said, crisply, 'I haven't mentioned it. I wouldn't need to. She can't very well help knowing. She's pretty bright — for her age.'

I winced a little over that last phrase. We were about through with our dinner while this distressing conversation was going on. I suggested that we have coffee in the library. It seemed that complete candor was in order now. I couldn't leave this matter dangling. It was too important.

Joyce drew up a low stool in front of my chair, refused the coffee, and folded her arms across my knees.

'I've hurt your feelings, Daddy,' she murmured. 'I was horrid.'

'No — you weren't horrid,' I said, 'but — you bewildered me a little. I've made no secret of my fondness for Helen. She is one of the most charming girls I ever knew. But — I haven't been romancing with her, if that's what you mean.'

Joyce put her face down into her folded arms and shook her head. Then, without looking up, she mumbled, 'I know you haven't, darling; but you're in love with her.' And when I did not reply promptly, she added, 'You know that.'

'My dear,' I said, 'it isn't always easy to supervise your feelings toward people. Some you dislike, for no very good reason, and they seem to sense it — no matter how much pains you take to conceal it. And some people you like, perhaps without knowing exactly why, and —'

'Daddy, don't!' said Joyce, thickly. 'If you

310

aren't going to talk honestly about it, let's drop it.'

'Very well,' I declared. 'If it gives you any pleasure to put your father on the grill, I'll admit that Helen is very dear to me. If I were fifteen years younger — ten years younger — I should try to win her love.'

'Try to win her love!' repeated Joyce. 'Are you blind? Or are you trying to spoof me?'

'Are you attempting to make me believe,' I demanded, 'that you think Helen Brent is fond of me — in that way? It couldn't be!'

Joyce straightened up, clasped her slim hands around her knees, and looked up steadily into my face.

'Are you being truthful, Daddy?' she asked, soberly.

'Never more so!' I declared, sincerely. 'Helen has never given me the slightest reason for thinking that she considers me otherwise than as a devoted friend — old enough to be her father. Doubtless it is because she has no father that she treats me with such tender solicitude.'

'She likes to be close to you,' said Joyce, reminiscently.

'Let's analyze that,' I suggested. 'When she was with us, last Christmas, and we were starting out to spend the evening, you probably saw Helen tuck my scarf closer about my throat; but that was the sort of attention a young person shows toward an elderly person. In fact, it defined our relation.'

Joyce smiled knowingly.

'But you are not an old man, Daddy. You swim, and golf, and drive like the devil was after you, and go everywhere performing tricky surgery. Helen doesn't think you need your throat bundled up.'

'You're on the wrong track, my lass,' I said, condescendingly.

'Well — maybe,' she conceded, arching her brows. Rising, she kissed me lightly on the forehead and sauntered toward the door. 'Have you read "My Antonia"?' she paused to inquire. And when I said I had not, she suggested that I do so. 'I am in the middle of it now,' she said. 'If you'll excuse me, I'll go back to it. You know how it is — when you're in suspense about a story.'

'Run along, dear,' I said, cheerfully enough. 'When you are through with it, I'll read it — if you can recommend it as a book that keeps you in suspense.'

'I didn't know you cared much for such stories,' drawled Joyce, a bit sly, as if she were inviting me into a commitment. 'I thought you liked stories that put you to sleep.'

'Not always,' I replied, gratified over the

change of conversation. 'Suspense is good for you, sometimes; helps to keep your blood in circulation. I don't object to a story that keeps me awake.'

'Well — I'll tell you one then,' said Joyce, slowly sidling through the doorway. 'Helen carries your picture in her card-case.'

I'm afraid my heart gave a strange little bump that wasn't the fault of my aneurism; but I decided not to be left sitting with Joyce's half-malicious valedictory.

'And what if she does?' I retorted. 'That doesn't mean a thing! If she carries my picture — and it's mighty sweet of her — she has about the same reason she would have for carrying the picture of her philosophy professor — or Uncle Percival, if he wasn't such a grim old icicle. For the present, Helen considers me as an anchor. She wants something substantial to lean on.' I realized, too late, that this final remark had not been happily selected.

Joyce, framed in the doorway, slowly nodded her head several times, in mock acceptance of my speech.

'Something to lean on,' she repeated. 'I've seen her do it.'

'Jealous?' I asked.

Joyce ambled toward me, her lips twisted into a pout.

'No — I'm not jealous,' she said, defensively. 'I think I'm rather glad. You've been lonesome — for years and years. I'm crazy about Helen. It would be gorgeous to have her here — always! Only — what peeved me was your taking this hoity-toity attitude, as if you were Moses — and I was nothing but — but —'

'The Ten Commandments,' I suggested, when she failed to complete the pass. 'Come here.' I wiggled a finger. She sat on my lap, and dabbed at her eyes. I pulled her down into my arms.

'I ought to be slapped,' she muttered, huskily.

'Me, too,' I admitted. 'I should have been more generous with my answers to your questions. But, darling, I really don't know the right answers. All that I can tell you is this: I do love Helen, and — that's the end of it. I'm never going to tell her, and I sincerely hope you won't. Because, if you do, we can never have her here again. Promise?'

Joyce raised up to look me squarely in the eyes.

'You mean — you don't intend to ask her to marry you?'

'Of course not!'

'But you two would be enormously happy!'

I shook my head.

314

'It wouldn't work,' I said.

'Poor Daddy!' Joyce patted my cheek.

Her tender words and the caress added several more years.

I deeply regret that this conversation occurred. It is very doubtful if Helen and I can retain the sweet relationship we have had. I should like to believe that Joyce will have sense enough to keep my secret, but I wouldn't bet much on it; and I shall not know — certainly — that she hasn't confided it. This doubt will make me self-conscious. Helen will sense it, and wonder why. Even if Joyce doesn't tell, Helen will feel this constraint. The situation troubles me.

I hope I'm not indulging in self-pity. But this precious woman has been good for me. It has restored my youth to have her close to me and be aware of her dear companionship. Aside from my work, my life — for many years — has been lonely. Surely no one would have begrudged me this beautiful friendship.

And now my child has unwittingly ruined it. If Helen comes here again, she will find me remote, austere, casual. I won't be able to resume our friendship freely.

When the tact was passed around, my daughter must have contented herself with a very modest serving.

Here goes for another sleepless night.

Joyce knew a story that would keep me awake.

Brightwood Hospital

July fifth, 1919, 9:30 P.M.

Late this afternoon McDermott and I were together in an operation. It turned out to be a fairly simple mastoid, and I did little but look on. Mac had thought he might run into something deeper. We were both glad his suspicions were groundless, and so was the patient who seemed almost as much interested in the case as we were.

It was a tedious affair and by the time we were into our street clothes it was six-thirty. Mac suggested that we have dinner here. It has been a long time since I have done that. We met Tim Watson, on our way down, and invited him to join us. Our table conversation was of considerable interest to me, and I am going to recapitulate it briefly. We were discussing the increasing disregard for law and order, and the probable outcome if this tendency is permitted to go on unchecked.

The subject arose as a corollary to our unanimous indignation over yesterday's inexcusable racket. There is a city ordinance prohibiting the sale or shooting of firecrackers,

317

but for the past week all sorts of noisy and dangerous fireworks were to be had almost any place in town. The patients at Brightwood — and we are far out in a residential zone where you would think we should be protected — were kept awake and on edge all night of the third and all day and all night of the fourth.

At the four corners of our grounds, which occupy the entire block, there are conspicuous signs reading 'Quiet — Please — Hospital.' It was generally agreed that there was more shooting in our block than anywhere else we had been, during this period.

McDermott insisted it was the signs, requesting quiet, that accounted for this annoyance. Mac thinks the rowdies see the notices and growl, 'To hell with your rules!' And light a cannon cracker the size of a rolling-pin, and toss it into the hospital grounds.

We asked one another, 'Who are these people? Where do they come from? Who breeds this stock?' These queries set us going on our serious talk about the mounting inconsiderateness of our time. It would seem that a certain element of our population is utterly callous to the fundamental claims of common decency. Tim thinks we are rapidly becoming a nation of boobs.

I do not think that I am personally acquainted with a man or boy who would deliberately throw a nerve-splintering explosive onto the lawn of a hospital. But there are such people. Who are they? How did they get that way? Do they derive from any particular species? Or are they just unclassified halfwits and hoodlums?

McDermott, who is I fear slightly prejudiced in favor of persons speaking something that resembles the English language, thinks we have been far too lax with our immigration restrictions; says the public's bad manners have been imported. While I do not share his certainty that this fully explains the growing impoliteness and disregard of the ordinary amenities, I do believe that the country is too heavily stocked with aliens who have no interest in the American way of living.

Now that bootlegging is rampant — as might have been expected, with the Federal Government in charge of prohibition enforcement — it is significant that the very large majority of the men arrested every day for liquor-smuggling and liquor-peddling are foreigners bearing other than English names.

Mac had an evening paper along with him, which he proceeded to spread out over the table and into the hollandaise sauce, and began drawing little circles around the names of persons figuring in today's crime news. 'Look!'

he said. 'See what I mean?'

It really was amazing! It appears that we are supporting an imported underworld composed of people who arrogantly defy our laws. In what other nation, inquires McDermott, would such a thing be permitted?

Tim thinks the war had a lot to do with the prevailing rudeness; says the demobilized soldiers, released from rigid restraints, are eager to exercise their liberty; thinks they enjoy the distinction of being 'tough guys.'

I ventured the opinion that the automobile has had much to do with making people inconsiderate. A naturally rude fellow will impose on other people, when he is behind the steering wheel of a car where they can't get at him. The bigger coward he is, on foot, the more bravely impudent he is, on wheels.

We still don't know what sort of people touched off the firecrackers around the hospital. But we do know that there is being developed, in this country, a contempt for law and the elementary civilities. I wonder if the big factories haven't something to do with it. Until the recent techniques of mass production came in, men in industry found joy in their work. The cabinet-maker produced a bureau; all of it. He designed it, fitted it together with skill, applied its hardware, varnished it, fetched it to market. Now, his son's contribution to the five thousand identical bureaus that the big furniture factory has contracted for, is limited to the job of feeding an automatic machine that dowels the boards with a punch — and a whack. You can't expect this young fellow to find any joy in that sort of occupation. He has to find his pleasure apart from his work. And he doesn't know how. He goes out looking for excitement. Firecrackers, perhaps.

I have made some notes on our conversation, tonight, because the problem we discussed is likely to grow more and more serious. Unless this increasing contempt for authority and indifference to the public welfare is effectively dealt with, the tendency may become a grave menace to the very life of this nation.

Evidently it is an easy step from impoliteness to vandalism, and from vandalism to disregard of life and safety. If we are not vigilant, there may come a day when life in this land will be cheap, and property rights insecure. *

When the hoodlum class has become sufficiently important, numerically, to be aware of its united power, it may either decide to

* Deaths by automobile accidents in 1919, 11,154; in 1922, 15,326. (R. M.) In 1938, 32,400. (Editor.)

make war on honest and industrious citizens at the polls, or stage a revolution.

For the past hour I have been in my office, talking with Nancy Ashford, who returned this evening from a two weeks' vacation in the country near Harbor Beach on Lake Huron.

One of our pet nurses, Cynthia Bates, hails from that neighborhood and is forever extolling the peace and quiet of the shore farms. Nancy, physically and emotionally worn by her heavy responsibilities, thought it might be good for her to escape into such a tranquilizing environment.

Her report was amusing. Nancy had the usual experience of the city dweller who, battered by the rasp of traffic and the suffocating contacts with the urban pack, seeks repose in the open spaces and among persons of simple life. The first day of this serenity is so delightfully healing to the bruised spirit that one doubts whether one will ever be able to return to the racket. And the first night, one sleeps like a baby — probably because well done up from a long journey. The next night — but I'll let Nancy describe it.

'The next night was mosquito night. They had a fiesta. And I was in the front row. Martha was sorry they didn't have electric lights

— I mean the house; not the mosquitoes — and so was I; for that meant I couldn't read in bed. There was a two candle power kerosene lamp on the table. I couldn't see to read by it, but it was just right for the mosquitoes to find their way about. And — so far as the peace and quiet went — I never heard so much noise; noises I wasn't used to. The katydids! My word! And the frogs! And the bugs!'

'Bugs?'

'Oh, no — not that kind. Martha is clean as a pin. I mean gnats and various things that fly around and sing — and carry hypodermic kits.'

'How was the food?' I inquired. 'You can generally get some very nice saddle-leather, at these country places, served with brown gravy.'

'The food was wonderful!' replied Nancy, fervently. 'Martha is a grand cook. I wish we could induce her to come to Brightwood. I've had about all I can take from Emmons.'

'Drinking again?'

'And surly — and impudent — and untidy.'

'Very well: get Martha.'

'She would like to come. I talked to her about it. But she lives with her brother. They're twins. They've never been separated. We would have to find a job for Perry.'

'That might not be hard,' I said. 'What can he do?'

'I don't know,' said Nancy, with a little sigh. 'Perry has a stiff knee that's gone to his head. It has made him sour as a pickle. He might be taught to help with the furnaces and mow the lawn and — odd jobs. He is handy with tools. Made his own motor-boat. Took the engine out of an old flivver.'

'Did you take a ride in it?' I asked.

'He didn't invite me. Perry's about as companionable as a — a porcupine. But Martha is a darling! And I can't see how she endures that lonely life up there with nobody to talk to but this sorehead.' Then Nancy went on to eulogize Martha's wide range of domestic accomplishments, and repeat her wish that the frustrated woman might be given 'a chance to live.'

'All right,' I agreed. 'Bring her on. We can find something for Perry. Maybe the change of scenery would be good for him too.'

So — we left it at that. Nancy hopes it will work out happily; and, for her sake, I do too; though it won't bother me very much, if it doesn't; I'm not responsible for what goes on in the hospital kitchen. It's Nancy's job.

I fear I have forgotten to report on the dinner party we had, a little while ago, attended by Natalie and Tim and Harry Wickes.

It was expected, at least by me, that Natalie and Tim would consolidate and leave Harry to the mercy of Joyce. From the first it was evident that Natalie and Harry have discovered their mutual indispensability.

If Tim has been in doubt whether to pursue his interest in Natalie, I think he may now set his mind at ease on that subject.

About nine, he put in a call to Brightwood, and regretted to learn that he had to leave us at once. I hope Tim is not going to fret, and I don't believe he will. I should like to see him in a home of his own. I wonder if he might like Dorothy. We must arrange to have them over together some evening.

Joyce heard from Helen today. Uncle Percival insists on her spending the rest of the summer at home. It's a very drab life for her. I wish we could do something about it.

AT HOME

August twentieth, 1919, 10:30 P.M.

On several occasions, during the past year or
more, I have talked vaguely with my good
friend, Fred Ferguson, about a small cottage
I thought of building on my few arid acres
overlooking Lake Saginack.

Fred has always made a little joke of it. As
the best-known architect in town, he doesn't
waste his time on such insignificant projects,
and he has doubted whether I would make
much use of a house in that uninviting region.

Last night, we found each other at the Columbia Club, and had dinner together. Mrs.
Ferguson was out of town, and Joyce is a guest
at Windymere over the week-end where
Bobby Merrick is entertaining a dozen young
friends from town. I wasn't keen on Joyce's
accepting the invitation, but I didn't care to
have a row with her.

Fred, as usual, wanted to know how the
little house was coming on; and when I assured
him that I still had the thing seriously in mind
he said, 'Why don't we drive out there tomorrow and look the place over — and make

a few pencil-sketches.'

I picked him up this morning about ten and we arrived shortly after one. The last two miles are off the highway on a narrow graveled road. I must say that the country round about is anything but attractive; a lot of dwarfed pine and brambles. Of course, everything is seared now with the usual midsummer drought. I felt a bit chagrined over the general appearance of my untamed property, as we turned into the ill-conditioned lane and proceeded slowly toward the unfenced west boundary of the tract which overhangs the water at an elevation of some eighty feet. Fred was saying nothing as we got out of the car and sauntered through the briars to the ledge. I rather expected he would remark, presently, that the situation was bad and that I had better not waste any money on it. He looked for a long time at the lake and the land, and then said, 'If you really want a little hideout, Doc, where you can rusticate in peace, I think we can build something suitable. It's a great view. And all you need, to make a lovely setting for your house, is a good job of landscaping, a deep well, and some competent person to keep up the grounds.'

We sat down on the parched grass and Fred continued thinking aloud. I might as well make up my mind, he said, that there would be a nice little item of expense — at the outset — for the engineering. There should be a low stone wall fronting the lake, and some grading and excavation necessary to make a safe and comfortable way down to a boat-house and swimming-wharf.

'But it will not be of much satisfaction,' he went on, 'if you think of it as a mere summer place. If you are willing to go into this thing right, build an all-year house and put some people in it who will take care of it and the grounds. If it isn't that important, I shouldn't do it, at all, if I were you.'

Then he began drawing some tentative plans for a house, part of it to serve the caretakers; two-thirds of it for the master, a couple of guest bedrooms, and — most important of all — a large living-room with a grand view. As the design unfolded, my interest increased. I need a place of this sort. I have stuck too close to my work.

'If you mean business,' said Fred, 'you would do well to have a good landscape man come out here and get some of your heavier plantings started. It takes a little time to do that.'

'I would probably not live long enough to see trees of any size,' I said.

'Not like the ones across the lake, certainly,' agreed Fred, pointing to the beautiful panorama on the western shore. 'The Fosters' grove of firs must be very old; big trees long before they built their place. Nick Merrick paid a pretty penny for his landscaping.'

'You built that house; didn't you?'

'Yes. It's a great place; don't you think?'

'Gorgeous! But I wouldn't want it. Too big.'

'Neither would I,' agreed Fred. 'I wonder if the old boy is happy in it.'

'Ought to be,' I said. 'He has everything; all the modern conveniences; fancy livestock, flower gardens, fresh air, the lake.'

'I don't think Nick makes much use of the lake,' drawled Fred. 'Young Bobby has a little fun, occasionally, in that big speed-boat. Have you seen him lately?'

I said I hadn't. Fred grinned enigmatically.

'Have you?' I asked, surmising that he wanted a little encouragement.

'Bobby's going to be a second edition of Cliff,' muttered Fred. 'A good deal brighter than Cliff — but a waster. They tell me he is doing a fairly good job at the University; finishes in February. But he goes at a pretty fast clip.'

'Does your Arthur see anything of him, over there?' I inquired.

'No,' snapped Fred. 'I put my foot down on that. He's no fit company for any young fellow with an ounce of ambition. Art was considerably upset because I wouldn't let him go to Bobby's house party that's on now at Windymere.'

'You must have your boy under good control,' I observed, 'or he would have gone, anyhow.'

'Oh — he knows better than to pull a trick like that on his daddy. However — I must say for the boy that he generally votes the right ticket. We haven't had much trouble with him. I've explained to him that we're not well enough off to let him grow up to be a bum. He has got his living to make. Young Merrick will never have to work.' After a little pause, he added, 'I expect that bunch, over there today, is plastered to the eyebrows.'

I made no reply for a long time; then I couldn't help saying, 'My Joyce is there.'

'Sorry,' said Fred, a bit flustered. 'I guess I spoke out of turn. However — I daresay your girl can take care of herself, all right.'

'I hope so,' I said. 'It's hard to know just what to do when these youngsters insist on having their own way.'

'Yeah — that's right, Doc,' said Fred, soothingly. 'Big problem.' He scrambled to his feet. 'Well — shall we call it a day — and go home?'

Our conversation had suddenly depressed

me. We drove another mile north on the graveled road, at Fred's suggestion, to see what the country looked like, further out. I hadn't been that far, before. Half a mile from my place we found an unoccupied house, not in bad repair, and sauntered around it, peering in through cobwebbed windows.

'Somebody tried to live here,' I said, 'and gave it up.'

'They probably hoped to make a living,' said Fred. 'Anyone who wants a house in this neighborhood will have to make his living somewhere else.'

We had some difficulty keeping our conversation alive, on the way home. It was still a bright day, but my own sky was overcast. I let Fred out at his house, and returned to the hospital to see if everything was all right. Or, perhaps my car proceeded over to Brightwood by force of habit. Or, perhaps I felt, subconsciously, that was the one stable fact left to reassure me. In any event, I went to the hospital, where things seemed unusually quiet. I did not talk to anyone.

I had my dinner at home alone. I suppose it was a good dinner, but I had no appetite. Afterward I began a letter to Helen, but found I had nothing in particular to say to her that I dared say. So I tore it up. Then I decided to write a few pages in this journal, but you can see that I am in no mood for that either. Life is very flat tonight.

Nancy has succeeded in bringing Martha Ruggles and her irascible brother to Brightwood. Martha is proving to be the jewel that Nancy had thought her. Grim old Perry who, for all that he is Martha's twin, appears to be about ten years her senior, is going to be a problem. Can't work with anybody. Thinks he is being made fun of, and I daresay he is.

He regards everyone with suspicion. Nancy thinks he is jealous of Martha's responsible position and growing popularity with our Brightwood family.

My heart goes out to the old codger. I think it's the stiff knee that has made him so stand-offish. If so, that means he is uncommonly sensitive. I have a notion he would respond to a little tactful attention.

Yesterday afternoon I waved a hand to him as he was hobbling across the grounds behind a big lawnmower. He paused, a moment, and regarded me with an impassive stare, but did not return my salute. An hour later one of the orderlies met me in a corridor and said, confidentially, 'This here new fellow, with the game leg, is out in the parkin' lot, a-tinkerin' with your motor. He's got the spark-plugs all out, a-fussin' with 'em.'

'I know about that, Danny,' I said, failing to add that I had just now found it out. 'And perhaps you'd better get back to your own job before it outgrows you.' I hate a tattler.

It annoyed me a little to have this report about Perry. I would have to tell him, too, to mind his own business. When I left the hospital, my car had more pep and snap than it had had for many a day. Perry had cleaned and readjusted the spark-plugs; probably had known they needed it when he heard the engine come into the lot.

I couldn't help chuckling over this droll affair. Perry is going to be worth cultivation, I think. Yesterday's episode is funny enough to make a dog laugh, but it has its pathos, too. Sour old Perry never gets an amiable word because he doesn't deserve it. I wave a hand to him, and he merely scowls at me. Then he ditches his lawnmower and goes out to do me a favor. I must see more of Perry, but I'll have to be very careful.

I think he has all the natural instincts of a squirrel. He could be trained to eat out of your hand, but it would be a mistake to pat him on the back.

BLACKSTONE HOTEL, CHICAGO

August twenty-eighth, 1919, 8:30 P.M.

I came here for a consultation with Russell. We had it this afternoon and I am going back to Detroit tonight. Russell really shouldn't have asked me over, for there was nothing to be done. A sixteen-year-old boy dived into a shallow pool. Anyone would know, from the character of the respiration, that the blow had fractured the odontoid process. You can't do anything about that.

Russell said, 'I know — but the family wanted to do everything possible.' And then he added that he wanted my confirmation of his own diagnosis. I told him I thought he could confirm that, in about three days, with an autopsy.

It was a great pity. They were very fine people, and the boy will be a sad loss to them. I can't get accustomed to these things. After the consultation, I had an hour's talk with the parents. They were bewildered; hungry for almost any kind of consolation. I am not sure that I gave them anything but my time and sympathy. I suggested that they have a talk with Dean Harcourt, after they have laid their boy away. They know he can't live more than a day or two. We gave them no false hopes. I do not think it is a kindness, in such cases, to offer any encouragement. And neither does Russell. The truth — taking it by and large — is more satisfactory than a lie, however kindly meant. You encourage a family to hope — when there isn't the ghost of a chance — and they keep themselves strung up almost to the breaking-point for a period of days; and then they have to take the blow when their nervous equipment is disabled.

I used, occasionally, to practice that sort of benign deceit, but stopped it when I realized — with a start — that it wasn't their own feelings I had been trying to protect so much as mine. I had thought I was being humane when I was only being cowardly. I didn't want to witness their grief. I wanted them to take their hard wallop when I wasn't present to see them writhe. You'll find, if you look into it, that your sympathies can play some queer tricks on you. There's a lot of fraudulent consolation offered by people who are merely trying to protect their own emotions against a distressing scene.

Somebody is in an awful mess, and you say, 'There, there; don't fret. Maybe this is going to come out all right.' And you damn-well know it isn't going to come out all right. It's already out — and it's all wrong! What you're really trying to do is to give them a little sniff of ether until you've had time to escape.

Of course it is a mistake to argue with grief, but it's a bigger mistake to dismiss it with 'Now, now; there, there.'

Pyle had an interesting patient at Brightwood, a few weeks ago; a serene and friendly little woman, who had been hospitalized for some deep surgery. Pyle asked me to call on her, when she was convalescent. In the course of our talk, I inquired about her family. She had lost a boy, an only child, when he was twelve. I said, 'That's too bad.' She shook her head and smiled. 'No,' she said, quietly, 'I've never felt that way about it. It was the great experience of my life — having him for twelve years. I live it over and over. Those memories are very precious. They comforted me so much when I was sick.'

I repeated this conversation to the Brownings, this afternoon. I told them they couldn't hope that their Lawrence would recover, but they had a right to hope for an early arrival of the day when their possession of him — for sixteen years — would become an enduring blessing. Mrs. Browning murmured, 'Larry has had such a short life.' I told her they might extend it by investing something — in Larry's name. Her husband, eager to comfort her, said they would do that; a gift to the hospital, maybe.

'Or, better, an investment in a person,' I suggested. 'Stake some worthy young fellow to an education that will fit him for constructive service — and that will be Larry, carrying on; Larry as a doctor, perhaps; Larry as a teacher; Larry as a violinist. Find a chap that can be trained to make people well, or informed, or happy. Then Larry will live for a long time yet.'

I never stepped out of a professional consultation before, to go into a lay consultation with the family. Perhaps I might not have done so today if I hadn't been out to the Cathedral this morning. I arrived here at nine, coming early on purpose to hear Harcourt. I have been under the spell of this, all day.

Harcourt is a straight and steady thinker. And everything he says sounds as if it was coming from Somewhere Else. Of course, the environment has a good deal to do with that. After you've been stilled by the impressive music and the ancient ritual, you drift into a sort of hypnosis which makes you peculiarly amenable to Harcourt's suggestions.

And yet he doesn't make the slightest effort to impose on your emotions. I can't quote the

337

text he used. There is a Gideon Bible here on the chiffonier, but that doesn't do me any good; for I have forgotten where the text was: something about 'The eye cannot see, nor the ear hear, the things God hath prepared for those who love Him; for He reveals them to us by His spirit.'

For a little while, the Dean talked very beautifully about one's aesthetic response to the God we find in Nature. It was a prose poem. God in the sunrise; God in the sunset; offering two entirely different revelations of Himself; the eastern view at dawn inviting joy and work; the western view proposing a tranquil thought of rest. 'That is what sunsets are made for,' said the Dean, 'to give you mental repose.'

If you use your imagination a little on this, you will get the Dean's general idea of God's appeal to the human eye; in the silent, patient majesty of big trees; in the august austerity of high mountains; in the confident onrush of rivers cascading toward the sea, and never coming back until — chastened and humbled — they return in quiet showers falling on still pastures and in snowflakes on the hills. That sort of thing.

Then he talked about God's self-disclosures to the human ear; in music, of course; and in the eternity-message of the surf; and in the cadences of a voice beloved.

These were aesthetic appeals, said the Dean, and nobody was to minify their importance. 'These messages,' he went on, 'are in the nature of spiritual oxygen. Without them, we cannot live as spiritual beings.' Then he talked a little about the properties and phenomena of oxygen. We have to breathe to live, and it's the oxygen that we're after. We can't get on without it, and we recover it from the air by breathing. 'When people become anaemic, spiritually, it may be for lack of oxygen. Perhaps there are no sunsets where they live. Perhaps they never see mountains or hear a waterfall. We get our spiritual oxygen through the eye and ear — and the other senses.'

Then he talked about nitrogen. You can't live without it, but you must work for it. You can't breathe it. It is not free. It is in the soil, in the plants, in the wheat, in the meat; but not free.

Spiritual nitrogen, on which the soul feeds, must be captured. You must invest, you must be willing to wait with the patience of a farmer, you must not quit sowing because there was a drought. But if you strive, God will reveal to you, by His spirit, some self-disclosures which He cannot give you in a sunset, or by starlight, or by music. 'Many people who can breathe,' said the Dean, 'are hungry.'

Then he talked about what one may do to acquire this needful nitrogen; the investment of one's life in the upbuilding of other people, the steady alignment of oneself with the forces that lead up and on; costly adventures, sometimes; the more costly, the more rewarding.

The sermon was in the nature of a strong stimulant. I wish I had easier access to this man. I have not met him personally, and I shall not seek to do so. He is — from the distance in feet and inches that has been between him and me — the most engaging personality I have ever seen or heard; but I shall not risk a disillusionment by asking for an introduction to him: I do not want him to inquire how the weather is in Detroit, or tell me he is glad I came to his church. I don't want anything out of Harcourt when he isn't standing in his pulpit with his black gown on. Maybe I should find him just as helpful, in private talk; but I am not going to venture the experiment.

Back in the country, when I was a youngster, they always inquired whether the candidating preacher was a good mixer. Maybe that was the reason the people never kept one preacher very long. He was a mixer, and while he mixed, the people starved to death spiritually. At least, I surmise they did; for they were always in rows with one another, which couldn't very well have happened if they had been spiritually alive.

The Shoreham, Washington

September seventeenth, 1919, 10 P.M.

I am in good spirits tonight, after a month or more of anxiety. Joyce is again in Helen's custody, and everything is going to be all right.

Their school resumed work today. I came down with Joyce, explaining that I had an errand in Baltimore, which is true, though I purposely timed my appointment there to coincide with her journey. She was candidly suspicious of my motive, and inclined to be resentful when she learned we were traveling together.

'I hope you aren't afraid I might elope with some stranger,' she said, ineffectually trying to be jocular.

'Not at all,' I declared, 'but I have to go down, anyway, and I shall be very proud to be seen in your company. Of course,' I added, pensively, 'if you're ashamed to have your infirm parent along, I can go on a later train.'

There wasn't much she could do, after that, but assure me of her great joy, so we planned the trip; and, on the surface, it was pleasant enough. But Joyce's surmise that, in my opinion, she needs a bit of supervision, isn't a bad guess. In fact she knows that I have been disturbed about her recent social activities. She has been playing around with a pretty gay set, seeing entirely too much of young Merrick and a chap named Masterson, who thinks he is going to be a story-writer.

I made an effort to learn something about the nature of these frequent engagements, some of which have kept her out late, but her accounts of their various diversions have been disquietingly sketchy, and her attitude on the subject decidedly cool. I have been less in Joyce's confidence, during the past couple of weeks, than ever before.

I think I once adverted, in this journal, to the very close relation between one's emotional states and certain types of heart trouble. I cannot too strongly insist that this is true. I have discovered, in my own case, that a few days of fretting will so intensify my heart disability that I am obliged to add that anxiety to the other worry.

My aneurism has bothered me so constantly, of late, that I decided to consult Ramsey at Johns Hopkins. I have an engagement to see him tomorrow afternoon. But I am feeling ever so much better, tonight; so very much better that I am half minded to call him up and cancel the appointment.

I know very well the reason for my sudden improvement. My girl is safe in Helen Brent's hands. I still have an aneurism — and it will unquestionably get me some day — but, to-night, I am fit as a fiddle.

Joyce gave herself the pleasure of teasing me, this morning, when I said I would go out to Chevy Chase with her.

'Why — how funny!' she shrilled. 'I thought you detested getting yourself messed up with a lot of fond mammas and old maid professors. There must be something else out there, dar-ling, that you want to look at. What could it be?'

I think she had repented a little, by the time we arrived; for she was prompt to find Helen, and when we met her attitude was intended to put us at ease. I feel assured, now, that Joyce — however scatter-brained on occasions — has not abused my confidence by reporting to Helen the conversation we had about her.

By special dispensation, the girls were permitted to come down-town to dine with me. It was a delightful evening. How quickly Joyce reacted to the gracious presence of her charming friend. Instantly, she dropped her recent rôle of blasé and world-weary cyn-icism — a part she is quite too flighty to play convincingly — and became what she is, and ought to admit being, an impressionable school-girl, with a wide knowledge of the movie stars, a low opinion of Trigonometry, and an insatiable appetite for chocolate fudge. She is about as sophisticated as a pet rabbit. I have been so exasperated over her silly attempts to be a bored duchess that it was refreshing, indeed, to witness her return to a becoming simplicity.

Joyce never does things by halves. Having decided to set her clock back, she came very nearly recovering her perambulator, which had the effect of increasing the three years between herself and Helen to about ten, and lessening by that much the chasm between her lovely friend and me. I think Helen was a little bewildered, at first, over this maneuver, but soon adjusted herself to my child's metamorphosis.

While we were lingering over our coffee, Joyce — who hadn't wanted any — said she was anxious to get a note off in the mail and thought she would go and write it, if we'd excuse her.

'I am greatly relieved, my dear,' I said, as Joyce moved off. 'She is a different person when she's with you.'

'I'm not conscious of doing anything to her,' said Helen.

'That's just it!' I said. 'You don't admonish or criticize. It's effortless. That's the charm of your influence. It's not because of anything you do. It's simply because you're you.'

Her lips parted in a slow smile and her eyes lazily met mine.

'You always say nice things to me,' she said. 'They build me up.' There was a little pause. 'You like to build people up; don't you?'

'You don't need any building up, Helen,' I said, sincerely.

'More than you'd think,' she replied, soberly. 'In my home, no one goes to much bother about it.' Then, impulsively candid, she added, 'I think I'm at my best with you.'

Perhaps she was hoping only to say something that would please me, but her tone was so obviously sincere that it stirred me deeply. I have been thinking seriously about it, since they left, a while ago.

Suppose it is true. Suppose that Helen really feels that way. I wonder if she might think that a constant companionship between us would give her a self-assurance valuable enough to compensate for the sacrifice she would have to make — of her youth.

Of course I would make a gallant effort to meet her age halfway. I think her comradeship might rub out a few of my years. She would unquestionably take on a quick maturity. But would it be fair?

I reason this all out, neatly, and almost persuade myself that the thing is possible, feasible, practical, commendable. And then the implacable figures — unadorned by any elaborate circumstantial extenuations — stand out like a problem in simple arithmetic. I am a fool for giving way to this desire. I shall not make a middle-aged matron of this radiant girl. It wouldn't be right. But — God! — how I need her!

And I am going over to Baltimore tomorrow to see Ramsey. The fact that my heart doesn't worry me tonight is of no lasting significance. I daresay the present apparent well-being of my heart is a simple psychological phenomenon, on the order of the bad toothache that suddenly lets up when one is on the way to the dentist.

I'll go to Baltimore in the morning. And I'll make an honest effort to put Helen out of my mind. The thing is impossible; and I may as well reconcile myself to that fact before I commit some serious blunder. As it stands, I can have her for a devoted friend. Perhaps I should be satisfied with that.

AT HOME

November twenty-seventh, 1919, 10:30 P.M.

Today was Thanksgiving. My chief grounds
for gratitude were provided by a telegram
from Joyce saying that Helen's attack of flu
— of which I was informed, day before yesterday — is very light, and that she is already
on the mend.

Helen is going home for a few days, to rest
up, according to Joyce's wire; though I think
she would be far better off where she is, in
the hospital. I had a big notion to telegraph
her to that effect, but decided it was none
of my business.

Joyce thought it better to remain in Washington through the Thanksgiving recess and
avoid the danger of picking up a flu germ on
the train, which I felt showed uncommon wisdom. I wish now that I had urged them both
to leave early and come here for the vacation.
We could have put Helen into Brightwood,
when she took sick.

This evening I had a little party at The Pontchartrain. I've had a private tip that this fine
old hotel is presently going out of business.

No announcement has been made yet, but it won't be long.

My guests were Natalie, Dorothy, Harry, young Minton — who has just come to Brightwood as assistant to Carter, and Nancy Ashford. My decision to invite Nancy was somewhat of a surprise to both of us. I never take her anywhere. Our business relations at the hospital require us to see so much of each other that I have thought it a safe policy to restrict our friendship to the contacts we have there. It would be so easy to set people chattering, if we went out together socially. I hate gossip.

Yesterday afternoon, in the course of a little conference with Nancy, she wanted to know whether I expected to be in town today. I told her I had no other plans, except for an informal dinner down-town with some young friends.

'Why don't you join us?' I asked.

'Sure you want me to?' countered Nancy, candidly.

'Of course!' I told her who would be there. 'Do you good to get out of here for a few hours.'

'Won't Doctor Minton think it's odd?' Nancy's eyes registered perplexity.

'Well —' I observed, loftily, 'Doctor Minton's thoughts haven't become very important around here yet.'

'Don't you like him?' asked Nancy.

'Sure!' I said, firmly. 'Only he has no right to do any thinking about anything at Brightwood until he has been with us for ten years, at least.'

'Very well,' said Nancy. 'Thanks. Shall I meet you down there — in Peacock Alley?'

'I'll come for you,' I said. 'About seven.'

'Don't be silly,' said Nancy, stringing out the last syllable derisively. 'I'll go down in a taxi.'

So — we left it that way. Damn it! If I'd had sense enough to ask Nancy Ashford to marry me, ten years ago, she might have done it; and we would have been immensely congenial. She would have taken Joyce in hand and made a normal, stable child of her. But Brightwood needed Nancy more than I did. If I were a little more wise than I am, I might propose this to Nancy — even now. But I doubt whether she would be the least bit interested. We have been associated in business too long to pitch our relations in any other key. We are very fond of each other — but — that's as far as it goes.

Nancy nearly took my breath away tonight. I haven't seen her in anything but hospital harness for a long time. She is certainly a stunningly beautiful woman, with that youthful face and white hair and trim lines. She was in black. It fitted as if she'd been melted and poured into it.

Naturally, she had the opposite side of the table. I admired the poise and assurance with which she accepted her hostess rôle. I was very proud of Nancy Ashford, tonight. Occasionally I caught her eye, and it came over me that she and I were very close friends; very dependent on each other; very much more intimately bound up together than I had thought. As a matter of fact, I haven't thought much about it — for a long time. We had our work to do. I wish I had a map of her mind.

Natalie, who sat on my right, showed me her engagement ring. It hadn't been bought at the ten-cent store. I suppose Harry will be paying for it over a considerable period. Natalie was starry-eyed. I think this match is perfect. Harry is thoroughly fine.

Dorothy, as usual, was very pretty, and self-contained. Dorothy doesn't say much, but her eyes are alight. Doctor Minton seemed to enjoy looking into them.

It was the traditional Thanksgiving dinner; turkey, mashed potatoes and gravy, baked squash, cranberry sauce, etc. I wonder what it is that a hotel does to a turkey that utterly relieves it of any taste, at all. Have you ever noticed that? It always looks fairly appetizing, and tastes like a lukewarm slice of linoleum.

I drove Nancy home, over her mild protest. We talked mostly about hospital affairs. When I let her out, she said, 'It's none of my business, but if I were you I shouldn't throw young Minton and your Dorothy Wickes at each other.'

'You think he's a trifler?' I asked.

'It wouldn't surprise me,' said Nancy.

'I hope he hasn't been making passes at any of our girls, here at Brightwood,' I growled.

'Oh no,' said Nancy, quickly. 'He is far too clever to do that. But — I think he feels pretty sure that women ought to find him practically irresistible.'

'Do you think Dorothy was impressed?'

'Well — Doctor Minton is a handsome young fellow, witty, amiable. Doubtless she enjoyed his attentions which, I thought, were quite marked. Don't take this too seriously, please. Only — as I said — if I were you I shouldn't contrive occasions to further their acquaintance.'

'Thanks for the tip,' I said. 'Your hunches are usually right.'

I wrote a letter to Helen tonight, inviting her to spend the Christmas holidays with us. Perhaps I shouldn't have done it. I have again and again explained to myself how imprudent it would be to pursue this hopeless friendship any farther. But, in the face of my sober judgment, I wrote the letter. I even pressed the invitation urgently. Heretofore, on similar occasions, I have merely added my hope to Joyce's that she would come for a visit. This time I told her that I was very anxious to have her come, adding that Joyce — of course — joined heartily in the invitation.

After I had written the letter I walked down to the corner and mailed it, which is certainly proof enough that I wanted to make sure my commonsense — possibly restored by daylight — will have no chance to deter me from committing this indiscretion.

At Home

December second, 1919, 9 P.M.

Joyce arrived home unexpectedly this morning. I was at the hospital when she telephoned from the house. She was sullen, sore, and uncommunicative. As soon as I could get away I drove home and queried her.

The story was hard to extract. She has not yet confided the full details, and may not do so. The most I can make of this half-hysterical, disjointed, incoherent report is that she slipped away from the school, just before dinner, the day before yesterday, and went down-town in a taxi.

At the Raleigh she met, by appointment, two local girls who had been expelled from the school, last spring, for insubordination. They were her guests at dinner, and afterward they went to a night club with three young men friends of the Washington girls, and danced. She showed up in Chevy Chase shortly after two, which she thinks is not very late for a young woman of her age to be out, but the management seems to have thought otherwise.

So they suspended her for the remainder of the year; and here she is, at home, apparently much pleased over her recollection of the things she said to the Principal before she left. I surmise that these final impudences were of a flavor to insure my daughter's future status in the esteem of the institution. It is very unlikely that they will ever take her back.

I tried to be patient and sympathetic as Joyce shrieked and blubbered her story. According to her view of the scrape, she has been persecuted. She had done nothing deserving of censure; much less suspension. It was just a few hours of innocent fun. She had been in respectable company, and behaving discreetly. These unwanted old prissies, instead of being cattishly jealous because a girl had been invited out of their stuffy little reformatory for some fresh air and lively music, should have been glad that at least one of their charges still had enough pep left to exercise her human rights — and so forth — and so on.

I knew better than to come to the defense of the school management, at this stage of Joyce's dramatization of her woes, and when I said, 'Too bad,' she shouted, 'How do you mean — "too bad!" I'll bet you don't mean it's too bad the way they've thrown me out! You mean I'm too bad, and it's too bad I am human, and too bad I like a little fun! That's what you mean!'

By two o'clock I felt that I had had about all of this that was good for me, and returned to the hospital. Before I left the house I heard Joyce telephoning to one of her girl friends whose acquaintance she made in the summer.

I came home early for dinner, this evening, hoping to find her in a less rebellious mood. She had left a note for me, saying she would be out for dinner. I suspect that I am now in for an indeterminate period of anxiety. I wish I knew what to do. I can't lock her up.

There is one comforting ray of hope. I had a letter from Helen today, in reply to my latest to her, saying she is almost well again and is planning to be with us through the Christmas holidays. Of course she had not yet learned of Joyce's misfortune. I hope this does not affect her decision to come, and I don't think it will: except possibly to make Helen more sure she should come — and see what may be done for our unhappy girl.

Nancy tells me today that our Perry Ruggles slapped old Danny Ulrick yesterday. She says there has been bad blood between Perry and Danny for some time. Yesterday Danny made some remark that annoyed Perry. There was no fight. Danny, having been soundly — and no doubt appropriately — slapped, immediately demobilized himself and went at full gallop to report his injury to the superintendent.

'I sent for Perry to come to my office at once,' said Nancy.

'And what did he have to say for himself?' I asked, with much interest.

'He didn't come,' said Nancy.

So — I suppose we will have to let Perry out of our organization. I shall try to see him tomorrow and find out whether there is anything we can do to save Martha. Nancy says Martha is much chagrined. But if old Perry goes, Martha insists that she will have to follow him.

I wouldn't have Nancy Ashford's job if it was the last bit of employment left in the world.

Carter told me this afternoon that he wanted me to be more circumspect with my digitalis. I had been feeling so well, for a few weeks, that I had let the dosage run down. I feel like an old man tonight.

At Home

December twenty-third, 1919, 4 P.M.

I have not been well for the past three weeks. Until yesterday, I have been going to the hospital in the mornings and coming home early in the afternoon. Joyce does not realize that I have been ill. This is not her fault, for I have made light of the fact that I am not pursuing my usual schedule of work.

She sleeps all forenoon, and is gone for the remainder of the day. A few times I have waited up for her, but she resents it and is frank to say so.

Yesterday things came to a little crisis with me. I passed out cold in the operating-room. It was an intracranial tumor — a long, tiresome, exacting task. Fortunately I had Tim Watson with me.

I have no recollection of fainting. When I roused, I was propped up in bed, with Carter counting my wrist. I suddenly remembered that I had been operating, and tried to raise up; but I was too weak. Carter said, 'You're all right. Take it easy. Watson's carrying on. You were all done but the sutures.

He can manage.'

'Queer,' I mumbled. 'Nothing like that ever happened to me before. Didn't have the slightest bit of warning.'

'It needn't happen any more,' said Carter, encouragingly. 'It was a long job — and you're not quite up to par. You'll be fit, after you've rested a little.'

'I think I'll get up now,' I said.

'Not yet,' advised Carter. 'I want you to stay right where you are for a couple of hours. I'll be back presently.'

I settled back on the pillows and noticed a hypodermic syringe on the table. The Bates girl was standing there. I said, 'What was that?' She pretended she didn't know, which was of course the proper behavior for her. I said, 'Hand it to me.' She did so, rather reluctantly. There was a minute particle of the solution adhering to the point of the needle. I touched it to the tip of my tongue. It was nitroglycerine. I hadn't fainted because of fatigue. It was a heart attack.

Carter drove me home about four, Minton following in Carter's car to pick him up. I didn't go to bed and Carter didn't insist on it; said I would be just as well off lounging on the davenport, not too flat. It sounded like good advice. Joyce did not come home for dinner.

I feel ever so much better, today, than for several days. I'm not fretting about myself. Carter said I should be quiet today, and he evidently reinforced his suggestion. I know the stuff he gave me has codeine in it. It accounts for my peace of mind.

Helen is coming tomorrow. I am not going to try to meet her. Joyce can tell her I had to be at the hospital. I hope I shall be well enough to entertain her properly. It would be too bad if her visit were spoiled. Perhaps I can keep her from finding out that I have had this little upset. If I am as much better tomorrow as I am today, maybe she will not notice. Joyce hasn't remarked about it. Gladys knows, but I told her not to say anything.

Joyce insists that she is very happy over Helen's coming for Christmas, but seems a bit embarrassed. Helen has been back at school and of course knows the story of Joyce's escapade. Perhaps they have had some correspondence about it: I don't know.

I am looking forward to tomorrow with mingled feelings.

AT HOME

Christmas Eve, 1919, Midnight

This is indeed a Merry Christmas! My heart is overflowing with joy!

I must try to record today's experiences in orderly fashion, but it will not be easy to do. Five minutes ago I parted with Helen at the foot of the stairs. I know that as long as I live the memory of that enchanted moment will quicken my pulse.

This morning I rose in better health than I have had for a month. I had a notion to accompany Joyce to the station. But I had told her that she was to meet Helen without me, and she had seemed pleased over the prospect. Perhaps she felt it was going to be easier for her if she had an hour alone with Helen, at the outset.

I drove to Brightwood. There had been a brain tumor operation scheduled for nine-thirty this morning but they had postponed it. I amazed my colleagues — and worried them, too, I fear — by announcing that I was going to do the operation. While we were scrubbing up for it, Tim said, 'Are you sure you want to do this? We can put it off a few days, you know. Give you a little more time to get your strength back.' I assured him I had never felt more fit. So — we went into it. My hand was never steadier. I think Tim and the nurses were relieved when I had finished. I know they thought I ought to be at home in bed.

It was after one before I could leave the hospital. For many years it has been my custom to give small Christmas presents to the nurses, orderlies, and all the help. Nancy always makes out these checks in figures consistent with the nature of the employment and seniority in service. The checks are enclosed in gay greeting cards and distributed during the morning of the day before Christmas.

It is difficult to account for the way some little traditions get themselves established. I suppose that the first time we issued these Christmas checks, some employee — eager to show his gratitude — came to my office at once to extend the season's greetings. And then all the rest of them followed suit.

At all events, I can expect — on the day before Christmas — that before I leave the hospital our entire outfit will swarm in on me with assorted felicitations and expressions of thanks.

This morning I forgot about it. I daresay

my absentmindedness was to be accounted for by my eagerness to go home and welcome Helen. Shortly after eleven, I was on my way out of the building when I met Nancy.

'You can't go,' she said, in a stage whisper. 'Have you forgotten?'

It suddenly dawned on me what she meant.

'Sorry, Nancy,' I said. 'I'm afraid it slipped my mind.'

'You feel all right; don't you?' she asked, anxiously. 'You mustn't stay — if you don't.'

I assured her that wasn't the reason. I had forgotten; that was all.

'Then you'd better wait,' she advised. 'They will be disappointed if you don't.'

I hesitated a little.

'Think so?' I queried. 'I was hoping I might get away early.'

Nancy shook her head.

'If it isn't something positively urgent, you ought to wait.' Nancy seemed to have something on her mind. 'You see,' she went on, slowly, 'there's a rumor going around that you're not very well. Everybody knows what happened. I think it will be just as well if they all have a chance to see you today, and find out for themselves that you're all right.'

I have always despised loose chatter and indiscriminate gossip. Nancy's report that there was a lot of buzz at Brightwood over my little collapse annoyed me.

'You saw to it that they all had their usual gifts?' I asked.

'Of course,' said Nancy.

'And now I'm expected to sit in my office, for a couple of hours, just to prove to them that I haven't had a stroke of paralysis — or something. Well — I don't like the idea.'

'But you'll do it,' wheedled Nancy, 'because I asked you.'

I turned about, took off my hat and coat, and trailed along after her to my office. Presently they began streaming in, the word that I was ready to receive them having got about quickly by the mysterious grapevine process of communication. I tried to greet them all with the usual exuberance, but I'm afraid the affair wasn't quite satisfactory. Most of them came to my desk with anxious, questioning eyes, as if they were trying to make a quick diagnosis. Their attitude perplexed me; chilled me a little. Some of them seemed almost strangers. I tried my best to be natural, probably overdoing it; and a few of the brassier ones showed an enthusiastic cordiality that was too strident to be spontaneous.

When it appeared that my large family had all been in, and I was making ready to leave — with the disturbing sensation that if they had been apprehensive about me before, they would probably be even more so now — grim old Perry Ruggles hobbled through the doorway and confronted me with a heavy frown. I was pulling on my overcoat.

'I ain't a-takin' it,' he growled, deep in his throat. He laid the check down on the desk, and pushed it toward me with a work-worn finger. 'I ain't been nothin' but a lot o' trouble to yuh.' It was plain to see that Perry had composed this speech with all the wormy abasement of the Prodigal Son. I could hardly keep my face straight. 'Yuh've paid me more'n I earned,' he rumbled. 'Ef it waren't fer Martha, yuh wouldn't hev me around, 'n' I wouldn't blame yuh. I'm no good here.'

I walked to the door and closed it, returned to my desk, and seated myself. 'Sit down, won't you?' I said. 'Let's have a little chat about it.'

Perry gingerly lowered himself into the chair, and sat on the edge of it, scowling inquiringly.

'Perhaps you haven't been entirely happy here, Perry,' I began, 'but that's probably because the work you have been asked to do has not interested you very much. You have known you were employed here because we needed your sister. I understand your feeling, and I know I should feel the same way myself. I have been trying to think of something more pleasant for you to do.'

Perry's lips were still pursed tightly but his brow had smoothed a little.

'I don't like it — in town,' he muttered. 'Neither does Martha, fer that sake. Ef 't-waren't fer Miss Ashford, a-bein' so good t' her, she'd go back t' the country with me.'

Suddenly I had an inspiration.

'Perry,' I said, 'I have a little place up on Lake Saginack where I am going to build a house in the spring; soon as the weather permits. I have had a lot of trees planted there, and shrubbery. How would you like the job of caretaker?'

Perry rubbed his jaw carefully, which I interpreted as a bargaining gesture. This, I felt, was enough progress for one session. And I was anxious to get away.

'What all would I hev t' do?' he asked.

'We can figure that out,' I said, rising. 'You stay here and try to content yourself for the present — and we'll talk about the other thing when we get around to it. And as for this little Christmas gift,' I added, 'I shall be more pleased if you take it. If you feel you do not deserve it, how about converting it into a present for someone else?'

Perry's upper lip lifted in amazement, and he blinked a few times. I suppose it was the first time that an idea of this nature ever collided with Perry. His expression was so amusing that I had to hold on tight to keep from ruining our delicate relationship.

'Didn't you ever do anything like that?' I asked. 'It's great fun.' Then — perhaps because I had already startled Perry with a strange suggestion, I thought I would see whether he could survive another harder jolt. 'It's even more fun,' I went on, 'if you give the present to someone who isn't expecting anything, and will be surprised.'

Perry drew a crooked grin and said he 'lowed almost anybody'd be surprised ef they got a present frum him. This struck us both as being very funny indeed and we laughed together. Perry's merriment was noisily uncouth, but short-lived. He quickly resumed his habitual frown, apparently repenting that he had let himself go in this unseemly manner.

'If you don't happen to know anyone to try this out on,' I said, 'I'd like to make a suggestion. Have you ever noticed this sharp-nosed little kid that comes every day with somebody's lunch?'

Perry eyed me suspiciously from under shaggy brows.

'Yeah,' he replied, unpleasantly. 'That's this here Ulrick feller's grandson.'

'He's certainly a ragged little rascal,' I remarked. 'I suppose everything he wears has been passed along to him, after it has been worn out by his brothers.'

'Yeah,' agreed Perry sourly. 'I guess so. Old man Ulrick has to feed a passel of 'em.'

I picked up the check and handed it to Perry.

'There you are,' I said. 'You go and see how much fun you can have with it.'

'Yuh mean — get some shoes, er sumpin, fer that kid?' Perry's tone was loaded with distaste. 'By Gar! That's more'n old Ulrick'd ever do fer any o' my kin, I'll bet!'

'I think you're probably right,' I said. 'I imagine that Danny has missed a lot of fun in his life. I suppose he has had his nose on the grindstone so hard that he never had a chance to give himself a treat.'

'Himself a treat?' echoed Perry, derisively. 'Yuh mean — I'd be givin' myself a treat ef I got this kid some shoes?'

'Of course,' I declared. 'I must go now, Perry. Good luck with your experiment.'

Perry blocked my way.

'Yeah — but see here,' he muttered. 'Ef I do that, old Ulrick will think I'm a tryin' t' be friendly like, and we ain't spoke fer weeks.'

'Oh, well, in that case,' I remarked casually, 'maybe you'd better not do anything about it. If it's more fun not to speak to old Danny than to get his grandson some shoes, let it go. I expect you're right. If you gave the shoes to the kid, old Danny would probably want to speak to you — and, of course, that would be annoying. Just forget about it, Perry. Bye-bye. Merry Christmas.' I went out and left him standing there.

On the way out, I met Nancy again. I had a broad grin on my face, and Nancy said, 'What have you been up to?' Perry was hobbling down the hall. She tipped her head slightly in his direction and asked, 'Have you, by any chance, been entertaining yourself at that poor thing's expense?'

I nodded, and assumed the guilty look of a child caught in the jam-jar.

'Does — does he know it?' asked Nancy, anxiously.

'I think so,' I said, soberly. 'And I believe he was entertained a little, too. Did you ever hear Perry laugh?' I asked.

'Impossible!' she declared. 'Want to tell me?'

'No,' I said. 'Not now. Merry Christmas, Nancy!'

Helen's greeting was very tender, giving me both hands, her smiling eyes full of sincere affection. I wanted to kiss her. Had my feelings toward her been simply that of a middle-aged parent, welcoming his child's best friend into his home, I might have done so. But I knew I could not pretend to exercise a doting father's privilege in greeting a young guest. If I kissed Helen, it wouldn't be a mere gesture of hospitality. So — I rejected the impulse, but retained her hands, and I am afraid that as I looked into her uplifted eyes she must have divined my wish; for she flushed a little, and seemed anxious to include Joyce quickly into our mutual expressions of happiness.

They were dressed for the street, Joyce having secured tickets for a matinée. It was suggested that they might be able to find a seat for me, but I declined, thinking it much better to let them be alone together. I was very happy. The old relationship between the girls had been resumed, and it was easy to see that Joyce was finding much satisfaction in readjusting herself to match Helen's poise and manner. The strained, half-rebellious expression had vanished from my child's mobile face. Helen exercises some strange witchery that transforms Joyce into a person of beauty and charm.

I spent the afternoon alone with my thoughts. It was good to feel physically fit again. It was good to see Joyce doffing her brittle affectations. It was very healing to my spirit to have Helen near me again.

It was almost six when they returned, tarrying before the open fire, for the temperature had dropped, and they were chilled. At Joyce's suggestion, we dressed for dinner. I was glad she had not wanted to go out. We met in the library at seven. I was proud of my dinner companions. They were very lovely. Joyce was in blue and Helen in coral.

Our talk skipped about, with no central purpose; no serious intent. When the dessert came on, there was a little lull in our conversation, and I remarked — quite fervently — that it was a very happy occasion; that it was delightful to have Helen with us. I surprised myself by saying, 'I don't see how we can ever let you go.'

'Why need she ever go?' said Joyce, turning fond eyes toward Helen. 'You're happier here than anywhere else; aren't you, darling?'

My heart skipped a beat. I hoped Helen would appraise the remark as one of Joyce's undeliberated disbursements, and make some rejoinder that would tag it as a spontaneous outburst of affection.

Helen did not reply, for a moment. A slow flush crept up her cheek, and she did not lift her eyes.

'See?' exclaimed Joyce, ecstatically. 'It's true! Let's keep her, Daddy!'

It was a pretty tense moment. At least it

was for me. And when Gladys popped in to tell Joyce that Mr. Masterson wanted her on the telephone I was pleased that something had intervened to remove her until we could tug the conversation back to firmer ground.

'Joyce,' I said, when she was gone, 'sometimes does her thinking afterward.' I chuckled a little, as if I had thought the situation mildly amusing. Helen, still pink, smiled, but made no comment.

'Of course,' I went on, drawing an aimless little design on my icecream, 'I couldn't imagine anything more wonderful — than to have you with us — always.'

Helen slowly reached out her hand and laid it on mine. I wrapped my fingers tightly about it, and searched her eyes. She gave a quick little intake of breath. I rose and drew her to her feet. She came into my arms, and I kissed her. Her response was all that a starved heart could wish.

After a long moment, I released her a little, and said, rather breathlessly, 'My darling — I have wanted you — so very much!'

'I know,' she whispered. 'It's all right.'

'Can you forget how many years there are between us?' I asked.

'I forgot that,' she murmured, 'a long time ago.'

I held her close to me again.

'Joyce will be coming back,' she said, softly.

'Shall we tell her — now?' I asked.

'Of course. She would know, anyhow. And we mustn't leave her out. That would spoil everything — for all three of us.'

What a sensible creature she is! I suppose that's the first and biggest reason I have for loving her. She intuitively understands. She knows what to do, what to say, how to say it, when to say it. She has *savoir faire*. *Savoir faire* is not an achievement, but a talent. You have it, or you don't. No amount of cultivation will give it to you. Helen possesses it in its perfection.

We resumed our places at the table. Joyce rejoined us, and asked airily what we had been talking about in her absence.

'Well — for one thing' — I tried to keep my voice steady — 'I repeated to Helen your wish that she remain with us — always.'

Joyce's eyes widened and she stared at us with curiosity.

'It was all your fault,' said Helen.

'You darlings!' exclaimed Joyce. She pushed back her chair, threw her arms around Helen's neck, and kissed her. Then she came to me, hugged me tight, kissed me — and cried like a little child; because she was excited, I think. I know she didn't cry because she was unhappy.

Arm in arm we went back to the library for coffee. Joyce, who had quite recovered her balance, said she didn't want any, and would be back after a while.

Helen said, 'I hope Joyce is going to like this idea.'

'After she gets accustomed to it,' I said. 'It's new to all of us.'

'Not to me,' murmured Helen.

'I mean — the idea that it has really come to pass,' I said. 'As for wishing it might happen, I haven't thought about anything else for a long time.'

'Yes,' she whispered. 'I know.'

My sense of well-being surged through me like a transfusion. I remembered an old text that I hadn't thought of for years, and repeated it, half to myself. 'They shall mount up on wings as eagles. They shall run and not be weary. They shall walk — and not faint.'

'Is that the way you feel?' asked Helen, softly, knowing the answer.

'Exactly.'

'That wasn't said of people in love,' she said, smiling, 'but of those who trust in the Lord.'

'Very well,' I said, 'I also trust in the Lord. He has been very kind — and I am on His side.'

Joyce came down, at eleven, in a fluffy dressing-gown, and asked us whether we were getting along all right without her chaperonage. I hope she isn't going to adopt this rôle permanently. It's bound to be an awkward situation if she poses us as lovers who need her mature counsel.

She left us, after a while, kissing us both and telling us not to sit up too late.

Helen and I practically discussed our future plans. I asked her if she could consent to an early marriage and she seemed entirely willing. I suggested a trip to Europe for the three of us, and she thought it a grand idea.

I put my arm about her and went with her to the stairway. I kissed her good night. She moved up on the next step, where she was on a level with me, and kissed me again.

I am very happy. Life has been very good to me.

AT HOME

December twenty-seventh, 1919, 11:30 P.M.

The three of us spent the evening discussing travel plans. Joyce is entering whole-heartedly into our program, seeming to be in full approval of our early wedding; and, of course, bubbling with enthusiasm over the prospect of our trip to Europe.

Helen goes home tomorrow. She had expected to remain until after New Year's Day, but feels now that she should not delay her preparations for our marriage which, we have agreed, is to occur on the eleventh.

It is really at Helen's insistence that we are being married so soon. I was content to wait until she had graduated in June. But she thinks that if I need her at all I need her now. Naturally we have talked over Joyce's problem candidly. Helen thinks that if Joyce is permitted to run at large here, for another five or six months, it may be difficult to reclaim her. She thinks, also, that my own worry over Joyce should be relieved at the earliest possible moment.

I do not know exactly how much sacrifice

it entails, on Helen's part, to give up school, this close to graduation. She assures me that she is glad to do it, and seems not to be fretting over it.

So we are arranging to be married in a fortnight. It will be a very simple wedding, with a half dozen friends in attendance. And on the next Thursday afternoon we sail on the Aquitania for Cherbourg.

In spite of Nancy Ashford's tactful but urgent warning, the other day, that all Brightwood was chattering about my ill health, it had not occurred to me that this anxiety had become a subject of formal discussion by the staff.

I had no operations scheduled for today, and did not arrive at the hospital until half past ten. After making a few visits on patients of mine, I put in a call to Ann Arbor and told Doctor Leighton I was going away presently on a two months' vacation. There are only three head cases here now, under observation, and waiting for surgery. Two of them Watson can handle alone. Leighton promised me he would look after the third, and any other cases which may show up, though I think Tim can give a good account of himself in all but a few problems. Leighton says he will be available whenever Watson wants him.

At noon, when I was preparing to leave, Nancy came in and said that Doctor Pyle wished to see me. I thought this odd, for I had encountered Pyle two or three times in the course of the morning and he had had every opportunity to talk. Apparently this was something private.

'Know what Pyle has on his mind?' I asked, casually.

'Yes,' said Nancy — but she did not elaborate and I respected her prudence.

'I hope it isn't anything that will detain me very long,' I said. 'I have an engagement at home.'

'Shall I see if I can find him?' suggested Nancy. 'Perhaps he can come at once — and get it over with.'

I said, 'Very well,' and Nancy slipped away. I confess I didn't like her employment of the phrase — 'Get it over with' — a stock remark with us when counseling agitated patients to submit to surgery.

Pyle seemed quite a bit flustered when he came in. Ever since I have known the testy old chap — and that is a very long time — he has had a funny trick of tipping up his lower lip, when embarrassed or bewildered, and gnawing absurdly at the tip of his diminutive goatee. In order to accomplish this maneuver, he is obliged to spread his mouth almost from ear to ear, achieving a mirthless grin that startles persons who observe this phenomenon for the first time.

He was pursuing this little whisker with his upper incisors as he took the chair opposite me, and I knew that something had gone wrong. Pyle had come on a difficult errand.

I gave him a cigar, lighted it for him, and said, 'What's the matter, beloved? You look as if you might have taken the wrong kidney out of somebody.'

'We must have a little chat, Hudson,' he began, ignoring my chaff. 'About your health. It's getting breezed around that you're in bad shape. Also that you insist on keeping up with your usual schedule. Now, if that goes on much longer, it is going to hurt you — and it might hurt Brightwood. We think you should take a vacation.'

'Who are "we"?' I snapped.

'The staff,' replied Pyle. 'All of us. It's unanimous. We met, afternoon before Christmas, and talked it over. Felt like traitors, of course. Hated to do it in your absence. Everybody was agreed to that. Everybody was sympathetic — and on your side — and wanting to do the right thing. I hope you will understand that. Nobody thinks you're done for. But we all feel that you should get away

— for six months, maybe. Rusticate. Travel. Play.'

Without giving me an opening, the good old boy carried on with his suggestions. He had a large envelope, crammed with cruise advertisements. Apparently he had gone to no end of bother to set up a half dozen tentative trips for me.

'Now, here you have —' said Pyle, spreading out a map of the world on my desk, and inching his chair closer, after the approved manner of a high-pressure salesman, 'Now, here you have a delightful tour around the world. Go west, stop at Honolulu, smell the flowers, listen to the marimbas —'

'You mean the ukuleles,' I put in.

'Do I? Very well, then. The ukuleles! And then you go to Tahiti! Think of that, Hudson! Tahiti! Marvelous! I confess I've always wanted to do that, but I've been so damned healthy that nobody ever thought of shipping me away for a rest. This will be a great thing for you, Hudson. Take your daughter along. Stop in Europe on the way back. Spend some time in Germany with the brain tinkers. Now — you do that! This is very important!'

Of course I knew it would be up to me to tell Pyle — and all the rest of them — about my plans for the European tour, but I hadn't quite got myself nerved up to confide about

380

the wedding. Perhaps this irresolution means nothing less than that I expected Pyle to be utterly disgusted when he learned of it. The fact that I was postponing the hour when this news must come to light disturbed me. I wasn't ready to tell him; not yet. I would organize a little speech, explaining it all, so he could understand how I happened to decide on matrimony. I couldn't tell Pyle that I had fallen in love with a girl young enough to be my daughter, but I could tell him she would be a steadying influence for my Joyce. And this would be true enough for all practical purposes. But I must have a little more time to consolidate my campaign of self-defense.

So — I heartily agreed with Pyle that I had been working too hard; told him I had plans made to build a cottage up on Saginack and go up there, for two or three days every week, soon as the nice weather came along.

Pyle gnawed his goatee, while I was elaborating on this, and it was easily to be seen that I wasn't making much of an impression. He interrupted me, presently, to inquire what was going to become of me — and all the rest of us — in the meantime.

I saw then that I might as well let him have it. I said, 'Pyle, I hope this won't knock you cold. I'm going down to Philadelphia, week after next, to marry my daughter's school friend, Miss Helen Brent.'

Pyle was stunned. If I had pulled a pistol out of my pocket and shot myself, I doubt if his strained expression of incredulity could have registered a bigger shock. I couldn't help grinning. I waited a moment for him to recover, and when it was obvious that the blow had struck his speech center, I went on to give him some details; told him about our projected trip to Europe — and everything.

He gradually came up out of his semi-conscious condition, and I gave him a fresh cigar. He bit the end off mechanically, and drew back a little, defensively, when I approached with a lighted match. I know he thought I had lost my mind. I laughed. And he finally found his tongue.

'Er — well,' he croaked feebly. 'That's very — surprising. Many happy returns.'

Then I began at the beginning and told him all about it, making no bones about the worry I had had with Joyce, Helen's remarkable hold on her, and the circumstances leading up to our recent decision. I don't know whether Pyle accepted any of it as reasonable, but when he left he was at least able to get away without assistance. At the door he wanted to know how much of this was a secret, and I told him it should be sufficient — for the present — to say that I was going abroad with my daughter. They could learn the rest of it when it happened.

Then, after some hesitation, he asked how much of the story he should tell to Mrs. Ashford. This distressed me a little. The fact is, I should have confided in Nancy at once. It isn't quite fair for me to have kept this a secret from her, seeing how close we have been, through all these years.

I daresay Pyle has had it in the back of his old head, for a long time, that Nancy and I would marry, some day. And I suppose it might strike him that such a match would be immeasurably more suitable.

'I'll tell her myself,' I said. And Pyle went out, and closed the door.

I called up Fred Ferguson, this afternoon, and told him I was going away for a couple of months, and wondered whether he could get the plans for my house in the country ready for me to see by the end of next week. He thought he could. I hope they can get going on it, so I can have some use of it during the coming summer.

This has been an eventful day and I am very tired. I am feeling the reaction from the difficult interview I had with Pyle. I suppose I should have sent for Nancy, after he left. I mustn't let much more time slip by until I tell her.

There is really no reason why I should feel any embarrassment about this. The relations between Nancy and me certainly do not call for any apologies. I never gave her any reason to think that we belonged to each other, except in the bonds of an invaluable business friendship. Perhaps I'm making a mountain of a mole-hill. Maybe Nancy has no such thoughts in her head. I hope not. Still, I wish I didn't have this to look forward to. Damn it! — why should I feel so sensitive about letting my friends into this secret? It's nobody's business — is it — whom I marry? I don't owe anyone an explanation. Perhaps I should have said something to Tim.

At Home

January eighth, 1920, 11:30 P.M.

This is undoubtedly the last entry I shall make in my journal until after our return from abroad. The day has been confusingly crowded with last-minute duties. I hope I have not forgotten anything of importance. Joyce and I are leaving tomorrow for Philadelphia where the wedding occurs on the morning of the eleventh. The time is growing short.

I am very restless tonight, and in need of diversion. To be quite frank, I might not otherwise be writing this. I have no inclination to read, I am not sleepy; besides, I told Joyce I would wait up for her, hoping it might encourage her return at a reasonable hour. She has gone somewhere with young Masterson.

There is no need for anxiety about the successful management of affairs at Brightwood during my absence. The staff is harmonious, loyal, efficient; and Nancy is at the helm. Nancy has given her full approval of my plans. There has been no constraint. I am glad of that.

I find that for many years I have been assuming that Brightwood, without my constant oversight, might promptly disintegrate. Of course I haven't been vain enough to say that to myself in so many words, but the bare fact that I have never felt free to take an extended vacation is proof that I felt the hospital could not get along without me.

It occurred to me today, after interviewing several members of the staff, that it wouldn't matter much if I never came back to Brightwood at all. When I bade good-bye to Nancy I remarked to that effect. Naturally she comforted my vanity by saying they would be simply marking time and hoping to keep things running smoothly until I returned.

I told her I had discovered a sin that the prayer-book had not taken into account. I recited what I could remember of the litany used at Trinity Cathedral in Chicago. This quaint confession had invited the good Lord to deliver us from all evil and mischief; from the crafts and assaults of the devil; from envy, hatred, and malice; but, I observed, it should also have prayed that we be delivered from indispensability. And in all seriousness I believe it disrupts a man's honest dealings with himself when — perhaps unwittingly — he begins to think that his home and his business couldn't possibly carry on without him.

Among the many callers who came this afternoon to extend their good wishes was my excellent old friend Caleb Weatherby. I had not seen him for nearly a year. He is spending the worst of the winter here. Before our return from Europe, he will have gone back to his home on Lake Moosehead in Maine. He had read in the papers that I was going abroad and came to pay his respects.

I cannot remember having spoken of him in this journal. He insists that I saved his life, and this may not be far from the truth, though the rescue was effected in a manner that may strike you as amusing. And if you have any fondness for baked beans, the story may make you hungry.

Late last fall, a year ago, Doctor Grant, one of our local physicians, called up one day to ask if he might bring in for observation a patient who had attempted suicide and was so deep in melancholia that he would probably finish the job at the first opportunity. Grant said the case history indicated a healthy and stable mind, until quite recently, and he felt that only a pathological condition could account for a depression so stubborn and dangerous.

Weatherby was brought in, the next morning, by his son. I did not at once see the old gentleman but had an hour with the son, a personable and fairly prosperous business man of thirty-eight to forty, who seemed loyally concerned about his father's plight.

He gave me the facts briefly. Weatherby, senior, had spent his life in Maine. He had always been active and most of his time had been spent out of doors, cutting timber, running a mill, making maple products. A few months before his wife had died. Weatherby, junior, and his wife had proposed to the old gentleman that he come to Detroit and live with them, because he was lonely and without employment. It was his first experience in a large city. After a few days, he began to be moody, taciturn, and glum. They tried to interest him in their own affairs, took him to the movies, made an effort to include him in their social life; but to no avail.

I thought I had a pretty good picture of the old fellow's dilemma. The problem of an old man, who comes to live with his son and his daughter-in-law, is much more serious than for the old lady who finds herself in the same circumstances. There are plenty of little things she can do to entertain herself, and small services she can perform which preserve her self-respect as a useful member of the household. She can knit stockings, sew on buttons, feed the baby, help in the kitchen on the maid's day out. There is very little that an old man can do. In the case of Weatherby, the enforced idleness and sense of dependence had made him loathe himself. He would sit for days on end, refusing to speak, and now he had gone to the limit of desperation by attempting suicide.

That afternoon I went up to my new patient's room. For a man approaching seventy, he was as fine a specimen of physical fitness as I have ever seen; nor have I ever seen anyone more stolidly depressed. He was sitting by the window, with his big, shaggy head in his hands, and when I told him who I was he did not look up. I sat down near him and began asking him leading questions but could get nothing out of him but grunts and growls and shrugs.

After a while he grew exasperated and barked out shrilly that I could go to hell with my questions, that he was tired of living, that he had lived too long, that he was only a nuisance, that he wished he was dead, that he was sorry the poison hadn't got to work before they pumped him out, that he was going to do a better job, next time; that it was none of my damn business how he felt, and would I go away and leave him alone?

I then resorted to the familiar technique of agreeing with him, which occasionally has the effect of making a functional — but almost never a pathological — melancholic rouse to his own defense. Slipping to the edge of my chair and pocketing my notebook and consulting my watch, to sign that I had lost interest and was about to depart, I ostentatiously stifled a yawn, the old man regarding me with sour distaste but with a trace of grim curiosity.

'You're probably right, Mr. Weatherby,' I drawled. 'You are sixty-eight. A man at that age is, as you say, a nuisance and far better off dead. Any old duffer of your years is practically worthless, even if he has fairly good health; and I suppose you've been puny and sickly, most of your life.'

That popped him! If I had touched off a cannon cracker under his chair he couldn't have responded any more promptly. It delighted me to see how mad he was!

As soon as he had yelled, 'Puny! Sickly! Me!' I knew there wasn't anything the matter with that fine old head. 'Puny?' he shouted. By Gemini, he'd bet he could take me outside and tie me into a hard knot! Then the glitter faded from his eyes and he suddenly subsided, with slumped shoulders, into his habitual gloom. But this did not discourage me. Apparently it had been a long time since he had blown the whistle, and the noise had startled him.

'Well,' I remarked, with an infuriating grin, 'we frequently find frail people making big threats. Now, tell me the truth, Mr. Weatherby, didn't you have quite a lot of lung trouble when you were a young man?'

This time he got down to business! 'Lung trouble! Who? Me? Hell!' Then he proceeded to inform me that at the age of fifteen he was doing a man's work in the woods; came from sturdy stock; his father had been killed by a falling tree at the age of seventy-six, still able to swing an ax with the best of 'em. Then he melted back into his chair again and scowled at the window.

'How did that happen?' I inquired. He shook his head crossly and did not reply. I thought I would try another bait. 'I saw your son,' I said. 'Sort of mean-looking fellow. Not much wonder you're tired of living with such a sour crab. I suppose his wife's a nagger. Probably that's what makes him abuse you. Two of 'em in cahoots to drive you out of their house.'

At that, he turned on me venomously. He'd have me understand that his son was one of the finest men in the world, and his wife had done everything to make him comfortable. And anybody who said she was a nagger was a dirty liar. Nobody could be any sweeter than Florence. Then the old man's eyes gushed sudden tears, and I saw that we were really making some headway. His hands were shaky as he filled his pipe, and his noble old nose was a-drip. He was still mad at me, but I knew now that I could make him talk, and felt it was time to conciliate.

'Of course I don't think your boy is mean,' I said, gently. 'And I don't think his wife is a nagger. And I know they both love you. But — you wouldn't talk to me, and I had to do something about it.'

He nodded, understandingly, and puffed in silence.

'And the fact is,' I went on, 'I never saw a healthier man than you are. You don't look as if you'd ever seen a sick day in your life. That probably comes from living in the woods. Must be a great experience to live up there in Maine. I wish you would tell me something about it.'

That was exactly what he wanted to talk about, and for the next hour he gave me a treat. In the coldest weeks of the winter they felled the trees and dressed out the timber. Then, at the first thaw, they reopened their little mill. It ran by water-power, and operated only for a couple of months while the early spring freshets made the stream bank-full. In the mill, they sawed up lumber and ground meal and feed. There was a fine maple grove, hard by. They gathered the sap and boiled it down. In the mill there was a big brick chimney and a huge fireplace.

And it was at this point that we came to the beans, which played so important a part in Caleb Weatherby's reconditioning.

'We used to bake beans in that fireplace,' rumbled the old man. 'And they were beans, let me tell you! No beans like that any more. People have forgot how to make 'em.'

'How?' I demanded. 'I like baked beans. But it's hard to get them cooked right. Too dry, I think.'

'There you are,' agreed Weatherby. 'Hard as buckshot, and dry enough to choke you to death. The way we fixed our beans: first we soaked 'em, of course, and then boiled 'em; put 'em in a stone pot, with plenty of salt pork, and salt and pepper and mustard, and an onion with a clove stuck in it —'

'And molasses,' I assisted, when he paused to recollect.

'Yes — but not sorghum. We boiled down the maple syrup until it was thick as sorghum, and poured in plenty; and then we did the thing that made 'em different! Level teaspoonful of ginger. Ever hear of ginger in beans?'

I hadn't, but it sounded all right, for I was hungry. It occurred to me that we might now tap the old torpid cistern again and see if we could get into it and bounce out of it.

'Look here!' I said. 'If you're really serious

about committing suicide, how about coming over to my house, some day, before you do it, and make up a nice big pot of those beans for me?'

The old man pulled a twisted grin and re-lighted his pipe.

'By Gemini — that's a pretty cool way to talk,' he growled, with a mirthless chuckle. 'You want me to make you a pot o' them Maine beans — and then I can go and kill myself, if I want to.'

'Well,' I explained, brightly, 'you said you were going to kill yourself, anyhow, and the beans do seem very good. I thought —'

'All right,' declared Weatherby, nodding his head. 'I'll just do that for you. When shall I come?'

Our Gladys has had the run of the house for so long that she lacks the discipline of a well-trained servant. She has had no illusions about her value to my establishment and talks back quite freely. Whenever our views have failed to coincide, I have promptly abandoned my position. Gladys is indeed a treasure; but, unfortunately, she has long since found that out. I confess it was with some diffidence that I informed her, in the morning at breakfast, that a fine old gentleman from Maine was going to spend the next day in her kitchen, making us a nice big pot of baked beans.

Gladys was a bit stunned at first, but presently recovered sufficiently to inquire what was the matter with her baked beans, and since when did we have to hire some old man to come all the way from Maine —

'Just a minute,' I broke in, firmly, though I suspected it was going to take longer than that; 'this gentleman is so lonely in Detroit that it has made him ill.'

'In the head?' inquired Gladys, remembering my specialty.

'Well — he's not insane, if that's what you're wondering. He has nothing to do, and he's tired of sitting around idle. But he does know how to make marvelous baked beans. And I want you to let him do anything he wants to do in the kitchen — all day tomorrow.'

Gladys sniffed and was about to deliver an oration. I had heard them before, and recognized the early symptoms. I held up my cup for more coffee and proceeded with my remarks. I told Gladys she had a chance to do something for this good man.

'Lots of people,' I went on, 'are going around half dead, and wishing they were wholly dead, because there's nobody to talk to about the only thing they're interested in. And one of the finest investments you can make, in restoring life to such wilted and discouraged people, is to make them see that this one thing they've got is important; worth doing; worth talking about. If you want to give yourself a happy day, Gladys, stand by this old man and make a big fuss over his ability to cook beans.'

'And keep the kitchen in a muss all day,' grumbled Gladys, quite truthfully, no doubt.

'Very well, then,' I capitulated, with a beaten sigh. 'If it's more important that you keep your kitchen nice and tidy, tomorrow, than to humor a lonesome old fellow who needs somebody to build him up and make him think more of himself, you just forget it.'

I waited for Gladys to retire to her domain, but she stood there thoughtfully scowling. Gladys is not pretty when she meditates.

'Of course,' I went on, mumbling through my toast, 'I said to myself, "Gladys will get the idea at once, and be glad to do it. Gladys will stand at the old boy's elbow and watch him mix up his mess, which she could probably do very much better — and she will oh and ah and be surprised — and pleased to learn; and that will make the old fellow so proud of himself that he'll be glad he's alive; swell up until he'll pop a button off his waistcoat." '

Gladys kept on standing there, after I paused, so I thought I might as well finish her off.

'But — that's all right, Gladys. I know how necessary it is to keep things neat and clean, and not be bothered by strangers that we don't know. After all, it's none of our business whether this old man's lonely or not. He has got some folks here in town. They can look after him.'

I pushed back my chair and left the room, but was in no great rush to leave the house. I knew that Gladys needed a little time to digest the dose I had given her. Sometimes I have wished I could administer an idea hypodermically. She was waiting at the foot of the stairs, when I came down.

'You can bring him,' she said. 'I'll treat him decent.'

'Thanks,' I said. 'I rather thought you might, when you had considered it a little more.' Then I added, confidentially, 'Now — you can either let this be a tiresome burden to you, or you can have a grand day. Don't try to pity this old fellow. He has probably had too much of that now. You just pretend to let him teach you how to make baked beans — and it will be the best day's work you've ever done — and the happiest, too, I'll bet.'

Gladys said she'd try, and grinned a little

over our conspiracy. I reflected, on the way to the hospital, that Gladys would have a chance to build herself up a little, too — an interesting by-product of my adventure.

I had told the nurse to send Mr. Weatherby over in a taxi next morning and he arrived at eight. Gladys had been instructed to soak the beans in cold water overnight. She was waiting for my patient when he came, and seemed pleased when he consented to have a cup of coffee with me in the breakfast room. Now that she had gone into this thing, she was going to do it right: I could see that.

'You'll probably have some time on your hands, Mr. Weatherby,' I said, 'and you are quite welcome to sit in my library and smoke your pipe and read anything that attracts you.'

He nodded, dignifiedly, and thanked me. Before I left the house I found an illustrated copy of Wallace Nutting's *Maine Beautiful*, and laid it in a conspicuous place beside the tobacco jar.

They were, as Mr. Weatherby had declared, great beans. I had not suggested that he remain for dinner. It had been a long, exciting day for him, and I didn't care to risk an anticlimax. I had him sent back to the hospital where, I learned later, he had eaten a good dinner and tumbled off to sleep without grousing about anything.

But Weatherby's melancholia had cut in pretty deep and I knew he would skid back into the same old mudhole if we didn't stay with him until he was safe on firm ground. Many worried people tinker with the idea of suicide, as a possible escape from their frets, and come through that phase of depression without serious harm; but if a man ever gets to the point where he actually tries it, you want to look out!

One pleasant day of bright endeavor wouldn't be enough to insure old Weatherby's life. I told him I should be greatly obliged if he would come again to my house, on Saturday, and bake a big pot of beans for a party I was giving to a few friends. I hoped the anticipation of this engagement would entertain him in the meantime.

Gladys had made no complaint about turning her kitchen over to the old gentleman, and I believed I could safely risk a repetition of my request. So, at dinner that night I gingerly ventured upon the subject, after informing her that nobody but herself knew how to cook creamed sweetbreads.

'I hope I am not imposing on you, Gladys,'

I said, 'but I should consider it a great favor if you would consent to have Mr. Weatherby come on Saturday and bake another pot of beans. I think this will be the last time.'

'Sure!' said Gladys, pleasantly.

'Was he very much in your way?'

'No — I liked having him here. He told me all about cutting down trees, and what they did in the mill.'

'That must have been interesting.'

'Not at first, it wasn't,' said Gladys. 'But I listened, like you said, and made believe I was interested, and pretty soon I was.'

'That's what makes people interesting, Gladys,' I said. 'You let them see that you're interested, and presently they begin to be interesting. Nobody can be very interesting,' I added, 'if he thinks the other fellow is bored by what he says.'

'It's funny, that way,' agreed Gladys. 'I had a real good time with Mr. Weatherby. And I think it did him a lot of good to talk.'

'You'll probably be wanting to try that on someone else, I suppose, now that you see how nicely it works.'

'Well,' admitted Gladys, confidentially, 'it was like you said. I had a good time. And it made me feel good — like I'd done something for somebody.'

'Gladys,' I said, 'you haven't told anyone

about this — but me?'

'And Mert,' she added.

'Of course — Mert. Now — don't tell anyone else. You have done a fine thing. You have helped that old man — perhaps more than you realize. And it has made you happy. Keep it a secret. Because — if you tell your friends what you did for Mr. Weatherby, and how pleased he was, and how pleased you are — you'll lose it.'

'That's funny,' said Gladys, doubtfully. 'You mean — if I tell about it I won't feel good about it, any more?'

'That's what I mean, Gladys,' I replied, soberly. 'And it is funny. But it's so. And the next time you do something for someone, and are very happy about it, don't tell anybody! Not even Mert; nor me.'

Gladys's eyes were wide with mystification. She slowly moved toward the swinging door leading to the pantry, and went through. Then she returned. Her eyes were now alight with discovery.

'That's what *you* do!' she said. 'I know now — about a lot o' things I've wondered at! For instance —'

I put up a hand, and shook my head.

'No, no, Gladys — if you please,' I said, firmly. 'You keep your nice secrets — and I'll keep mine. Then we'll both be glad.'

The Weatherby beans were getting to be very important.

The next experimental pot of beans was ready for me at six o'clock on Saturday. I sent Mr. Weatherby back to his son's home, that night, to spend Sunday. I had kept in contact with his son, advising him to make the old man talk about his youthful experiences, and send him back to Brightwood on Monday.

I had Gladys wrap up the pot of beans in a small blanket and we put it in a big wooden bucket. I had asked Pyle to join me at The Pontchartrain for dinner, and went down a bit early with my strange luggage.

It is barely possible that you may remember Louis, the famed *maître d'hôtel* at The Pontchartrain. Louis is beyond all question the best cook in town, a product of the Cordon Bleu, insufferably snobbish, and quite forthright with his cold contempt of patrons who think of food as something to sustain life. I have known Louis for a long time and he has done me the honor of his friendship.

He was standing stiffly at the door, in his evening dress, when I appeared at the Gold Room, carrying my bucket. I drew him aside and guardedly muttered into his ear.

'I have a hot pot of Weatherby baked beans in this bucket, Louis,' I confided. 'Perhaps you know about them; made according to an old Maine logging-camp formula; Weatherby's. I got wind that the old man was in town visiting his son; happened to do a little favor for him, and he paid me off by baking these beans. I want them for dinner. Doctor Pyle will join me here presently.'

'Oui,' said Louis, bowing. He signed to one of the bus boys and the beans made off toward the kitchen.

'And Louis,' I continued, 'if you have a minute, taste those beans. You know, it occurred to me, today — this grand old fellow is retired now, and hasn't much to do — if you could say, on your luncheon menu, about twice a week maybe, and on Saturday nights, that you were serving the famous Weatherby beans, made by Weatherby himself, in your kitchen, after an old formula concocted in the logging-camps of Maine, where maple syrup was easier to get than sorghum —'

'Merci,' said Louis, bowing. I could see that the thing had bit him.

Monday afternoon I drove Mr. Weatherby down to The Pontchartrain for an interview with Louis, and he held forth there on Tuesdays, Thursdays, and Saturdays — as beanster-extraordinary — until the warm weather came along. Then he went back to

Maine and opened up a little roadside place where he served nothing but 'Weatherby's Baked Beans — with brown bread and other suitable accessories. I had insisted that he stick to the bean motif; and, seeing that the beans had saved his life, he seemed glad enough to do so.

'And print on your menu,' I advised, 'that you may be found, during the winter season, baking beans at The Pontchartrain. That ought to fetch 'em.'

He is spending the roughest part of the winter in his son's home where, he told me today, he is entirely contented. The novelty of Weatherby's beans has worn off, at The Pontchartrain, and the old gentleman is not working there now; but he is glad enough for a little rest, he says.

'Had a mighty busy summer,' he reported. 'I am fixing up the place a little, this season, and taking on a couple more girls to help. Ain't as spry as I used to be.'

And that, I noticed by his gait, is true. He ain't as spry as he used to be; but, at least he hasn't killed himself, and I don't believe he is going to. He inquired, warmly, about Gladys, and said he had had a Christmas card from her. His beans did more for Gladys than he realized. Her little investment in Weatherby has given her something new to think about.

The old man told me today that I had saved his life. He was not effusive, however, and made the statement calmly. I assured him I had been abundantly rewarded by his friendship.

Perhaps you may think that this narrative is too trivial to be worth recording, but I want you to know that I put a great deal more into old Weatherby's salvation than appears on the surface. To justify Louis's experiment, I talked Weatherby's Baked Beans to all my friends until they thought I was losing my mind.

Several times that winter, when I had occasion to get a few men together for a business luncheon, we met at The Pontchartrain and I insisted on their having beans. Tim Watson was in on a number of these affairs. One day he said to me, 'I'm so damn tired of Weatherby's beans that if the old fellow doesn't commit suicide pretty soon I think I will.'

It is two o'clock, and I am going to bed. I wish my girl had come home. I do not like these late parties. It will be a great comfort when I can put Joyce into Helen's keeping.

BRIGHTWOOD HOSPITAL

August sixth, 1921, 11 A.M.

Doubtless it has often occurred to you, while deciphering this journal, that the book was not only a private repository for certain experiences and impressions which I did not care to share with any of my contemporaries, but was in the nature of a little sanctuary where I might solace my loneliness.

For many years, this journal has served as my most confidential friend, and many a long evening has been made endurable by the somewhat laborious game of burying these observations in the code.

You will not think it strange, therefore, that since my marriage I have had no inclination to resume this eccentric pastime. Helen's sweet companionship has completely filled my life. I have had no temptation to slip away by myself, in the late evening, to document the events of the day; though there have been plenty of occasions when the events were even more worthy of record here than some of the items you have read.

I have not given this journal a thought for

a long time. And I might not be writing these words, today, but for the fact that I want you to have access to a few of the thoughts expressed yesterday in Chicago at the funeral of my valued friend, Doctor Clark Russell.

Before I attempt to recover these significant words, let me sketch briefly the present state of my various interests. I pursue much the same program of work as formerly, except that I have been assigning to Watson most of the post-operative care. The personnel at Brightwood is practically unchanged. Doctor Minton is not here. The Ruggles twins are taking care of my place in the country. Pyle is on a vacation cruise in the South Seas.

Helen has gone to Philadelphia, suddenly summoned by a not very explicit telegram from her cousin Monty who appears to have got himself into some scrape which he prefers to discuss with her in person. She did not want to go, but she would have fretted about it; so I told her she had better set her mind at ease. She left on Thursday night, and will not be back until Monday or Tuesday.

As it turns out, my advice was not very good, and Helen will probably be sorry she went; for Joyce, who had decided to decline an invitation to spend the week-end at Windymere, impetuously changed her mind, and is out there now. Young Merrick has just arrived home from France and is having a party. I tried to persuade Joyce not to go. Perhaps it will turn out all right, but I dislike the prospect of Joyce's getting interested again in the fast set that Bobby Merrick gathers about him.

I fear that, little by little, Joyce is exerting her independence of Helen's quiet and affectionate supervision. Perhaps we should all have foreseen that Helen, in the rôle of stepmother, could hardly retain the influence she had as a comradely schoolmate.

I am lonesome and restless today. In a few minutes I am going to drive out to Flintridge and spend the week-end. It is very peaceful out there.

Russell's death was very sudden. I had seen him, only a couple of weeks ago, and he was in his usual health. It is hard to think of him gone.

Dean Harcourt conducted the funeral service in Trinity Cathedral. I think it was the most impressive affair I ever attended.

Of course my emotions were easily accessible, for the loss of Clark Russell is a serious grief to me. Moreover, I have a great admiration for Harcourt, and whatever he says carries much weight.

There is something about the Cathedral,

too, that inspires me. I have had several up-lifting experiences there. In my regard, it is indeed a holy place.

It was very quiet, when we took our seats. It was after four o'clock, and the declining sun was flooding the rose window in the apse. The candles on the altar glowed.

The Dean was led into the chancel by his curates. He sat down in a tall Gothic chair, his face impassive, serene, saintly. I think Harcourt has suffered much pain. He has probably paid a pretty high price for his nobility of soul.

The casket stood at the head of the broad, stone-flagged, central aisle, covered with a pall. There were no flowers on it. People who come to the Cathedral for the last time are not expected to bring their floral displays along. You needn't fret because your cheap little bouquet won't make much of a showing. Trinity Cathedral, like God, is no respecter of persons.

The organ played 'Lead, Kindly Light.'

Dean Harcourt read the ritual.

I understand that it is not customary for any additional remarks to be made in an Epis-copal Church on such occasions. But, when the Dean had concluded the formal reading of the funeral service, he talked quietly, for a few minutes, about the eternal life.

This was — as I have said — the most impressive thing I ever heard, and the memory of these simple words is haunting me. I have not come out from under their spell.

If we are immortal, at all, said the Dean, we are immortal now. If we are to survive, the future life will be a continuation of our life now. It will be different only in respect to its larger freedom, and the chief attribute of that freedom will be our escape from the dread of death and transition.

'We all have our ambitions,' said the Dean, 'and many of them lack fulfillment. Our houses burn up, our ships go down, our bubbles burst. All our ends are uncertain but this. Whatever we may or may not come to, this is inevitable. It is the shadow that clouds our sky. Our friend has emerged from that shadow.'

The Dean did not specify any of Clark Russell's scientific contributions to medicine and surgery or his other well known philanthropies. Perhaps he knew that every one of the five or six hundred people present was fully aware of Russell's invaluable career. But, by implication, he recognized this exceptional service.

'It is given to some men,' he said, 'to achieve immortality in two worlds. They go hence — but they linger here. This is very fortunate for them. They have earned a right to live on — Here and Elsewhere. We shall not weep for them. They do not need our tears.'

Of course I realize that my written impressions of this inspiring event cannot convey the full flavor of Dean Harcourt's quiet words; but, to me, they were august!

I seem still to be in this other-worldly mood. I can't shake it off. The Dean's sonorous sentences were punctuated by impressive silences. Two or three times I thought he had finished, and I was sorry. I hope this doesn't sound like cant — but what this man said was nourishment to my soul. I could feel it building me up! It was majestic! How it would have stirred Russell!

It seems that at five o'clock, every afternoon, no matter what is going on in Trinity Cathedral, the chimes in the tower play the 'theme-song' of this great institution — the tune to the ancient hymn, 'O God Our Help in Ages Past, Our Hope for Years to Come.'

The Dean closed the service while the big bells were booming this soul-stirring confession of faith. The air was vibrant with these tones while he recited Browning's imperishable lines, 'So — if I stoop into a dark, tremendous sea of cloud, it is but for a time. I press God's lamp close to my breast: its splendor, soon or late, will pierce the gloom. I shall — emerge — one day!'

And the great bells in the high tower carried on, 'Our Shelter From the Stormy Blast — and Our Eternal Home.'

The employees of THORNDIKE PRESS hope you have enjoyed this Large Print book. All our Large Print books are designed for easy reading — and they're made to last.

Other Thorndike Large Print books are available at your library, through selected bookstores, or directly from us. Suggestions for books you would like to see in Large Print are always welcome.

For more information about current and upcoming titles, please call or mail your name and address to:

THORNDIKE PRESS
PO Box 159
Thorndike, Maine 04986
800/223-6121
207/948-2962

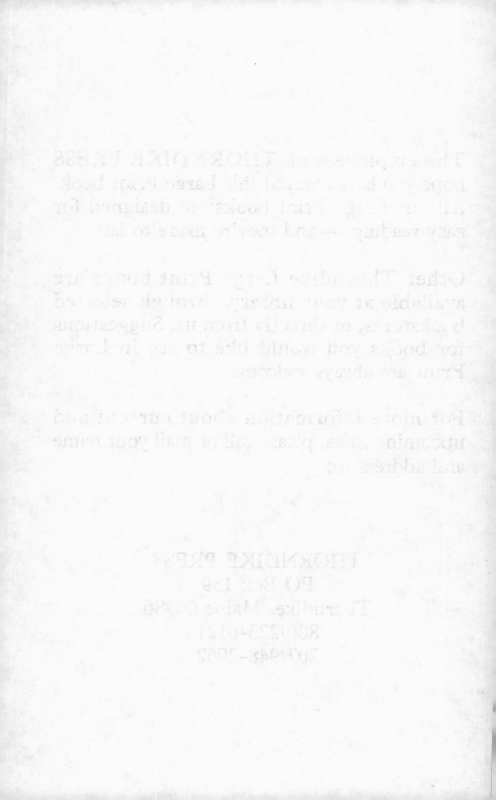